Destroyed from Within

A novel

Carmen Welker

Printed in the United States of America

ISBN 978-1-62374-013-9

First edition, Jun, 2014

sapphirepubs.com

Dedication

This book is dedicated to:

- ❖ My loving and supportive husband, Bill Welker, who is my soul mate on every level!

- ❖ The six million Jews who died in Europe's concentration camps, and to those who survived to tell the world.

- ❖ To those who have overcome physical or mental handicaps and hardships of any kind, including my good friend, Rhonda Pirtle who – through her love for our Creator has slain myriad obstacles in her path.

- ❖ Every person who has ever been physically, sexually or mentally abused.

Cover Image:

- ❖ Thanks to Michael Gora of Middle Bass Island, Ohio, who made a special effort to provide the photo of the one-room schoolhouse used to represent the converted one-room schoolhouse in this novel.

- ❖ The colorful "explosion" overlay licensed by ©Can Stock Photo Inc./oneo

Romans 3:10. As it is written: There is none righteous; no, not one: 11. And none that understands, nor that seeks after Elohim. 12. They have all turned aside together and become reprobates. There is none that does good; no, not one. 13. Their throats are open tombs and their tongues treacherous; and the venom of the asp is under their lips. 14. Their mouth is full of cursing and bitterness; 15. And their feet are swift to shed blood. 16. Destruction and anguish are in their paths: 17. And the path of peacefulness they have not known: 18. And the Fear of Elohim is not before their eyes. (Aramaic English New Testament)

Table of Contents

Chapter 1

Enter the Beast

Ephesians 6:11 And put on the whole armor of Elohim so that you may be able to stand against the strategies of the Accuser. 12 For our conflict is not with flesh and blood but with principalities and with those in authority, and with the possessors of this dark world, and with the evil spirits that are under heaven. 13 Therefore put on the whole armor of Elohim that you may be able to meet the evil (one); and, being in all respects prepared, may stand firm. (AENT)

* * * *

Satan just walked through the door!

Becca winced as these words resonated in her mind, and for a fleeting moment, she feared she had spoken them out loud.

To cover her embarrassment, she quickly extended her hand in greeting to the tall, ruggedly handsome cowboy who had just entered the renovated old, one-room school building that now served as a Messianic Jewish synagogue.

Something about him seemed oddly familiar, and it wasn't a good feeling. As a matter of fact, had she not been standing at the door in the capacity of "greeter" this morning, she might have been tempted to walk in another direction, just to avoid him.

"*Shalom*, and welcome to Beit Yisrael," she said with a radiant smile. "I'm Rebecca Ritter. Becca...."

"R. B. Lambert," the man replied in a husky voice that emanated from the deepest regions of his diaphragm. "My friends call me Rex." His brilliant blue eyes bored straight into her soul, briefly mesmerizing her with their intensity. "Beautiful dress," he went on. "Great color on you...teal. Goes well with your dark hair."

"Well, thank you." Contrary to Rex's intentions, his compliment made Becca cringe. She had dated many philandering types over the years, and always ended up hurt. Ever since her marriage to Liam a couple of years earlier, she had turned into the quintessential no-nonsense "happily married" woman, and she felt quite uncomfortable whenever men tried to come on to her. Allowing her welcoming smile to wilt, she dropped her gaze and hoped the guy would just move on.

Nevertheless, much to her chagrin, Rex stayed put and kept ogling her. "My God, girl," he said after some moments, "has anyone ever told you, you look like Reba McIntire?"

"Ah...no, you're the first," she said as she handed him a copy of the synagogue's weekly bulletin. Rex's mustachioed smirk and the "I'm awesome!" attitude exuded an arrogance that Becca found repulsive; but, as someone who had worked in public relations for most of her life, she knew how to maintain her dignity around difficult people. "Anyway, welcome and I hope you'll enjoy our Rabbi's teaching."

"Well, I hope so, too, little lady," he replied. Without so much as a peek at the bulletin, he tucked it away inside the black cowboy hat he was holding in his left hand, and

2

squinted his eyes to scan the brightly lit little sanctuary with its rows of plain, cedar wood pews lined like soldiers at attention before a simple, matching podium on a slightly raised platform at the far end.

Had he bothered to read the short "History of Beit Yisrael" section on the back of the bulletin, he would have learned that the renovated old school house had briefly served as a Methodist church that failed and went into foreclosure. Its present owner, Rabbi Orlando Dominguez, who happened to be vacationing in Missouri at "just the right time," bought the building via a "short sale" some sixteen years ago and turned it into a Messianic synagogue.

"Hmm. Never been to a Messianic synagogue before," Rex remarked – adding with a silly grin: "...So, does that mean there are some 'messy antics' going on in here, or am I getting my hopes up for nothing?"

"I'm not even going to dignify that with a response," Becca replied curtly.

Without missing a beat or losing the smirk, he craned his neck to toward the staircase immediately to the left of the entrance. "Boy," he said, "this is a really tiny place! I see your restrooms over there under the staircase, but I don't see any kitchen, so where's the smell of baking bread coming from? Upstairs, I guess?"

"Yes, the downstairs is the sanctuary, and the loft area upstairs is our 'catch-all' which serves as the Rabbi's office, kitchen, conference room, and kids' playroom."

"Cool! Small and homey. I like it!"

Becca couldn't help but notice how much he resembled the "Duke", John Wayne, in his earlier years, with, maybe a little Clint Eastwood thrown in. Deeply tanned and muscular, with shiny black hair, he seemed to be in his late forties or early fifties. He clearly knew he was an attractive man, and made no effort to pretend otherwise.

Still, there was something about him....

"So, you been a member here for very long?" he wanted to know.

"I've been a member for three years, and my husband started coming just before we got married a couple of years ago."

The cowboy's grin turned into a theatrical frown. "Oh, shoot, you have a husband," he said, as if the disappointment was tearing him apart. "Well, dang, that's too bad! The good ones are always taken."

"Well, most people in our age group usually are married...."

"Aw honey, what do you mean, 'our age group'? I doubt you're anywhere near as old as I am! I'm guessing you're not even out of your thirties yet?"

Realizing that Rex had no intentions of moving on, Becca decided to steer the conversation in another direction. "So, where do you normally go to church?" she asked in a deliberate monotone.

"No place right now," he replied, his voice low and deep - a ploy apparently designed to make him sound as macho as he thought himself to be. "Been looking for a church home, but haven't really been able to settle on anything. I just moved up here from Albuquerque and bought a 200-acre ranch over toward Norwood. Tried a few churches in Springfield and Ozark, but so far, I've been out of luck. Nothing seems to fit, know what I mean? Anyway, I saw your quaint little place as I was driving by last week and thought I'd see what you all are about."

"Well, we're glad you dropped in. I'm sure you'll find us a little different from other congregations, but you'll get used to us eventually. That is, if you decide to make this your church home."

Taking a small step backward, she motioned for him to enter the sanctuary so he could mingle with the few "early birds" who were already inside. But, to her dismay, Rex remained rooted to the spot.

"Honestly, I'm hoping I'll like it here," he continued. "I really need to settle somewhere because it's no fun being new to the area and not having anyone to fellowship with. Shoot, I even attended that Baptist church down the road in Seymour, but, dang, those people are crazy! Way too rigid for my taste! Baptists are all stiff and puckered up all the time, like they've been eating sour grapes or something. Everything's a sin to them and we're all going to hell!"

Becca found herself grinning. Rex was right - Baptists could definitely be "stiff and puckered up" sometimes. But, she had been "saved" in that particular little Baptist church a few years ago and, even though she had grown away from the Baptist belief, that little church and their amazing pastor held some fond memories.

"I know what you mean," she said with a chuckle. "But, just so you'll know, we tend to be a little 'puckered' over our belief here at Beit Yisrael, too. You'll quickly come to realize that we're different, because we're actually not a 'church', *per se*; and...well, actually, we're not Christians, *per se*, either...."

The look on Rex's face was comical as her words sank in. Straightening to his full height, he peered down at her and frowned. "What do you mean you're not Christians?" he barked. "Your marquee says, 'Affirming the Jewish Messiah'. That makes you Christians."

"Well, yes, but while we do believe in Jesus, we are also Torah observant, which means we're *not* Christians *per se*. We are Torah observant Believers in Messiah Yeshua. We are a Messianic Jewish synagogue."

Rex shrank back. "Okay, darlin', two things," he said soberly. "First of all, to be honest with you – and don't ask me why, because I won't tell you - I personally have an aversion to anything Jewish, so I don't really want to hear about that aspect of it. And secondly, you're assuming I know what Torah is. I mean, to me that silly word was taken straight out of that old Jap movie, 'Tora, Tora, Tora!'"

Becca sighed as she shook her head. Every *Shabbat* there was at least one person who ended up challenging her about her faith, and this week, it was turning out to be R. B. "Rex" Lambert. Knowing from experience that the mere mention of Torah always incited verbal riots, she decided to keep it simple. "Just go to our website when you get home," she said. "The address is in the bulletin."

"Well, can't you just quickly outline it for me in a couple of sentences?"

6

Attempting to hide her frustration, she looked down to smooth her dress. "Torah consists of the first five Books of the Bible which contain all of God's Divine Instructions to His people. That's what's called Torah, and that is what we adhere to."

Rex's patronizing smile had totally faded. "Really?" he croaked. "So, you believe in that Old Testament stuff? Christ...I didn't realize that. I don't even know how the hell I'm supposed to respond to that!"

Something in his expression didn't feel right to Becca. She *knew* that look from somewhere, and it was more than a little upsetting.

"God Almighty, woman, you're talking about the *law*!"

Several people in the immediate vicinity turned to look in their direction, but Rex ignored them and kept his focus trained on Becca. Once again, his eyes were drilling into her soul; only this time instead of conveying interest in her feminine attributes, they were pregnant with contempt.

"Lady, wake up!" he went on. "We're under grace! *Nobody* has to work for their salvation anymore!"

Not wishing to cause a scene, Becca kept her tongue in check. She understood that, like most, he didn't know the first thing about Torah, and further discussion would be futile. He was just another "gawker" wandering in and out of various churches, trying to find a place that best catered to his personal theology.

Beit Yisrael had had more than its share of those types. At first they were always thrilled with the uniqueness of the services and the newness of the "Jewish music and liturgy";

only to ultimately decide - once they figured out that God has some rules to follow - that this "Jewish stuff" wasn't for them....

"Okay, I understand your frustration," Becca retorted. "But we are who we are. I'm sorry that you're disappointed, and I wish you well in your ongoing search."

Hoping this would be the end of Rex Lambert, she punctuated her words with a curt smile and then turned her attentions on a tall, gangling young lady who had just appeared in the doorway and was making her way into the sanctuary.

"Hey, Cassie," she said, purposely turning her back on Rex who was still showing no signs of leaving. "How's your week been?"

Cassie briefly waved as she breezed past. "Can't talk now," she said. "Need to see Rabbi Orlando before the service."

Becca's hopeful smile wilted as she watched the young woman scurrying down the middle aisle toward the head of the sanctuary. Cassie always seemed to have a crisis of some kind and Becca found herself wondering what it could be, this time.

"That must be Rabbi Orlando, huh?" Rex remarked as he watched the young lady receiving a fond embrace from a portly, mustachioed Hispanic man standing behind the podium. "He that chummy with everybody?"

"He's a very loving guy."

"So it would seem." Rex casually watched Cassie and Orlando for a few seconds longer, and then suddenly turned to gawk at Becca with a stare so intense it sent shivers down her spine. "Well, so what do you think, sweet cheeks?" he said. "Should I stay or go?"

"I was under the impression you were leaving."

A grin played at the edge of his mouth as he fiddled with his cowboy hat. "Feisty," he said, "I like that!"

"Hey, Becca!" a young teenaged girl called as she hurried past. "Have you seen my brother come in yet?"

"Not yet, hon, but I'll let him know you're looking for him when I do."

Rex quietly watched the girl join a circle of teens mingling nearby, and then turned back to Becca with a resolute gaze.

"Well, hell, Miss Becca," he proclaimed loudly, "since I'm here, I might as well stay and see what this Torah stuff you mentioned is all about." Gently elbowing her in the side, as if she were an old buddy, he added: "...And, anyway, if you and that sexy lady, Cassie, over there are any indication of the type of women I'll find in here, I'm gonna be one happy camper, right?"

"What I hope you'll find here, Rex," Becca replied dryly, "is God. Beit Yisrael isn't a dating service or a social club. We just want people to learn to get themselves right with God. That's *all* that matters."

Rex's expensive smile - although transparently disingenuous - was dazzling as he reached down to give her chin a demonstrative tweak. "I'm already right with God, little Miss Reba," he said with a wink. "Matter of fact, me and

Jesus are tight. We are the best of friends, don't you worry about that!"

Becca instantly recoiled. For just a split second, Rex's face seemed to morph into a hideous, twisted mask of evil, leering down at her with lust of such intensity that it caused her knees to buckle. It wasn't Rex she saw, but a ghostly figure inhabiting the space that was Rex's face. It was transparent, yet very real; its green, squinty eyes filled with a raw hatred too deep for the human mind to fathom. On its cheek was the faint outline of a Swastika.

You little Jewish bitch! a disembodied voice screamed in Becca's mind.

Her jaw dropped when she realized she *knew* that voice! That voice belonged to somebody she…. No! No, no, no! No, she decided, it was nobody she knew.

Yet, there was no mistaking that somehow, she had been transported to another point in time, to a place where terror reigned and fear held her hostage. *You're a dirty little Jew whore, just like your mother!*

Eyes wide with shock, she merely stood there and gawked. The sensation of Rex's fingers on her face had sent electric tremors into the pit of her stomach that literally took her breath away.

"Get off me!" she managed, backing away as if she had been burned. Her breath came in ragged gasps and she stood quaking, gaping up at Rex in confusion and disbelief.

Rex stared at her, his face reflecting confusion. "Whoops," he said, "did I do something wrong?"

Becca opened her mouth to speak, but nothing came out. Not knowing exactly what to do next, she cut her eyes toward her husband, who was busy doing something with the sound system near the stage toward the front of the sanctuary.

Hot tears slid down her face as she stood, wondering what had just happened, and wanting nothing more than to escape Rex's overwhelming presence.

Moments later, she found herself outside in the parking lot, gulping the brisk Fall air. To keep from being seen, she hurried toward the back of the building where she stood with her arms crossed, trembling, breathing, staring at nothing in particular in the multi-colored woods. Fall was her favorite time of year, and right now, the reds, oranges and browns and yellows were especially bright. Way too bright....

Random thoughts, impossible to bridle, crashed violently through her mind like stormy waters against a rocky shore. One question kept forcing its way into the forefront: *What just happened in there?*

Angrily swiping at the freely flowing tears, she realized she was just as surprised by her strange reaction as Rex seemed to have been. It was no secret that she was prone to unexpected bouts of rage sometimes. God knows Liam had been at the receiving end of some of her outbursts. But she had never, in her whole life, heard voices before....

Being physically touched in the face by this pushy stranger with demons dancing behind his eyes had totally unhinged her. Rex's seemingly innocent gesture had unleashed some-

11

thing evil and ugly and terrible; something completely unexpected, incomprehensible and utterly terrifying.

The sound of approaching footsteps caused her to turn around. Her face fell when she saw it was Rex.

He stopped a respectable distance from Becca, cowboy hat in hand, appearing quite contrite. There was no trace of arrogance in his countenance at all now.

"Becca," he said apologetically, "I'm sorry. I don't know what to say except, please forgive me for whatever I did wrong. I was trying to flirt and then you cut me off, and then you started that Torah stuff, and I got mad, and then I was trying to be funny.... I guess I messed up somehow, and I'm sorry. I don't know what else to say."

The two stared at each other for several long moments when Becca, still trembling, broke the silence. "Okay," she managed hollowly. Her mouth felt dry and uncooperative, and it was difficult to form words. "I...I'm sorry, too. I may have overreacted...."

Rex discharged a loud snort. "Ya think?" he replied. "That's an understatement, lady! All I did was touch your chin, and you acted like I had jumped your bones and raped you, or something!"

"You're a good girl, Rebecca! Such a pretty little thing! Come here and sit in my lap, Schatzi...."

Becca shrank back; she felt like screaming! Who or what was inside her head?

Fahrvergnügen!

"Stop it!" she cried, covering her ears as the word reverberated in her mind.

Rex balked. "Stop what?" he demanded. "Geez, what is your problem?"

"...Nothing...."

"Girl, you're spooky!"

Fighting back a new onslaught of tears, Becca simply stood there, glaring at the man who had single-handedly managed to ruin her entire morning.

"I'm sorry," she whispered. "My mind is...off today."

"Yeah, so it seems. Good grief, woman!" Waiting in vain for her to say something else, he muttered, "So, okay...can we start all over again and pretend this never happened?"

"Sure," she replied faintly. She just wanted him gone, out of her sight. The sooner, the better. "Just don't ever touch me again."

"Oh...you don't like being touched. Yeah, I kinda gathered that. So well, then...I guess I'll just head back inside and have some coffee and mingle."

He turned as if to leave, then hesitated and gazed back at her, a coy smile playing across his lips. "Uhm, just so I can be clear in my own mind," he began slowly. "You're so very married that I'll never have a chance with you, right?"

Becca produced a searing glance that left no room for misinterpretation.

"Gotcha. Okay. Just kidding," he said, backing leisurely away. "But I want you to know I'm real hurt, because women don't usually turn me down."

"Well, you've been turned down now, so deal with it! Just go away!"

"Whoah! I just *love* me a feisty woman!" she heard him say as he turned to leave.

Becca's legs were leaden as she painstakingly made her way toward the front of the building to resume her duties as greeter. Her strange encounter with Rex had left her completely drained and out of sorts, breathless and exhausted.

Hoping to be able to present a "normal" façade in light of what had just transpired, she returned a wave to a familiar young couple in the process of extracting their little girl from the back seat of their car.

"Hi guys," she cried with a voice that didn't sound like her own. "Enjoy the service today!"

Everything is fine, she told herself, knowing full well that it was a lie. Something…some sleeping *thing* had been awakened.

And she could tell – no; she knew beyond a shadow of a doubt! – that "thing" wasn't about to allow itself to be subdued!

Chapter 2

As "Fate would have it"....

Matthew **6:**33 *But first seek the Kingdom of Elohim and His righteousness and all these things will be added to you.* (AENT)

* * * *

"I don't think he's saved," Becca said with resolve as she clicked her seatbelt into place. Usually, she and Liam stayed after the service to help clean up. But today, she insisted they let someone else do it. She simply didn't have the energy.

She had not even been able to pay attention to Rabbi Orlando's teaching today. Her strange encounter with Rex had thoroughly drained her, totally shattering her concentration. She had gone through all the motions of singing along with the Worship Team, and lovingly touched the ancient Torah scroll as it was making its traditional trek through the congregation in the arms of one of the Elders. But she couldn't remember hearing the teaching at all. Her mind simply wasn't in it.

"What?" Liam asked. He, too, seemed preoccupied and deep in thought.

"I said, I don't think he's saved."

"Who?"

"The 'Duke,'" Becca replied. "Rex. The jerk who caused me all those problems this morning."

"Oh! Sorry. Yeah, that guy is just plain bizarre! Wish I could have been there for you, sweetie," Liam said as he backed the car out of its slot and pointed its nose toward the road. "I hate that someone managed to get you so upset."

Becca's throat filled with tears, and she quickly swallowed. "Upset?" she cried, trying to conceal the raw terror she felt in her gut. "Honey, I got totally weirded out! I actually heard voices in my mind when he touched me! Dark and evil voices….There was this one word I heard that practically had me jumping out of my skin."

"What word?"

"*Fahrvergnügen,*" she said hesitantly, adding a forced laugh to show that she recognized the absurdity.

"What?

"I…I know it sounds crazy! It's just something from my past that my father used to say, and it has a really bad connotation. I really don't want to talk about it."

Liam raised an eyebrow as he turned to give her a comical look. "I remember that term from the old Volkswagen commercials! It means 'driving enjoyment', or something like that, right?"

She shuddered. "Yes. Yeah…Liam, please, let's not talk about it, okay?"

Liam gave his wife a sympathetic smile, and reached over to gently place his hand on her knee. "Don't worry, babe," he said. "I understand. Everything will be all right. This Rex guy probably won't return, anyway. I mean, after you told me about him this morning, I watched him like a hawk and I could tell he wasn't interested in Orlando's teaching at all. He was just perched there like a bump on a log, scoping out the room the whole time. I don't know what he was looking for, but it definitely wasn't God. Anyway, I doubt that he'll be back, so just try to forget about him and chalk it all up as a bad day."

"Easier said than done," she mumbled. The woods outside the window on this stretch of Highway BB were a colorful blur as the scenery raced past. Becca loved this area. Some 40 miles east of Springfield, the region was basically Amish country, and it had a quiet ambiance that had served to soothe her frayed nerves when she found herself at wits end five years ago after her divorce from "Husband Number Four."

She had come to Seymour on a whim one Sunday morning with a girlfriend who was "church hopping"; and, on that particular day they had ended up at Webster County Baptist where the pastor happened to have that "just right" message. Something in Becca's mind had clicked and she suddenly understood who Jesus was.

After that, she became an avid "church-goer" who couldn't get enough of Scripture. She read her way through the entire Bible in just a few months, and studied everything she could get hands on, vowing to live her life according to God's will, from then on.

Once those "scales" had been lifted from her eyes, Becca realized how badly she had messed up the first 40 years of her life by doing things according to "the world" and how she had been constantly "looking for love in all the wrong places"; she wasn't about to live the second 40 years on that same merry-go-round!

Unfortunately, she had lost all her friends over her newly found faith. And even to some of her new friends – Christians – she seemed to come across as "holier-than-thou" because, unlike most, she dove headlong into her spirituality, and truly *lived* her life for God. It hadn't taken long to realize that most people didn't give themselves to God completely. They chose to keep one foot in the carnal and the other in the spiritual, constantly trying to reconcile the two.

It also didn't take long for her to fall in love with Pastor Wesley Price and his wife and their congregation, and she immediately became a member. Eventually tiring of traveling the distance from Springfield to Seymour every Sunday morning, she decided to quit her job as an ad executive at a local television station, and took a position as a journalist/ad designer at the Webster County Crier. Although it was a huge step down in pay, she didn't mind, because she had never been happy with the stress-filled environment at the TV station, anyway; and somehow, this new and unusual lifestyle change "felt right."

There was no doubt in her mind that she had made the right decision. The slow pace in Seymour had presented her with many things, including the perfect opportunity to "deflate" from her tempestuous past, which included a string of bad relationships, all of which had left her broken-hearted and wondering if there wasn't "something wrong" with her.

For reasons she couldn't fathom (although she had her suspicions that it had something to do with her pervert of a father) she had always been attracted to the macho, abusive type. And after dumping her last husband, Larry, an alcoholic with a violent temper and a roving eye for other women - and the occasional man - she had decided she was done dating...and she was not about to ever get married again! She had finally found the key to filling that "little hole in her soul" and she was perfectly fine with idea of becoming "an old maid."

Once she "got saved," the bottom line was, her heart belonged to Jesus, and for her, there was no turning back. Webster County Baptist in that tiny "hick town" of Seymour, Missouri, it seemed, was the perfect oasis to rest her weary soul.

"I'm a little bummed, myself, today," Liam remarked, jerking Becca out of her reverie. "I'm happy Orlando chose me to be an Elder, but I've got the distinct feeling that he thinks I'm his personal slave."

"Oh-oh," she said. "What does he want now?"

"Well, today he asked me to record all his teachings every week. I'm now expected to record, edit and post them on the website. *And* he wants them on there by Saturday evening, if possible. Every week he finds something new for me to do."

"Oh great," she cried, throwing up her hands in disgust. "There goes our whole weekend!"

Liam shrugged, his face reflecting anguish. For a brief moment Becca was ashamed of herself for not noticing her husband's plight before. She had been, as was often the case, too wrapped up in her own emotions.

"Honey, I'm so sorry," she said. "I don't understand why he's doing this. He's leaning on you for everything! I love our synagogue, but my goodness...."

"Well, he does it because he knows I can and will get things accomplished. I just wish he would stop piling things on. It's getting ridiculous! Not to mention, his teachings aren't *that* great...."

"Yeah, plus we're just a tiny synagogue, not some mega-church. Why would anybody outside the congregation care about his teachings?"

"I don't know, sweetie. I guess I need to bring that to his attention one of these days." Emitting a great, shaky sigh, Liam beheld his wife and presented her with an anemic smile.

"All I know," he went on, "is that weekends are becoming a real chore. I can't get to anything else anymore except synagogue stuff. I've been hoping to get some projects outside the house – such as getting rid of that silly humped bridge in our driveway, but I just can't find the time. Between my job and the synagogue, my entire life consists of nothing but work."

Becca frowned. "It kinda defeats the purpose of the Sabbath, huh?" she said. "Perhaps you need to learn to say 'no!' I mean, come on - there are three other Elders. Why can't they pick up some of the slack?"

"Well, honey, Leroy is ninety-five years old and can't do much of anything at all, you know that. He's just a figure-head. And the other two...well, they're too busy with their own lives."

"Oh baloney, Liam! Arnold is a retired computer programmer who doesn't do a thing except invite people over to his house for get-togethers! He could certainly volunteer to do some of the Wednesday evening Bible studies, or something. Or, why can't he record and post Orlando's teachings? He knows how to do that stuff."

"Well, his wife is sick a lot."

"So? Julie is sick because she's a heavy smoker who refuses to give up her precious cigarettes! Why should that be your problem? And what about Fred...he's doing nothing these days. He's been sitting around moping at home since he was laid off from his job last June."

"Well, he's feeling all depressed. And it doesn't help that Annie is forever lording her 'I'm the bread winner in this family' stuff over him."

"Oh, stop making excuses!"

"Well, look, Fred doesn't know much about computers, and certainly not editing media files, so he's kind of useless in that department."

Liam peered over at Becca and shrugged. "Well, surely can you see why Orlando hits me up for everything?"

"Yeah. Because you're gullible!"

"And you aren't? He uses you just as much as he uses me."

"That's not true!.... Well, okay, maybe a little," she added with a chuckle. "I can't bring myself to turn him down whenever he approaches me with that irresistible smile and hang-dog look that says, 'Becca, I really need your help and you're the only person I trust'."

"Uh-huh. And there's our dilemma! We're both too willing to help out, and he knows it. But, anyway, I promise, at the next Elders' meeting, I will open my mouth and let them know that I simply have too much on my plate now, and that it's time for some of the others to help out."

"Good...because I'm tired of sharing you with Orlando! You're married to me, not him!"

Liam gazed at his wife with an impish smile. "I've been meaning to talk to you about that," he said. "I thought maybe we could ask Orlando and Lora to move in with us. That way, he could have access to me every night when I get home from work, and you could have Lora to talk to when you get lonely."

"Yeah, great idea!" she replied, grinning. "I'm all for it. As a matter of fact, I think we should ask the Elders and their wives to move in, as well. That way, they could all sit around and chat and sip coffee while they watch you jump through Orlando's hoops."

"Sounds like a plan."

"And maybe you should quit your job, so you can be available to him twenty-four, seven."

Liam tossed back his head in laughter. "I'll submit my resignation on Monday!" he said.

Becca's face beamed as she gazed her husband. She loved the sound of his voice, and everything else about him. Liam was truly God's gift to her, after a lifetime of endless ups and downs. Liam, with his sweet, easy-going personality and understanding nature, had helped to center Becca, whose high-strung and impetuous nature occasionally caused her to become upset over the smallest, most benign issues.

A smile played across her lips as she remembered the sunny Saturday afternoon in late March nearly three years ago when they met at Wilson's Creek Battlefield Park on the outskirts of Springfield.

Liam, an Air Force colonel in Springfield for a weekend meeting, was out jogging on that day; and Becca - for no other reason than to do something different on that particular weekend - had been out walking her Miniature Schnauzer along the myriad paths and hiking trails snaking their way through the park. It had been an unusually grueling week at work at the Crier and she was desperate to get away.

As "fate would have it," her life was to change drastically that Saturday...in the vicinity of a cannon that served as a marker for the position of the Pulaski Light Battery during a Civil War battle. Ironically, she and Liam would probably have never spoken, had it not been for Becca's "fur person" whose sniffing of the grass around the cannon was interrupted by the sound of someone's feet crunching on the gravel.

Becca winced when she saw the dog's ears perk, because it meant someone was coming and she would have to put him back on his leash. But, before she had a chance to do that, he charged, barking frantically at a jogger who had appeared on the trail. She watched the man freeze in his tracks momentarily, before tentatively reaching down to pet the little gray and white bundle of jumping joy. Seconds later, he was seated in the grass, scratching the dog's ears and receiving some slobbery kisses.

"I'm so sorry!" Becca called out as she hurried over. "Don't worry, he won't hurt you."

"Yeah, I can tell he's real tough and ferocious," the man replied, laughing. "How do you manage to handle a beast like this all by yourself?"

"I'm safe as long as I do what he tells me! His every wish is my command."

"What's his name?"

"Spike."

The man's eyes widened. "Spike?" he said, grinning. "You named a Miniature Schnauzer Spike?"

"Yeah, well, it came to me one evening as I was sitting home alone sharing a bottle of wine with me, myself and I."

The man's laugh echoed through the woods as he began to roust himself. "Been there and done that, and got the T-shirt and the matching hat!"

"Oh, really? Well, you must have the same friends I do!"

"Sounds like it." The man stared at Becca for several moments, clearly searching for something else to say. Kinda hot out here today, isn't it?" he finally offered.

"Yeah...for March."

An awkward silence ensued as the two strangers admired each other. Becca liked his unassuming presence. There was nothing presumptuous or arrogant about him. Dark-haired, slightly balding and handsome, he had a kind face that exuded extreme intelligence, and beautiful light blue eyes that could only be described as "genuinely sweet."

"Do you have a dog?" she asked, for lack of anything else to say.

He shook his head. "I rent an apartment in Kansas City near Whiteman Air Force Base. No pets allowed."

"Oh. So, you're not married?" The words had simply slipped out and she felt a blush creeping along her neck. Normally, she wasn't this forward, but she wanted to keep the momentum going.

The man nodded, and moments later, they were exchanging "horror stories" about their former spouses, and discussing their respective careers and even talking about their favorite "Oldies" songs.

Fifteen minutes passed before the conversation began to wind down. "Well, now we know everything about each other except for our names!" Becca said with a girlish giggle. "I'm Becca Day. And you are?"

"Liam Ritter," he said, happily shaking the hand she held out in greeting.

"Oh, that's German! Cool! My...my...father is German."

Liam put his hand up to his mouth, and employing a stage whisper, he confessed, "Rumor has it my ancestors may have been German Jews, through my father's side.

Although Dad didn't care about his ancestry and was not even religious, Judaism has always held a fascination for me. As a matter of fact, I graduated from a *yeshiva* before I joined the Air Force. I once had aspirations of becoming a Rabbi."

Becca's eyes lit up. "You're a Rabbi?" she asked, unable to hide the joy in her voice.

"Technically, yes. I believe Judaism is the most on-the-mark religion in the world. But, I always felt there was something missing, somehow – same thing with Christianity - and that's why I decided against leading a congregation."

Becca positively beamed as she scrutinized her new friend. "Oh Liam," she cried joyfully, "I can tell you *exactly* what you were missing!"

Seven months later, they were married at Beit Yisrael, with Orlando officiating the ceremony under a "chuppah" - a cloth canopy, a Jewish *tallit* - held aloft on poles attached to its four corners. It was a beautiful little ceremony with most members of the small congregation present to witness the union.

Liam's grown son, Jason - an instructor at the Defense Information School at Fort Benjamin Harrison, served as "best man" and Becca had asked the Rabbi's wife, Lora, to be her Matron of Honor. Lora, owner of the 'Everything You Need and More" store at a Springfield Mall, had graciously provided all the flower arrangements and decorations.

By that time, Liam had retired from the Air Force and taken a job as chief of Information Technology Security for the Springfield City government, and together he and Becca bought a beautiful little "Southwest ranch-style" house on 20 acres, nestled in a hilly, wooded area ten miles southwest of Seymour. Life was good!

The only thing she didn't like about the house was the weird little Oriental, humped camel-backed bridge which served as the entrance to the long driveway that snaked toward their home. It simply clashed with the Southwest style of the house; not to mention, it looked silly and out of place, hunched over the narrow creek that ran alongside the highway.

Liam's cellphone jarred Becca back to present day.

"Hi Mom," he said loudly, flipping on the speaker so Becca could join in.

"Where have you been?" the old woman demanded.

"At synagogue," Liam replied. "You know we go to synagogue on Saturdays."

"Oh, yeah, that's right. Ever since you married that Jewish woman...."

"I've got the speaker on, Mom. Becca's here, too." Liam gave his wife a sideways glance as he rolled his eyes.

Becca simply smiled and nodded. She knew Liam's mother didn't like her, mainly because of her "strange belief." Neither did Liam's older sister, Donna, who became cold and distant the day Becca asked her to stop the endless forwarding of dirty jokes via email.

"Hi, Nola!" Becca shouted. "How are you doing? How are things in Boone these days?"

"I'm fine. Just wantin' to touch bases with Liam today. There's nothing much goin' on here. Iowa is Iowa. Weather's fine. Gettin' cold. Donna's here visiting me right now."

"Hi, guys!" Donna's voice crackled in the background. Obviously, Liam's mother had her speakerphone on, as well.

"Hey, sis," Liam said. "What are you doing at Mom's? Have you and Darrel decided that West Virginia needed a break from you two?"

There was a slight and awkward silence, then: "I left Darrel. We're getting divorced."

"Aw, sis, I'm so sorry to hear that. What happened?"

"I don't want to talk about it. It doesn't matter. Anyway, I'm spending a couple months here with Mom until I get my head straightened out. I guess I'll leave after Christmas and then go back home. Darrel should be all moved out of the house by then."

"Is there anything we can do?" Liam asked. Casting a glance at Becca, he silently mouthed, "That's divorce Number Six!"

"Nope. Not a thing."

"I have an idea!" Becca chimed in. "Since I've never met either of you yet, how about Liam and me coming to Boone for Christmas so we can all finally meet and really get to know each other?"

"I thought you don't do Christmas," Liam's mother cut in.

"Well, that's beside the point," Becca replied. "We can still come and visit. It will be fun, and maybe it will cheer up Donna."

"No, don't make a special trip just for me," Donna said.

"It wouldn't be any trouble at all. Liam and I are due for a vacation, anyway, and so we might as well...."

"I don't think you get it, Becca!" Donna screeched. "I don't want you to come! You guys are still basically newly-weds pawing at each other, and here I am, going through another divorce. I don't need to be around that."

Becca and Liam exchanged stunned glances. "Donna," Liam said, "We're middle-aged. We don't go around pawing each other."

"I don't care! I'm going through a divorce, dammit! I can't stand to see you happy right now!"

"What?"

"...You know what I mean. You guys are blissfully happy and lovey-dovey, and I don't need to be around.... Well, I just need to be alone with Mom right now. I don't need people trying to cheer me up or pumping me for information."

Hurt and disappointment were etched deeply on Liam's face. He looked as if he had just been slapped. Not knowing what else to do, Becca reached over to pat his knee in hopes of providing some comfort.

She was painfully aware how much he wanted to be loved by his emotionally absent mother, and how much he longed for any sort of affirmation or approval from his older sister. But that never happened. Neither his mother nor his sister bothered to do much more than to keep in touch by phone, always leaving no doubt that their call was simply a matter of obligation. They hadn't even made the effort to attend the wedding two years ago, each citing their own respective lame excuse.

Unfortunately, Nola and Donna were the only family Liam had, since his father had died of colon cancer many years before. But they might as well be dead, too, since neither one of them ever bothered to reach out to Liam or even acknowledge his existence.

Regardless, Donna's callous comment had cut to the quick, and Becca found she could not allow her to get away with it.

"Well, Donna," she snapped, "I guess that's that, then. I'm sorry I even mentioned it. Liam and I certainly don't want to intrude on your pity party. And we *sure* don't want you to see us happy!"

Whatever Donna's response might have been, Becca didn't hear it; she was no longer listening. The pain reflected in Liam's face was breaking her heart, and she wished she could reach through the phone to tear Donna's hair out.

Nola and Donna both were experts at manipulating a conversation toward the negative, and this time Donna had gone overboard. This was the "last straw" and Becca decided she was done trying to fit into Liam's little family. For her, the conversation was over, perhaps permanently.

The incident at the synagogue this morning had taken its toll, and she simply had no more fight left in her. To keep

Liam from seeing the rage in her face, she tossed her angry gaze out the window and brooded, leaving him to deal with his dysfunctional family.

"Well, Donna," she heard Liam say over the mad hammering in her temples, "once again, you've made your hatred of me crystal clear. Point taken. Goodbye."

Chapter 3

"Mommy, are you dead?"

---

1 Peter 5:8 Be sober and guarded because Satan, like a lion, roars and goes about and seeks whom he may devour. (AENT)

* * * *

Ow, my head! Where am I? It's dark and it stinks....My eyes are open, but I can't see! Aching all over. Hard to breathe....Hurts to swallow; throat feels raw and swollen.

I hear car horns blaring! People talking and laughing; ordering food?...I'm not at home; where am I?

Oh! A light from above. Someone opened a door! A door above me? How can that be? Ow, my eyes! A silhouette. I'm trying to talk, but my throat hurts so badly! Ow! Oh, my head, my head. WHERE AM I?

Someone is lying here beside me. Mommy? Mother? You're all blue...and cold. You're so cold! Mommy, are you dead?

Becca awoke with a start on Monday morning. Sweat beading on her brow, she sat up and gasped for air. The dream had been so real. It was as if she had really been there, in that dank, dark, smelly place!

"Mommy," she whispered, wiping a tear from her cheek. "Oh, Mommy...."

33

As consciousness fully set in, she realized Liam was already in the kitchen, brewing coffee.

"What's the matter, sweetie?" Liam asked, as she entered, bare feet padding on the cold, hardwood floor.

"I had another nightmare," she said, sinking into his arms. "Just a stupid dream."

"Wow! You're trembling so hard, honey! "What did you dream about?"

"I don't remember exactly. I was in some dark, nasty place, hurting all over."

"Here," he said, handing her a cup of hot, steaming coffee. "This will make it all better."

Becca set her cup down on the counter and stretched. She had a slight headache, which wasn't unusual, as she had suffered headaches all her life. Rubbing the back of her neck with her hand, she gazed upward at the high, vaulted ceiling of her beautiful Southwestern-style home, briefly admiring the open design of their house.

It was a "Pueblo" style house, with the kitchen residing at its center, various exits spilling out all around into the dining room, living room and fireplace room, and one hallway that led toward the bedrooms at the back of the house. She had fallen in love with the house from the moment she laid eyes on it. Life was good! Finally....

Minutes later, she and Liam were perched on the living room sofa, watching the morning television news. It was the usual - strange weather patterns around the world causing horrendous devastation, another school shooting, violence and decadence being forced on the world as "normal".... It was, as Liam liked to label it: "The Books of Daniel and Revelation unfolding before our very eyes!"

"So, what's on your agenda today, sweetie?" he asked as he poured their second cup of coffee.

"Today, I get to cover the yearly Mennonite Fall Festival and Benefit Auction over at the Mennonite church. It'll be an all-day event."

Liam rolled his eyes and grinned. "Hmm, sounds real exciting! Wish I could go with you."

"Lying's a sin, honey," she said with a throaty laugh. "You wouldn't last until lunch with all that 'old time fun' - the sack races, the egg rolls, and hay rides and the games that don't involve one single computer or new-fangled contraption!"

Chapter 4

The serpent rears its head

Ephesians 6:12 For we do not wrestle against flesh and blood, but against the rulers, against the authorities, against the cosmic powers over this present darkness, against the spiritual forces of evil in the heavenly places. (ESV)

* * * *

The next few days, filled with too much work for Becca, virtually became a blur. By the time Wednesday evening rolled around, both she and Liam were exhausted from their respective jobs. Liam was growing tired of the long commute to Springfield every day, and Becca was simply worn out from the endless interviewing and writing and newspaper folding and preparing the bundles for their weekly mailing.

Plus, this week, she had been playing "receptionist" and doing all the ad design by herself, as two of her co-workers were out with the flu. And now her boss was talking about the possibility of producing a quarterly magazine, as well, and he wanted Becca to spearhead the entire project.

When she and Liam entered the synagogue for the mid-week Bible study, they found quite a crowd. Usually, the Wednesday evening classes were sparse, with only a handful of people attending. But tonight, there must have been close to fifteen or twenty people.

"Wow," Becca said, snickering. "We're turning into a virtual mega-church. Somebody must have told them you're not teaching tonight."

"Oh, very funny!" Liam replied with a grin. "But I'm too tired to care. All I know is, tonight I get to just sit back and relax and let Orlando do the talking."

Moments later, they were seated next to Elder Fred and his wife Annie who was, as usual, peering over her glasses like some stern old school teacher, fiddling with her gray, waist-length hair. Fred, a balding wisp of a man, stood to briefly hug Liam and Becca before retreating back into the invisible shell he had built around himself since being laid off work as a mechanic.

He was undoubtedly ashamed of the fact that he and his wife were forced to subside on her meager income as head cook and waitress at a small diner in Seymour.

"So, what's new with you guys?" Annie asked.

"Working way too hard," Becca replied. "It's been a crazy week. And you?"

"Well, Fred is still looking for work. I guess I'm doomed to remain as the only bread-winner in our house."

"Oh, hon," Becca said, patting Annie's hand. "It won't be forever. Just keep the faith and keep praying."

A few minutes later they were joined by Elder Arnold and his wife Julie. Becca silently prayed that Julie wouldn't sit too close because she always reeked of cigarette smoke; but, to her dismay, Arnold and Julie sat directly in front of her and Liam. There would be no escaping the stench tonight.

For some reason, both of them looked older and more haggard than usual. The lines in Julie's pale face were exaggerated by the harsh neon lights suspended from the high, wooden crossbeams and Becca found herself wishing she had the intestinal fortitude to confront Julie about that nasty smoking habit of hers.

"Good Lord, are you okay?" Annie asked Julie in her no-nonsense, direct style. "You're lookin' a little down in the mouth today."

Without turning around, Julie replied, "I've got lung cancer. It's terminal."

Becca's hand flew to her mouth as she and Liam exchanged glances. Not knowing what else to do, she reached over to touch Julie's shoulder. Although she had never admitted it to anyone else except Liam, she had known that this would be Julie's fate. Julie was a non-stop smoker who knew about the dangers of smoking but insisted she couldn't quit. From what Becca could tell, Julie had never even bothered to try. Still, it was a shock to hear the news.

"I'm fine," Julie snapped. "Don't baby me; just leave me alone."

Arnold, half turning to face his friends, gave them an apologetic look and simply nodded to show his appreciation for their support.

"You know we'll pray for you guys this evening," Liam said. "And we'll have the whole synagogue praying over you this coming *Shabbat*."

"Orlando will be talking about it this evening, instead of doing a regular teaching," Arnold replied somberly. "We told him as soon as we got the news this morning."

All eyes were drawn to the front when Orlando tapped on the microphone. As always, he was a huge presence in every respect. A very tall and rotund man who kept his bushy mustache well-trimmed and his long, dark hair tied back in a ponytail, he literally seemed to fill the front of the sanctuary; not only with his physical being, but with his bubbly personality and unabashed spirituality. Although he originally hailed from Juarez, Mexico, there was hardly a trace of an accent when he spoke.

Standing beside him was his wife, Lora, a handsome, full-figured woman with perfectly coiffed, highlighted, short hair. Tonight, she was wearing an expensive tweed and leather pantsuit that unmistakably came from one of the more expensive shops in Springfield. Usually, on Wednesday evenings Lora sat in the audience, but apparently things were going to be different this evening.

Annie leaned over and whispered in Becca's ear. "Isn't she kinda overdressed for a Wednesday night? The rest of us are in jeans, for crying out loud."

"She must be rolling the in dough and wanting us to know it," Becca replied. "These days, she's a got a new outfit on almost every time I see her."

"Hmmm. Must be nice."

"Shalom mishpocah," Orlando said, his voice rich and low. Becca always loved the sound of his voice and she imagined that that is what God Himself sounded like. "Hope you all had a great week so far!"

In response, there were several scattered "amens" and one little boy whining, "My sister hit me on the playground yesterday!"

"Well, I hope you didn't hit her back," Orlando replied. "Did you forgive her, like God would want you to?"

"No," the little boy replied with a giggle. "I threw poop at her!"

Once the laughter settled down, Orlando pulled his *tallit* over his head and said a little opening prayer, first in Hebrew, then in English. When he looked up, his eyes were bright with tears.

"Folks," he said, "we won't be talking about this week's Torah portion tonight. Instead, I want us to gather around Arnold and Julie Dean, because they received some terrible news this week.... And the news is that Julie has terminal lung cancer."

Several scattered gasps could be heard as all eyes turned toward Julie who sat silent and broken. No one said a word.

"So, here's what's going to happen," Orlando went on. "I want Arnold and Julie to come up and sit in the chairs I've placed up here in the front, and when I turn the lights down, I want you all to come up and pray for them and love on them for awhile."

Minutes later, after everyone had had a chance to hug the couple, they gathered around in a circle to hold hands and participate in silent prayers. Every once in a while, someone would pray out loud. Several cried openly, placing their hands on Julie as she wept.

Occasionally, they could hear the repetitive mantra of the congregation's "odd fella" - the coverall-sporting Harry Malone, chanting his annoying "Humminah, humminah, humminah" (his idea of "tongues" - which he always delivered in rapid, monosyllabic fashion). Harry also believed God had told him to stop bathing for two years, and after a month of this, his stench was becoming a major problem.

Finally, Orlando's deep voice filled the air, putting an end to Harry's incessant chanting. "Heavenly Father, I thank You so much for this day," he began. "Thank You for blessing us with it and in it another opportunity to serve You. Thank You for being the light in this dark world. We thank You for the enormous blessings that You bestow upon us. Thank You for sending Sister Julie into our lives. Father, she needs you now and we humbly come before You to ask that you comfort her. She is a good woman who doesn't deserve this horrible disease. And we pray this in the Mighty Name of Yeshua *haMashiach*, Jesus Christ. Amen."

"May I ask a question?" a strong, resonant voice bellowed. The man's words, emanating from deep within his diaphragm, reverberated in the sanctuary.

Becca's heart skipped a beat and she instinctively drew nearer to her husband. She and Liam were standing with their backs to the door, but she knew even before she turned around to whom the voice belonged.

Fahrvergnügen!

"Yes, Rex?" Orlando said as all eyes turned toward the man sitting alone in the row nearest the entrance of the synagogue. "Welcome, brother! I didn't realize you had joined us tonight."

"Yeah, I came in while you all were standing around praying, and it took me awhile to figure out what you were doing. For those who don't know me, I'm the new guy. Last Saturday was my first time here.... I'm really sorry to hear about your illness, Julie."

"And what do you have to ask us, my friend?" Orlando said softly.

Rex remained seated with one arm slung casually over the back of the pew, while smoothing his mustache with his other hand. "Well," he said, "As much as I hate to bring it up, I'm just wondering who y'all are praying to. I hear you praying in the Name of Jesus – whom you just referred to by another name; but I understand from listening to your sermon last Saturday - and what that sweet little Becca lady pointed out to me - that you also believe you should adhere to the Mosaic Law. Seems to me, you can't do both."

Becca leaned over to whisper in Liam's ear. "Oh God," she said, squeezing his hand. "Here we go again."

"Well," Orlando said, "we are a Messianic Jewish congregation, and we call our Savior by His given, Hebrew name."

"Well, yeah, whatever. Just wondering, does that mean you're all Jews or that you all have converted to Judaism, or what?"

"Some of us have Jewish blood, but nobody here was raised as a Jew. Most of us are Gentiles grafted in through the Blood of the Lamb."

"I see. But you all believe you need to work for your salvation."

Orlando's face reflected a mixture of confusion and irritation. "No," he said, making no effort to hide his annoyance. "Nobody here works for their salvation."

"Well, then why do you believe you need to keep the Law?"

"It's not the 'law' we keep," Orlando replied. "It's Torah, God's instructions to us for righteousness; our blueprint for moral, holy living. And we don't *have* to keep Torah; we *get* to keep it!"

"That's not true," Liam whispered in Becca's ear. "I've discussed this with Orlando before! From what the Bible tells us, we *have* to keep God's Divine Instructions. We can't pick and choose at will!"

"Well," she said in hushed tones, "as you know, he's got his own ideas and is stuck on his own interpretations."

Rex sat quietly for some moments, seemingly contemplating Orlando's words. "You *get* to keep it. Hmmm, interesting," he said. "So, why don't you go out back and kill a goat for Julie and pray that its blood would please God enough to want to heal her? That's what they used to do in the olden days, right?"

Liam released Becca's hand and made his way through the small crowd.

44

"Rex," he said, with all the patience he could muster as he walked down the aisle, "tonight is really not the time to talk about this. Perhaps you could pose your concerns at one of our Elders' meetings? We'd be happy to answer all your questions there."

Rex nodded as he slowly rose. "Oh sure. Yes, of course you're right," he said. "I'll do that." Pulling his lips into a tight, sheepish grin, he made his way past Liam and stopped in front of Julie who was still seated in her chair next to the podium.

"Ma'am," he said gently, taking her limp hand in his and kissing it, "I cannot tell you how sorry I am that you have cancer, and I will pray for you at home tonight."

Julie lifted her tear-stained face and peered up at Rex through the curtain of white hair that had fallen over her eyes.

"You just stay strong," he admonished. "Look to Jesus for your salvation. Don't worry about this silly Torah junk right now." Straightening to his full height, he turned to leave, then stopped abruptly and turned to face her once more.

"I am always stunned to see these things happening to good people," he said. "I just don't understand why God would allow a beautiful lady like yourself to end up with such an awful disease. Makes you kind of wonder whether there really is a God, doesn't it? My god, even little kids get cancer and whatnot. How fair is that? I can't help it; I just wonder sometimes."

Becca, shuddering with rage, felt like screaming! No longer able to remain silent, she took a few steps forward and glared up at him. "What are you doing, Rex?" she cried. "We live in a fallen world, for heaven's sake! Stuff happens. Babies are born deaf, diseased or crippled and are dying of starvation all over the world. Do you really believe God is *doing* this to them?"

Rex's gaze was calm and steady. "Could be," he replied with a carefree shrug. "I don't really know, and neither do you. The Bible tells us He controls everything. That being the case, I'm guessing He *gave* Julie cancer."

"Stop being a jerk, Rex! He didn't *give* Julie cancer! She ended up with cancer because she smokes!" Becca cringed as she heard the words slip from her mouth. She hadn't meant to say them; they had simply skidded out. Hoping to redeem herself, she quickly added: "Julie has cancer because she…because she lives in this fallen world!"

"Jerk?" Rex said with a grin. "Whoah! Really? You're a feisty little thing, aren't you? Not very godly of you to resort to name calling…but, regardless, I stand by what I said. If He really cared about His people, He wouldn't allow them to suffer. It's almost like He doesn't care."

Trying to stay her rising fury, Becca balled her hands into fists and took a deep breath. "I don't believe this," she said angrily. "On one hand, you spout off Jesus; and on the other, you're making silly allegations. You make no sense, whatsoever!"

"Well, I'm just calling it like I see it."

"Well, perhaps you need to do some more Bible study so you can see things differently! From what I can tell, you know just enough about the Bible to be dangerous!"

Rex's nostrils flared as he observed Becca. "Dangerous?" he said. "Little lady, you really need to work on your anger issues. You're not a very nice person, sometimes."

You little Jewish bitch! How dare you talk back me?

Becca flinched at the voice in her head. "And you need to learn some basic social skills!" she said, feeling as though she sounded strangely weak and small and insignificant.

"I need to learn some social skills? You're the one standing there, yelling!"

Suddenly she felt Liam's arms encircling her from behind. "Babe, just let it be," he whispered in her ear. He knew his wife well enough to recognize that she was nearing her "point of no return."

Just then, Orlando, a tense smile pasted on his face, stepped in between them to halt the sparring. He was nearly as tall as Rex but twice as wide; and he was not easily intimidated.

"Brother Rex," he said in a soothing baritone, "perhaps it would be better if you went ahead and left us alone right now. Emotions are high and this isn't helping our sister, Julie."

Silence reigned as the two men momentarily stared at each other. Rex's face reflected a blend of anger and indignation as he fought to get his temper under control. Then, quite suddenly, his shoulders relaxed and he flashed his pearly whites at Orlando.

"Sure," he said. "I'll be off now. Didn't mean to cause a ruckus here. I still feel it's a shame that God would allow

Julie to get cancer. She seems like a really nice lady. It makes no sense at all, does it? Y'all have a good night now."

As he headed toward the door, he remarked without turning around: "And God Almighty, Rabbi Orlando, I wish you'd tell that guy in the coveralls to take a shower. He's stinking up the whole place!"

His words remained hanging in the air like dead autumn leaves blowing on a breeze. Arnold broke the awful silence when he rose to help a sobbing Julie to her feet. "Thank you all for praying for us," he said. I think we'll just go on home now so my sweet bride can rest."

Julie, who had hardly said a word since she entered the synagogue, suddenly cried out in anguished tones. "I don't know why God allowed me to have cancer, either!" she yelled. "Like Rex said, it's not fair! It's just not fair! I'm a good person!"

"Hon, come on," Arnold coaxed as he ushered her toward the door. "Don't do this to yourself."

The heaviness was almost unbearable as others followed suit and began to leave. No one said a word. Just as Liam and Becca prepared to head out, Orlando approached and clapped Liam on the shoulder.

"Brother Liam," he said, failing at his attempt to sound enthusiastic. "Have you thought about my request to record and post my teachings?"

Liam pressed his lips together and shook his head. "To be honest with you, Orlando, I haven't had much of a chance. I've been super busy at work."

48

"I understand. I really would like my teachings to start going up as soon as possible, though."

There was no mistaking the authority in Orlando's voice. This was not a request; it was an outright command.

"Actually," Liam replied hesitantly, "I was wanting to talk to you about that because...well, I'm not sure I can even fit it *into* my schedule. What you're asking entails a whole lot of work."

Orlando's face fell and his voice, when he spoke, reflected disappointment. "Well, okay. I understand. I was just hoping I could depend on you."

"Well, of course, you can depend on me! But you need to remember, I also have a job to go to and a boss to please. All this additional work for the synagogue is starting to eat up my weekends!"

"Well sure, I realize that, brother, but...."

"No 'buts', Orlando!" Becca cut in sharply. "Liam does *everything* around here!"

Orlando winced. "Yes, he does a lot," he replied. "It's just that Liam built my website and you guys have everything at your disposal at home." Brow furrowed, he cast a pleading glance at Liam. "You know I appreciate you both so much, and I was hoping you would want to help build up our synagogue as much as I do. But, I'll understand if you can't find the time."

Recognizing that Orlando was clearly playing his manipulation games again, Becca cast a quick glance in her husband's direction and bit her lip. She knew her husband was a "servant" type who would do anything for anybody. But she could tell that Orlando was pushing him just a little too far. Liam had his limits, and he was about to reach them. And so was she.

"I'll do my best," Liam replied with a heavy sigh. "But truly, Orlando...this has got to stop. You're starting to wear me out."

Orlando's eyes lit up and he clasped Liam's hand in gratitude. "I knew you would see it my way!" he cried. "I can always rely on you, my dear, dear brother. Your work will not go unrewarded."

"Honey, we should go," Becca said irritably as she tugged on Liam's arm.

"Oh, just a minute!" Orlando cried. "Before you go, Liam, I was wondering...well, I was thinking perhaps you could also figure out a way to put a 'pay per view' thingy on my videos?"

Liam's eyes widened in disbelief as his gaze shot first to Becca, then back toward the Rabbi. "You want people to pay for your teachings now?" he asked, incredulously.

"Well, just those on the Internet who don't have a church home."

All eyes turned toward a noise coming from the restroom area. "It's just me!" Lora said jauntily as she glided over to join them. "I heard your question, Liam, and my response is, why not? Everybody's doing it. It will generate some more income for...for, you know, for the synagogue. People aren't tithing very much these days, and it's hard to make ends meet. It's a good thing my store is doing well, because the meager income from the tithes in this place just isn't cutting it anymore. As you know," she added as if the words left a bad taste in her mouth, "My husband's income relies solely on tithes."

Becca held her tongue as she quietly eyed Lora's expensive pantsuit. Obviously, this "pay per view thingy" had been Lora's bright idea. It didn't seem to matter that it was yet more work added onto the mountain of work Orlando had already piled on Liam!

"Hmm," Liam said testily. "I suppose you want us to collect the money for you and cut you a check every week?"

"Well, yeah," Lora replied. "However that works; weekly, bi-monthly. I don't know, and it doesn't matter. Whatever is easiest for you."

Liam rolled his eyes and shook his head. "Okay," he snapped crossly, "that's really quite enough now! I know my spiritual gift is service to others; but this is getting ridiculous!"

"But, brother…."

"No…no, please, Orlando. Don't say anything else. Just let us go home now."

Before anyone had a chance to say another word, Liam took Becca by the arm and ushered her out the door.

Chapter 5

"Give us a break!"

James 1:31 Let all bitterness and anger, and wrath, and clamoring and reviling, be taken from you along with all malice: 32. And be affectionate towards one another and sympathetic; and forgive one another as Elohim by the Mashiyach (Messiah) has forgiven us. (AENT)

* * *

Becca's cellphone rang as she was walking to her car after interviewing an Amish bishop who had been charged with animal abuse - for literally beating his dead horse, which had collapsed in the summer heat at the side of the highway several months earlier.

Her caller ID revealed it was Orlando. She scowled as she slid into the driver's seat, because the Rabbi was the last person on earth she wanted to talk to right now. Last night's conversation had left her on edge, and she was in no mood to discuss anything going on at Beit Yisrael.

"Becca," Orlando began, his attitude humble and apologetic, "I just tried to call Liam, but got voice mail. Thank God I managed to get through to you, at least! I just wanted to tell you guys that I'm really sorry about last night. You know I have no one else to turn to besides you and Liam. You're my best friends!"

"I don't want to hear it!" Becca shouted angrily. "Liam and I have had quite enough with this nonsense, and it needs to stop! We love Beit Yisrael, but our good natures are being abused now. It seems you've found in us a couple of suckers who are at your every beckon call! It's bad enough that you've been using us to death, but now your wife is thinking up things for us, too? I'm sorry, but Liam and I find that very upsetting!"

"I know, I know, and I promise there will be an end to it. It's just that, right now, there are some things I would like to get accomplished...."

"Well, you're going to have to figure out a way to accomplish them without us, Orlando, because we're about ready to walk out of your life!"

"Wait! No, Becca! Sister...hear me out. You and Liam are a godsend! I truly believe God sent you to Beit Yisrael for a reason! You're both such hard workers and dedicated servants and I don't know what I would do without you. I *can't* do it without you!"

Becca gritted her teeth and slammed the car door shut a little harder than intended. "Perhaps it's time someone spelled it out for you," she said after some moments. "You don't seem to understand exactly how much Liam and I do! We have built and maintained your website. We also create weekly newspaper ads for you - and, as part of our tithe - we've even been paying for those ads."

"I know all that...."

"Liam has been doing most of your Wednesday evening teachings and takes over for you whenever you're not there on *Shabbat*. He handles the sound system and creates the visuals...he does everything, Orlando! And now you want your teachings posted on the website, along with a 'pay per view thingy' account that you want us to monitor! How much more do you expect of us?"

"Becca...."

"I'm sorry, but I'm just really angry with you! We have no life anymore because of you!"

"I know, Becca, I know, and I promise to back off. I've got some major plans for Beit Yisrael, but I'm dealing with some personal issues, so please hang in just a little while longer."

"Well," she said with an undertone of sarcasm, "your 'major plans' are ruining our life! We're *volunteers*, Orlando; not paid workers!"

"Okay, okay, I know. I am sorry, okay?"

"Well, you should be!"

Silence hummed on the line; and Becca feared that Orlando was about to hang up on her. She loved him, but it was time he learned that friendships require boundaries. He was going to learn to respect those boundaries, or risk losing their friendship. After some moments, she heard him emit a great sigh of frustration.

"Sister Becca," he said, sounding very tired. "I don't wish to argue with you, okay? I hear what you're saying, but I'm at a breaking point, too. I get enough flack and harassment from my wife on a daily basis, and I don't need you adding to it! So, please back off, okay? This is not why I called you today."

Becca shifted uncomfortably in her seat. Her suspicions, it seemed, were true; there was trouble in Orlando's paradise. Lora wasn't the easiest person to get along with, and if the tithes were indeed waning, then chances were, they were only adding to his stress, because Lora was extremely high maintenance.

"Well, I'm sorry," she said. "Didn't mean to upset you. But surely you can understand my frustration. You are a bottomless pit of demands! Beit Yisrael has become a fulltime job for us and it needs to stop!"

"Okay, *fine*! I understand!" Orlando snapped. "So, are you going to post my teachings on the site, or not? If you really don't want to do it, I'll figure out some other way. I certainly don't want to be guilty of abusing anyone."

Fighting another wave of resentment, Becca closed her eyes and rested her head against the back of the seat. She did not want to fight with Orlando, and she did not want to lose his friendship. She just wanted the endless requests to cease so she and Liam could start resuming a normal lifestyle. Subtle hints had not worked.

"Well," she said, her voice quaking, "you know we will do as you ask. But please, after this, give us a break, okay? We're tired and we're overdue for a vacation. At least get someone else to do the Wednesday evening teachings, or something. And perhaps someone else can handle the sound system on *Shabbat*. Gosh, the Sabbath is meant for rest, not for wearing ourselves out!"

Orlando's voice was filled with relief when he spoke again; and he sounded as if a tremendous weight had been lifted from his shoulders.

"Well, okay," he said. "That settles that. Thank you, sister. And, oh! The reason I was trying to call Liam was to tell him that Arnold called this morning to inform me that he and Julie were quitting Beit Yisrael. Julie is apparently having problems with her belief in God now, and she wants nothing to do with Him or us right now."

Becca shook her head as Rex came to mind. Her eyes narrowed at the thought of the "Duke" and the problems he had caused in the congregation within just a few days' time.

"That truly saddens me!" she said slowly. "It reveals that Julie didn't know God or His Word, in the first place…wow! I guess she's just been going through the motions all her life."

"Well, we don't know that…."

"Those who have the Holy Spirit inside love Him, no matter what, Orlando. They don't blame Him for their ills or drop Him like a hot potato when things go wrong."

"Well, we're all on different parts of His Path."

"Boy…that Rex!" she went on irritably. "He led Julie down this road. He's brand new and already causing trouble! I hope he gets tired of us soon and decides to go somewhere else!"

"Rex? No…I doubt this was his doing. But I agree, I wish he hadn't said those things."

"Of course, it's Rex's fault, Orlando! You heard what he said to Julie last night. Oh, wow…I knew he was trouble the moment he walked in the door!"

She briefly thought about sharing last Saturday's "vision" incident that occurred when Rex touched her chin, but abruptly forced the thought from her mind. Orlando evidently had his own problems, and he didn't need to be bogged down with hers.

"No, I wouldn't say he's trouble," he retorted. "I think he's just lost. He just needs to become familiarized with Torah, that's all."

Becca started to respond, then thought better of it. She remembered Lora telling her once, that Orlando had no discernment when it came to people because he was able to see only the good in everyone.

"Anyway," Orlando continued, "I wanted to tell Liam about Arnold and Julie, and to ask him what he thinks of the idea of adding Brother Chad as an Elder. I spoke with Chad a while ago and he said he would be happy to handle the sound system every other week, at least, and do some of the Wednesday evening teachings."

Becca grimaced. "Chad Kretschmar has three little kids," she exclaimed. "Are you sure he won't have tons of excuses to get out of doing those things? I'm just saying that, because every Elder at Beit Yisrael seems to have tons of excuses, and I can already see which one Chad will use...."

"No, no. Chad is truly a good guy. He's very reliable. He assured me nothing would get in the way of his duties."

"Well, okay. I hope so, for your sake and ours," she mumbled.

Becca felt exhausted and headachy when she hung up. Her entire life, lately, seemed to consist of nothing but stress, and she wanted more than anything to just go home and lie down.

Unfortunately, her boss had asked her to run over to Webster County Baptist to take a few pictures at their bake sale and maybe get a few quotes from Pastor Wesley Price.

Chapter 6

"I don't miss Christmas"

***James 1:**22 But be doers of the Word, and not hearers only; and do not deceive yourselves.* (AENT)

* * *

Although the day had started out sunny and cool, it quickly turned dreary, overcast and cloudy. By the time Becca arrived at Webster County Baptist, the rain was coming down in sheets. Pasting on her best passable smile, she entered the beautiful new church building.

The booths had been set up inside, and her nostrils were instantly assaulted with delectable aromas. Even though Christmas was well over a month away, holiday music mingled with the excited voices of children who were running from booth to booth to partake of the free cake and cookie samples.

Several people turned to wave at Becca as she passed. Some gave her a hug and told her they had been missing her since she left the congregation.

She found Pastor Wes in the sanctuary, baby-sitting his wife's booth. His bespectacled face lit up when he saw her and moments later, he came out from behind the table to gather her in his arms to give her a loving, fatherly hug.

"Hey, kiddo," he said, "how's my favorite little girl doing?"

"Oh, I'm hanging in there, Wes. How are you guys? From the looks of things around here, I'm guessing you're doing great!"

"We are; yes, we are! Webster County Baptist seems to be getting popular these days. We've got around three hundred members right now, many of them coming up from Springfield."

"Wow! Congratulations! I'm so happy to see you guys growing!" They both laughed when she added: "Better watch it, or you'll end up being some decadent mega-church!"

The small talk continued as Becca shot a few random photos of Wes and his booth and some nearby tables. Afterwards, she took at seat near him and simply relaxed in his presence. She dearly loved this man who had led her to the Lord and helped her to begin her new life as a believer. When she first came to his church, she had never read the Bible and had no clue how to begin navigating her way through it. Wes, seeing he had had a "babe in Christ" immediately took her under his wing and introduced her to the various workbooks designed to show her who God was, what He expected of His people, and how to live a holy life, according to His will.

Unfortunately, the more she studied, the more questions she encountered - most of them having to do with God's original commands and ordinances that the church was definitely *not* keeping. Her endless questions to Wes had included some basic, common-sense inquiries: Since we are all "one in Christ," why don't Baptists keep the commanded Seventh

Day Sabbath, which, on today's calendar, falls on Saturday? Who decided to change the day to Sunday? Where did Jesus ever say His death would serve to abolish the Seventh Day Sabbath or His seven Festivals, all of which seem to point to Christ? Why do Christians celebrate Christmas and Easter - neither of which can be found in the Bible - while ignoring His Festivals, which are *commanded* in the Old Testament where we actually see the "thus saith the Lord" scriptures, and which is the *foundation* of our faith?

Why, she had asked him one day, are Baptists allowed to eat pork and shellfish, when God clearly stated in Leviticus that they were "unclean"? From what she could tell, the "unclean" things were the world's "garbage disposals." Jesus was our final *sin* sacrifice; His death didn't serve to change His Father's food laws! And since we have the Holy Spirit residing within, aren't we kind of forcing God to "eat unclean" things with us whenever we dine on pork and shellfish? He never said He came to change His Father's Divine Rules! He said He came to proclaim the Kingdom and do everything His Father commanded....

Becca's every question received one of two answers: Either, "That was just for the Jews," or, "Let's take a look at what the Apostle Paul said." It got to the point where Becca felt Paul was Wes's god, because for him the writings of Paul took precedence over what Jesus taught and what the Father had commanded. Wes stopped answering her questions when, one day, she pointed out that Paul had written something profound in Romans 3:31 - something that nagged her day and night and caused her to believe that Christianity had somehow misunderstood his writings. Paul had posed the question: "Do we then nullify the Law (Torah) through faith? May it never be! On the contrary, *we establish the Law!*"

"So, which is it, Wes?" she remembered asking on that fateful day. "Is the law nullified or established?"

She had never forgotten the look in Wes's eyes as he spat, "For God's sake, Becca, get over it, will you? Jesus nailed the Law to the cross! The sooner you realize that, the sooner you'll become a good Baptist!" - to which she had responded: "I don't want to be a 'good Baptist'; I want to be a good follower of what Jesus taught and what His Father commanded!"

Wes's voice jerked her back into the present. "So," he was saying, "how does it feel to be an old married lady?"

Becca's pixie face brightened. "Oh, Wes, I never knew marriage could be like this!" she cried. "Liam is just awesome! I'm so happy! He's kind and loving and supportive...and totally understanding of my strange moods. He's truly a gift from God!"

"Well, he seems like a great guy, and you're a really cute couple. It was a beautiful little wedding. I wish you had let me marry you guys, instead of that Rabbi. But, oh well...I got over it. Anyway, you should bring Liam to listen to my sermons some Sunday. He might like us!"

"I'm sure he would. The thing is, our Rabbi keeps us so busy that our weekends are usually filled with work. He's got some big plans for Beit Yisrael, and he's using us to help him accomplish them."

Wes frowned and the lines in his face creased, reflecting grave concern. Becca knew how he felt about the Messianic faith, and she silently prayed that he would refrain from challenging her right now. God only knew how tired she was of defending herself at every turn. Everywhere she went, there was someone who felt the need to challenge and harass, and to tell her she was in a cult – all because she wanted to obey God instead of man and man's myriad theologies.

When she first broke the news to Wes about leaving his church for a Messianic congregation, he did everything in his power to change her mind. In the end, when it became clear she was not going to budge - and for the sake of their friendship - he backed off and "agreed to disagree and leave it at that."

She was relieved when he promptly changed the subject and asked about the membership at Beit Yisrael.

"It changes from week to week," she replied, "but, including the usual 'one-time' visitors, we usually end up with anywhere from fifty to seventy people for each service."

"Wow, that's pretty good for a Messianic synagogue!" Wes said. "I didn't realize so many folks around here would be interested in that stuff."

Cringing over his choice of words, she managed to preserve her smile. "Well," she said, "like in your case, many come from Springfield. People like to hear Orlando teach. He's really good.... Not as good as you, of course," she added with a grin, "but pretty good!"

"Yes, Orlando seems to be a very a nice guy; and he can't be all bad, since was a former Baptist preacher! I just don't understand what possessed him to cross over to Messianic

Judaism! But, oh well, maybe I'll show up one of these days to hear him teach. If nothing else, at least I'll get to see you again."

"No, I don't think you'd like it, Wes. You would last all of five minutes before coming unglued and yelling, 'You're under the law!'"

Wes grinned as he dropped his gaze toward the floor. "So, kiddo," he said, "do you miss Christmas? We've got a nice Christmas program coming up."

A shudder ran along Becca's spine, but she managed a weak smile and shook her head. "No! No, I don't miss it at all, Wes! I've never liked Christmas. I think I told you that before. In my childhood home Christmas consisted of endless fights and arguments spawned during my father's drunken rages. He endlessly taunted my Jewish mother with the 'this is Christ's birthday' stuff, until it came out of our ears."

You Jewish bitch! You should have burned in the ovens!

"Ah, yes, we did talk about that, once. Sorry, I forgot."

"Ironically," Becca went on, "Mother was an atheist; a very secular Jew who couldn't care less about God or the Bible. Father-dearest was basically an atheist, too, but he loved to throw her Jewishness into her face.... So, no, Wes, I don't miss Christmas!"

You have no clue how much I hate you and your little Jewish brat bastards!

Rex came to mind as she spoke, and she quickly closed her eyes in hopes of dousing his image.

Fahrvergnügen!

"Wes," Becca said as she tried in vain to suppress the anger that the Christmas memories had evoked. "Just the mere mention of Christmas drives me up the wall, and I have to say, I'm feeling a little peeved right now. I really wish you hadn't brought it up!"

"Okay, well, I'm sorry. I forgot...."

They both sat silently for some moments, each lost in their own thoughts as they stared off into the milling crowd. Finally, Becca said - knowing full well that her comments would only serve to annoy her former pastor: "What upsets me most about Christmas, Wes, is that it's *not* Christ's birthday! And Santa Claus is one of the first lies we tell our children...."

Pastor Wes gave her a sideways glance. "Yeah, yeah," he snapped irritably, "I know, I know! I've heard it all before, Becca, and I'm not going there again. That Messianic stuff has clearly done a number on you, and for you, there's no turning back. I get all that. But I'll never pretend to be happy about it. I feel like I failed you somehow."

Becca, doing her best to keep a strange array of emotions in check, reached over to touch his hand. "I love you, Wes," she said tenderly. "You haven't failed me at all. You did your job by leading me to the Lord. But you know I don't belong here at First Baptist anymore. God grew me away from man-made faith. I'm sorry, but that's how I feel about Christianity."

"Well," he replied, emitting a long and shaky breath, "as I told you before, I think God calls His Jews back to Torah;

that's what I think happened to you, Becca. You can't help yourself."

"Wes," she said, gazing at her beloved former pastor. "Think about the comment you just made! If Torah is so bad, as you keep insisting, then why would God call the Jews back to it? Why would He have two different sets of rules – one for His natural and one for His adopted children?"

"Okay, Becca, let's just drop it. You know we can't talk about these things without getting upset with each other!"

"In the Book of Numbers He makes it clear that *all* who accept Him are to do exactly as His people do! Aren't Christians His people, too? Or does God only expect the Jews to be holy?"

To indicate that he didn't wish to hear anymore, Wes made a comical show of putting his hands over his ears. "Can't hear you!" he said loudly. "Not interested."

Becca suddenly found herself angry, but decided to keep her comments to herself. Nothing she could say would cause Wes to understand the truths God had led her to see.

"It was truly nice to see you again, Becca," Wes said, rising to indicate his desire to end the visit.

"Wes – come on! Please don't be mad at me, okay? I want us to remain friends."

"Well," he replied, keeping his gaze lowered, "I'm not going to tell you I'm not disappointed. You were my prize pupil! I have never in my life seen anyone like you; I've never seen anyone grow as fast as you did! I could literally *see* the change in you as you studied and grew! And yeah, I'm not ashamed to admit I really hated to see you end up in this Messianic belief. I think you've made a huge mistake!"

"I'm sorry I disappointed you," Becca said, as she gathered her camera and notebook and tucked them under her arm. "But Wes, you need to know, I didn't do this lightly. I begged God to show me what it was that I was missing in church, and He showed me *very* vividly...and I knew the first time I ever set foot in Beit Yisrael and heard Orlando speak, that this was where I would find the answers to all my questions. And I did."

Linking arms with Becca, Wes slowly walked her toward the door. "I've been meaning to ask you," he said, "how the heck did you end up there, anyway? I've always wondered that because I know nobody from Webster County Baptist ever mentioned or suggested that place!"

Becca hesitated, as she knew he wouldn't like her answer. "Remember that Sunday I came into your office and told you I had just had a vision of Webster County Baptist burning down, and you laughed at me? Well, I was right, wasn't I? I knew it was a vision and that it would come true. I've had visions since I was a child. But you wouldn't believe me. And then last year your church burned to the ground due to some electrical problem and now you're in a brand new building."

Wes gave a reluctant nod. "Oh, I think that was just a coincidence, hon. Your supposed vision had nothing to do with it. The visions and prophecies stopped a long time ago with the prophets of old and the Apostles."

"Well, whatever it was, it's how I ended up at Beit Yisrael. I had a vision while on my knees praying one day. I had been begging God for months to show me what it was that I felt was missing in church, and suddenly, clear as a bell, I saw a little white building on a knoll just off the highway, with a small marquee that said 'Beit Yisrael'. I looked it up on the 'net, and soon found myself walking through their front door. And I've been there ever since!"

Wes remained guarded as he opened his arms for a hug. "I think you're crazy, kiddo," he said. "But I'll always love you. And if you ever change your mind about all this Torah nonsense, you know you'll always have a home back here at Webster County Baptist."

"Thanks," she said with a smile. "And thank you for allowing me to take pictures of your bake sale and your beautiful new church. They will appear in the next edition of the Crier."

"It was great seeing you again. You and Liam come join us some Sunday!"

Becca's eyes were brimming with tears as she headed toward the parking lot. She knew she would be eternally grateful to Wes for his part in God's grand plan for her.

But she also knew with every fiber of her being, no matter how many attacks or hardships came her way, that she could never go back to the typical Christian belief. There was no doubt in her mind that God had her exactly where He wanted her to be!

Chapter 7

Friday afternoon "hen session"

Proverbs 11:3 *The integrity of the upright guides them, but the crookedness of the treacherous destroys them.* (ESV)

* * * *

"Oh, that man is just too much!" Lora cried, laughing so hard that tears had begun to form little pink rivulets in the expensive, thick rouge on her cheeks. "Rex was standing there in the doorway, flirting with...you? Oh, Becca, I'm going to start calling you 'Reba'! That's just too funny! Reba and the Duke!"

Becca grinned, lovingly eyeing each of her friends in the informal ladies' get-together, which was by now jokingly dubbed, "The Friday Afternoon Hen Session." The group, meeting at a popular bookstore featuring a small Starbucks Coffee restaurant in Springfield, had been created approximately a year ago, and originally consisted of her and Lora, Annie, Julie and Cassie. Julie hadn't joined this week's get-together for obvious reasons, and in their opening prayer, the ladies remembered to ask God for mercy and *shalom* for poor Julie and her cancer problem.

"Well, Lora," Becca said, "it was an experience I'll never forget - especially that weird vision he caused me to have. I don't think you or Annie were there yet, or I would have called someone over to help me out." Grinning at Cassie, she said, "I was hoping when you came in that I could somehow get your attention, but you were in a hurry to talk to Orlando and kind of left me hanging."

Cassie, adjusting her rectangular, gold-rimmed glasses, bequeathed Becca with an inquisitive glance. Her lips were tightly pressed together as she put down her coffee cup. "What do you mean I 'left you hanging'?" she lamented. "How was I supposed to know you were in trouble?"

"Oh, I'm just kidding!" Becca replied, mentally kicking herself for forgetting that Cassie didn't have much of a sense of humor. An unmarried virgin at the age of 35, Cassie was an odd and not very bright person who tended to become offended easily, and to amplify the most innocent of comments or situations.

"Well, I had to see Orlando about a private matter," Cassie said. "I have a new boyfriend...and, well, I didn't just want to take him to synagogue without Orlando's approval."

"Oooh, another new boyfriend!" Lora said, eyes sparkling. "Inquiring minds want to know the details! Fork 'em over!"

"Why would you need Orlando's approval?" Becca asked. In her mind's eye she couldn't imagine a "normal" man being attracted to poor Cassie, and it was actually kind of sad to see her struggling so hard to find a mate. In the past, she had brought all kinds of unsavory characters to synagogue, announcing they were engaged to be married after just a few days or weeks of dating. The men were always rejects of society, homeless or struggling somehow because the world was supposedly "against them, keeping them from their dreams," and Cassie was trying to save them all.

"Well, okay, I'll tell you," Cassie conceded. "But don't judge me, okay?"

"Just tell us and get it over with," Annie said in her lackluster, no-nonsense style. "So, you've got another new boyfriend. Why are you making it sound so mysterious?"

"Well, because he...he's got a past."

A hushed silence fell over the little group as they all stared at Cassie, waiting for her to continue.

"He just got out of prison and I wanted to ask Orlando if I could bring him to synagogue."

"Prison?" Annie half shouted. "What did he do, kill somebody?"

"No! He was wrongly accused of something."

"Of what?" Annie demanded. "Geez, spit it out already!"

"He...he was accused of...of messing with a child."

"Messing?" Lora asked. "You mean he's a pedophile?"

"No. He said he was *accused* of it."

"Well, he was obviously more than just accused if he landed in prison!"

Cassie's face turned crimson. "Well, I believe him," she retorted. "He assures me he's innocent, and that's that. Someone lied and an innocent man went to prison for it!"

"How old was the child he supposedly messed with?" Annie wanted to know.

"...Two."

Becca felt as though the air had been knocked out of her lungs. "Two?" she cried, gawking, slack-jawed, at the poor, deluded young woman who was so desperate for love that she was willing to give the benefit of the doubt to someone who was convicted of child molestation. "A two year old lied about someone sexually abusing her?"

"No, her parents lied about it!"

"So, how was he convicted, then?"

"Supposed DNA evidence."

"Yeah, okay, *supposed* DNA evidence...." Becca said, unable to disguise her frustration. "Maybe you're willing to believe his story, Cassie, but I don't! That guy is *not* coming to our synagogue! Not as long as I'm a member there." In her peripheral vision she noticed the surprised looks on the faces of her friends.

"You can't say that, Becca," Cassie whimpered, her eyes welling with tears. "You're not God, you're not the Rabbi and you're not the final authority!"

"There are children in our congregation, Cassie! Someone like that can never be trusted around little children again. Ever! People like that don't just stop."

Come here, Becca, sweetheart! Fahrvergnügen time!

Becca winced. Heart stuttering in her chest, she clasped her trembling hands in her lap and swallowed the curdled spit at the back of her throat. It was all she could do to control the rage that simmered hotly in her gut.

"Wow, Becca!" Annie said. "You okay, kiddo?"

Her nod was almost imperceptible. "Cassie, I'm really sorry," she said when realized that all eyes were on her. She absentmindedly reached up to rub her temples in hopes of warding off the threatening headache. "I really don't think it's fair of you to ask our congregation to accept someone who was convicted of raping a two year old. What I'm trying to say is, I know that if you were to bring him to synagogue, I personally would always sit there wondering whether he's fantasizing about one of our little ones."

"He doesn't do that, Becca!" Cassie countered angrily. "He's a Christian now and he's changed! Who died and made you his judge?"

"I'm not judging! I just know from…from experience that a leopard doesn't change its spots. Pedophiles can't be trusted. End of story."

Cassie's lower lip trembled as she glared at Becca. "You don't know that! You don't know Rowdy!"

"His name is Rowdy?" Annie asked incredulously. A grin started to form, but she quickly repressed it.

"So, Cassie," Lora interjected, "just out of curiosity, what did Orlando tell you?"

Deliberately cutting her eyes toward Becca, and with an obvious air of contempt, Cassie related that Orlando said he would bring it up at the next Elders' Meeting so they could make a joint decision.

"That means it won't be up to you, *Becca!*" she said defiantly. "You seem to have some real hang-ups, lady. Perhaps it's time to see a shrink?" Without bothering to wait for a reply, she rose and stomped off in a huff before anyone had a chance to protest.

Lora took a hold of Becca's hand to stop her from going after Cassie. "Let her go," she said calmly. "There's nothing you can say right now to make her feel better. I agree with you; we don't need a convicted pedophile in our congregation. Unfortunately, Orlando will probably allow him in. He's such a wimp...."

"But, I'm so sorry I snapped at her," Becca replied. "I...I shouldn't have been so vicious towards her. I can be such a schmuck at times!"

"I totally agree," Annie said, snickering. "You went above and beyond the call and got just little too judgmental, in my humble little opinion. After all, we don't know the guy! He's apparently paid his dues, and if he truly has turned to Christ, who are we to deny him entrance into our congregation? Maybe we would be exactly what he needs to help him keep his focus."

Becca swallowed hard. Annie was, of course, right; but truly - anyone who could rape a small child was evil and nothing less than immediate castration could fix that. The mere thought of a convicted pedophile being around the precious kids at Beit Yisrael drove her to the point of insanity. There was no way she would ever be able to deal rationally with Rowdy if he were to join the congregation....

"You're right," she managed, once she found her voice. "I pray the guy has changed; and Scripture tells us we are to forgive those who have repented and turned to God. But in the meantime, Annie, can we be certain that he really has changed and is doing things according to the Bible? Do you really want him hanging around your little grandkids? Do you mean to tell me that, if he were to sneak upstairs during the service – even though there is always an adult with the kids - you wouldn't be compelled to follow him to make sure he's not getting too close to your little grand-daughter?"

Annie raised an eyebrow. "Well, yeah," she conceded. "I would definitely be keeping a watchful eye on him."

"My point exactly!" Becca had more to say but, instead, she dropped her gaze. "I have to apologize to you all," she mumbled. "I should have kept my mouth shut. I'm just so sorry about Cassie....I could just kick myself!"

"Oh, don't worry about it," Lora chirped gaily. "Just forget about her and leave her alone to pout. She's weird and she doesn't add anything to our group, anyway." With an impish grin, she added: "So, let's just get back to bashing Rex, shall we?"

Becca gawked at her friend, disappointment written on her face. "That wasn't very nice, Lora," she mumbled. "And we weren't bashing Rex."

"Well, I'm sorry, but I just like to tell it like it is, okay?" Lora commented with a throaty laugh. "Gosh, Becca, lighten up, will you? And for your information, I'm not saying we are going to bash Rex; I'm just suggesting we simply share our thoughts about him! Boy, you're such a prim and proper little thing. Snap out of it, will ya?"

Her hand traveled up to her neck to adjust a pricey, long string of pearls that had fallen off to one side. Her long, acrylic fingernails had been painted a pearl color to match her necklace, with a tiny diamond pasted in the middle of the nails on both of her index fingers. The forest green, baggy sweater she wore today was designed to discreetly cover her midriff bulge.

"Actually, as bizarre as this is going to sound," Lora went on, "I have to say, I think Rex is excruciatingly handsome and sexy. He's got a gorgeous face and a body to match – oh my gosh! And a smile that just makes your heart flutter!"

To illustrate her feelings, she batted her eyes and made a fanning motion with her hand. "Oh, those gorgeous blue eyes with that pitch black hair. Oh man, they are just to *die* for! He reminds me of some Indian god or something."

Becca made a face. "Oh, get a grip!" she said. "You're a married woman! And, honestly - after what I told you, and after the Julie incident, you are still able to think of his physical assets? He's a horrible person! You saw, first-hand, what he was capable of!"

"Well, sure," Lora retorted. "But just because he's a little strange and has a crappy character doesn't mean he's not hot. Come on, Becca, admit it! Doesn't he look like some Indian chief, or like some hunk in a fairy tale? He's got that dark and brooding, regal thing going on. Sorry, but I find that to be a real turn-on!"

Scrutinizing her friend with total disbelief, Becca shook her head. "So how does Orlando feel about Rex?" she said, in hopes of steering the conversation in another direction.

Lora's response was a startled, questioning gaze. With a dismissive wave of her hand she replied, "Who cares what Orlando thinks? He's a spineless toad. He's got absolutely no discernment when it comes to people. I can tell you right now, he's not going to do anything about Rowdy, or Rex. My God, he hasn't even done anything about that stinky 'God told me not to bathe for two years' nut job, Harry Malone! People have left Beit Yisrael because of him, for crying out loud! Mark my words, Becca – and get used to the idea – all three of those guys will be in the congregation until the Rapture comes, because Orlando doesn't have the intestinal fortitude to open his mouth!"

Becca exchanged silent glances with Annie who apparently hadn't appreciated Lora's crass comments, either. How could anyone speak like that about their husband, especially a godly man like Orlando? It was true that Orlando was lacking in leadership and management qualities, but he was a nice guy who loved God.

"Orlando's not a spineless toad!" she muttered. "Gosh, Lora, how can you say something like that?"

The sound coming from Lora's throat resembled an old dog's bark. "Oh good lord," she said, "here we go again, Miss Holier-than-Thou! Believe whatever you want, okay? I know my husband! He's a weakling and a coward who does whatever it takes to avoid confrontation. He's just not much of a man, and that's why he ends up spending most nights in the guest room."

Biting her bottom lip to keep from responding, Becca again exchanged a furtive glance with Annie. The conversation had taken a wrong turn somewhere and it was making her uncomfortable.

"Okay, I saw that look!" Lora exclaimed loud enough to draw the attention of the folks at a neighboring table. "That's the second time in the last minute, and I don't appreciate it! I thought you were my friends and I could tell you anything. But, I guess not, so I'll just quit while I'm ahead."

Glowering, she snatched up her coffee cup and took a long, hard swig. "I'm going to the restroom," she snapped after some moments. "Feel free to gossip about me behind my back!"

Becca and Annie quietly watched Lora disappear into the rows of books until she was completely out of sight. Neither said a word as they pondered the events of the last few minutes.

It was Annie who finally broke the silence. Acting as though she had been poked in the backside, she suddenly ceased fiddling with her long, gray hair and straightened, and leaned forward to place her elbows on the table. "You're quite an anomaly, you know that?" she said.

"Me?"

"Yeah, you. I've been sitting here thinking about you and how you react to certain things. You come across like some little tough broad, but yet, you're excruciatingly delicate and sensitive. You're witty and can be really funny at times, yet there's something profoundly sad in your eyes. It's hard to figure you out because you're so...I don't know, secretive, I guess is the right word."

"Sad and secretive?"

"Yes! You were quite obviously sad just a little while ago when you mentioned something about that 'vision' Rex brought out in you. Although you tried to cover your feelings, I could tell that the whole ordeal really tore you up! There's something in you that you're trying very hard to hide, even from yourself. Between the Rex thing and your reaction to Cassie's new boyfriend, I can tell you've definitely got some issues. I think Cassie hit the nail on the head when she said you have hang-ups."

Becca forced a grin and shrugged. "No, no hang-ups," she said. "Issues, yes; hang-ups, no. I know exactly why the subject of pedophilia makes me angry. But I'm not sure why Rex affects me the way he does. That's the true anomaly! There's just something about him that triggers me, Annie. I don't know. He kind of reminds me of my father, for some reason...which is weird, because he looks nothing like him! But he's got certain behaviors I find absolutely repulsive."

"Oh? You don't like your father?"

"No! No, I don't...."

Come here, Becca. Daddy wants you....

Annie waited patiently for some moments, and then began making a drumming sound on the table with her fingers when it became evident that Becca wasn't going to elaborate.

"Well, I don't know what else to say," Becca explained, shrugging. "And I don't really want to talk about him."

Emitting a dramatic sigh, Annie tilted her head to the side and stared at her friend. "Girl," she said, "getting any information out of you sometimes is like pulling teeth. But, I totally get it. What you're trying to say without actually saying it is that Daddy-dearest was a pedophile."

Lora, who had just returned from the restroom and was about to nestle into her seat, tossed a questioning gaze at Annie. "Whose Daddy are we talking about?" she demanded.

Annie raised her chin, sat back in her chair and folded her arms across her flat bosom. "Becca's father. It became clear to me by the way she reacted when Cassie told us about Rowdy. She turned every shade of purple there is!"

"Becca's Daddy is a pedophile?" Lora quipped with raised eyebrow.

Blushing, Becca dropped her gaze and took another sip of her tea. "Okay, yes, my father was a pedophile," she admitted. Her hands shook slightly, and she quickly lowered the cup and smiled at the women in hopes of assuring them that she was psychologically intact. "And yes, he sexually abused me – actually he abused me *and* my little brother. That is why I freak out over sexual issues that involve kids. Y'all happy now?"

"You have a brother?" Lora asked, posing the question as if it were an accusation. "You've never mentioned a brother before!"

"Yeah. His name is Ray and he is.... Well, he's not in my life right now. And I'm sorry if I've been coming across as secretive about my past, but the thing is, I truly can't remember much about my parents. I can hardly remember what they looked like because I don't have pictures. They were all burned up in a house fire when Ray and I were kids. My mother died when I was fourteen, and my Dad disappeared right after the fire, and left us to be raised by my mother's parents. There's nothing to relate about my family, and I don't know whatever happened to my father. Perhaps the big, bad, blond Arian god went back to Germany; I just don't know, and I don't care. And that's why you never hear me talking about my childhood."

Lora's eyes bugged. "Your father was German?" she said. "Oh, my gosh! How cool! More details, girlfriend! More! More!"

Becca sighed. "Okay, look," she said, "the only reason I'm going to share this with you is so you'll be better able to understand why I became unhinged over Rowdy. After this, I would appreciate it if you don't ever bring up my family again...."

Unsure as to where to start, she quickly provided some sketchy details of how a stubborn and arrogant German soldier named Klaus-Dieter Behringer, married her gorgeous, American Jewish mother, Rachel.

"Mother told us she met Dad when she was stationed in Northern Germany with the Women's Army Corps, back in the early Fifties," Becca related. "She was a translator and some kind of a communications specialist, and he was a soldier in the German Army. Dad said he was only too happy to leave Germany because he was fed up with the government, and that's how he came to end up living with Mom in Ash Grove, Missouri."

Lora, always thirsty for gossip of any flavor, was absolutely hypnotized by Becca's story. "That is so awesome!" she warbled. "Maybe you should try finding him on Google or something! I mean, who knows? Maybe he's on the Internet somewhere and you guys could be reunited. I could help you look!"

"No!" Becca yelled, her eyes flashing. "What do I have to do to make it clear that I don't *want* that sick pervert in my life! He abused all of us for years, and then deserted us kids altogether! That was a *good* thing because all the sexual abuse ended when he left. I'm thrilled that he left! I don't want to find him!"

You wouldn't be here if your Jewish slut of a mother had burned in some oven!

"Wait!" Annie cut in. "Okay, so let me get this straight. If your parents married back in the early Fifties, that means you must not have come along until much, much later."

Somewhere in the back of her mind, Becca realized she had been sitting there, nervously shredding her paper napkin into myriad tiny pieces.

"Correct," she said. "Ray and I didn't come along for about twenty years. For some reason my mother couldn't get pregnant. But then, all of a sudden, along came little ol' me, and five years later, Raymond."

"That's just plain bizarre," Annie remarked. "And your father raped *both* of you? My God! And neither of you ever told on him? Why didn't your mother stop him?"

Anger once more began to roil in the pit of Becca's stomach, and she tried in vain to push it away. "I don't know, Annie!" she snapped. "I just don't know, and I don't care to dwell on it. This is exactly why I don't like to discuss my personal business. All it does is to spur on endless questions, and force me to talk about a childhood I would rather forget!"

Oven fodder!

Becca flinched as Klaus-Dieter's words resonated in her mind. With an unsteady hand, she quickly took another sip of her tea to obscure the shock that was surely reflected in her expression. In her mind's eye she could still see the "blond Adonis" sitting across the table from little Raymond, admonishing the poor kid for not holding his fork right, or for not cleaning his plate fast enough. She could see Klaus-Dieter's hand flying across the table to thump Ray's little forehead when he gagged on a mouthful of something he didn't like.

In Klaus-Dieter Behringer's house you lived to please to Klaus-Dieter. You liked the food Klaus-Dieter liked, you liked the TV programs Klaus-Dieter liked, and you laughed at Klaus-Dieter's jokes. You took your life into your own hands if you dared to displease the green-eyed German monster in *any* way....

Suppressed tears began to flow as Becca remembered her often absent mother, Rachel, who was constantly putting in overtime at the company where she worked. She wasn't home often enough to notice that her own daughter, at the tender age of five, had become her husband's sex slave....

Upset with herself for having shared her sordid story, Becca leaned back and blew her nose and peered guiltily around the room to see if anyone else in the restaurant had witnessed her outburst. Fortunately, most were engaged in their own conversations, perusing a book, or absorbed in their own thoughts.

Annie gently took Becca's hand in hers. "Honey, I'm really sorry," she said. "It's all my fault. I started it. But honestly, I think you probably needed to talk about it. There's obviously some festered stuff in you and that's why that idiot, Rex, is able to affect you like he does."

"Oh, baloney," Lora said. "You're making Rex out to be some weird catalyst for Becca's mental issues. She just doesn't care for the guy, that's all. Hopefully, that will change and everything will be all right, in the end!"

Becca closed her eyes and shook her head. Lora's voice was beginning to grate on her, and it was time to call it a day. The dark mood spurred on by the strange conversation, was heavy, unshakable, impenetrable, and the only way to shed it was to get up and leave it behind.

"Let's go home, girls," she said irritably. Her head was pounding now, and it was becoming too difficult to remain civil for much longer. "The sun is about to set and *Shabbat* is just around the corner. Time to forget about the world and all our cares, and just concentrate on God."

Chapter 8

The destruction begins

Micah 3:11 Her leaders judge for a bribe, her priests teach for a price, and her prophets tell fortunes for money. Yet they lean upon LORD and say, "Is not LORD among us? No disaster will come upon us." (NIV)

* * * *

On Saturday morning, to ensure she would not run into Rex, Becca asked Annie to act in the capacity of "official greeter." In the meantime, she stayed close to Liam, who was busy showing Chad Kretschmar how to work the sound system, as Chad, a brand new Elder, had agreed to share that responsibility.

The smell of food cooking on the stove in the tiny kitchen area upstairs had permeated the entire building and she smiled at the thought that Annie was apparently planning on showing off her culinary skills today. Annie liked to be the center of attention at her monthly *onegs*, the Sabbath meals that took all morning to prepare, and followed fellowship. "It kind of defeats the purpose of Sabbath rest, doesn't it?" Becca had asked her one Saturday – which netted her nothing but a disapproving scowl from Annie, with the admonishment to go and mind her own business.

"So, hey, how are you guys doing this morning?"

Becca didn't have to turn around to know who had come up behind them: It was Harry Malone, the incessant "humminah" chanter, his sweaty bouquet preceding him and filling the air with an overwhelmingly pungent, foul stench.

"Did y'all have a good week?" Harry wanted to know.

"I did," Chad replied cheerily, his sweet azure eyes sparkling. "My oldest had his 9th birthday and so we went camping up at Lake of the Ozarks and spent a few days. It was great to get away from my pizza business for awhile!"

Becca could tell Harry was smiling because his teeth were showing through the scraggly, long mustache and beard he had been growing for several months - ever since "God told him" not to shave or bathe for two years....

"Good for you guys!" Harry said. "Where are the three little munchkins, anyway?"

"Upstairs, in the playroom with their Mom," Chad replied."

"So," Harry said addressing Becca and Liam, "how goes it with you guys?"

"We're doing just fine," Liam replied curtly. His lips were pressed together and Becca could tell he was trying his best to keep his composure.

"You mad at me, bro?" Harry asked.

Several seconds passed as Liam kept fiddling with one of the knobs on the sound system. Finally, he looked up and said, "Harry, please don't view this as me being mean, but you've got to bathe. People are talking...."

Harry, clearly miffed, straightened, raised his chin and stuffed his hands into the pockets of his dark blue coveralls. "Not gonna happen," he said firmly. "I told you, God forbade it!"

"Well," Liam went on, making every effort to come off as gentle, "while I totally appreciate your desire to please God, I honestly don't think He told you not to bathe. He is clear, throughout the Bible, about how much He wants us clean in body, mind, spirit and deed...."

"Not gonna happen!" Harry repeated. "I love you for being honest enough to come out and say it, Liam, but I am not going against God!"

"I understand, Harry. I do. But please think about this: Do you really believe that God wants you to repel people with your body odor? Come on, Harry, there's no way to escape your smell anymore! This is a small building and, brother; your smell permeates the whole place! There's no way to get away from it!"

Chad, a very quiet young man who normally didn't have much to say, approached Harry and placed a loving hand on his shoulder. "Brother," he said gently, "I personally saw some newcomers last week turn around and leave because of your smell. What you're doing is just not right. If you don't start bathing and acting like a normal human being again, you will drive everyone out of here and Beit Yisrael will fold. Is that really what you want?"

What was visible of Harry's face turned bright red, and Becca found herself feeling sorry for the man. Harry wasn't some crazy vagrant; he was a computer programmer employed by the same company as Liam. But for some reason, he was hooked on the notion that he wasn't supposed to bathe. She was glad that both Chad and her husband had the courage to confront him about it.

"Harry, we love you," she chimed in. "Please listen to your brothers. It's true that you are starting to drive people away."

"Orlando hasn't said anything to me," Harry retorted indignantly.

"Well," Liam remarked, "we have discussed it in an Elders' Meeting, and trust me, Orlando is on the same page."

"Well, I realize you Elders in your starched shirts and ties make all the rules," Harry snapped as he turned to leave. "But, I'll wait for Orlando to say something. Until he does, I'm not bathing!" Briefly facing Liam, he said with an undertone of cynicism, "I got laid off at work yesterday, and I'm guessing it's for the same reason, but I'm not budging! *God* tells me what to do; not the world!"

"Wow," Chad exclaimed as he watched Harry saunter off and take a seat toward the back of the sanctuary, near the entrance. "That guy is definitely not playing with a full deck."

Liam shook his head as began to concentrate once more on the sound system. "Thanks for backing me up," he said. "I'm glad to have you as an Elder."

Becca's face fell when, out of her peripheral vision, she noticed Rex walking through the door, black cowboy hat in hand. Today, he was wearing a tan jacket with Navy blue jeans. Annie, smiling up at him, handed him the weekly bulletin and told him to enjoy the service.

Unlike the previous Sabbath, he didn't hang out by the door; he simply smiled and ambled over to greet a circle of ladies engaged in an animated conversation near the restrooms. Minutes later, they were all laughing at something Rex had said.

Becca was able to discern the pleased look on Lora's face when she emerged from the ladies' room and saw Rex. Not wasting a second, Lora joined the group, squeezing herself into a spot directly beside Rex, who gave her a casual hug, as if they were old friends.

Shaking her head in dismay, Becca trudged up the aisle to stand beside Annie at the door. "Can you believe that?" she whispered, indicating the group with a slight move of her head.

"I'm absolutely astounded," Annie mumbled, keeping her voice low. "But it really doesn't surprise me. The girls all think he's gorgeous. Especially our Rabbi's wife…."

"Yeah, I know! Annie, honestly…on one hand, I totally understand and agree with Lora that Rex is a nice-looking, charismatic man. But he's also a total jerk."

"True. I've been watching him and I don't think he means to be a jerk, on purpose. He just is the way he is. I don't think he even realizes how he comes across. Know what I mean?"

Becca nodded. "My guess is, he was raised that way. I'd be willing to bet he had an aggressive, arrogant father that he looked up to and emulated; and a doting mother who spent her days spoiling him to death and telling him how awesome he was."

A chilly breeze blew in as Cassie opened the door and came inside. A tall, young red-haired man wearing a light blue denim suit was at her heels. Cassie's countenance became stony when she noticed Becca.

"Welcome, stranger!" Annie said, handing the man a bulletin. "What's your name?"

The young man adjusted his horn-rimmed glasses, then reached out his hand in greeting. "I'm Rowdy," he said, beaming.

"Oh!" Annie exclaimed. "Cassie has told us so much about you."

"All good, I hope," he said, gingerly taking Cassie's hand in his.

"...Oh, yes," Annie replied with a forced smile. "All good!"

Cassie, eyeing Becca with raw disdain, threw her shoulders back as she made her way past. "Orlando said I could bring him," she said icily. "Deal with it!"

Becca silently watched as Cassie and Rowdy found a seat toward the middle of the sanctuary.

"You okay?" Annie wanted to know. "You look a little green around the gills."

"I'm just stunned," Becca managed. The color in her face had risen to such a hue that it rivaled the deep purple, lacy trim of her beige pantsuit. "Truly. I am stunned! The guy is a convicted pedophile! Did Orlando call Fred to seek his input about this guy?"

"Nope."

"Well, he didn't ask Liam, either!"

"Well, my guess is, he gave in to Cassie. Lora is right; Orlando isn't very...well, whatever. The only thing we can do is now is to keep an eye on our little ones. Thank God the kids' room is upstairs! We'll just make sure he never goes up there."

For a brief moment, Becca felt as if she were frozen in time; everything stood still. The overhead lights seemed a little brighter while, at the same time, the immediate vicinity felt slightly out of focus and "fuzzy."

"Come here, Becca; give me some sugar...."

"No! No, Daddy. No!"

"Oh yes, yes, yes.... You know better than to shy away from me"!

"No...."

SLAP! "Don't fight me, little girl! You know better than that!"

A noise coming from the podium doused the vision and she stood, trembling in its wake. There was no use in denying that both Rex and this weird Rowdy character had set Satan loose in her mind. She simply had to find a way to deal with her feelings....

"Shabbat shalom!" Rabbi Orlando said, his greeting booming over the loudspeakers. "Are you all ready to be blessed this morning?" Over by the sound system, Liam - with Chad watching intently - hustled to turn down the volume.

A resounding "YES!" filled the air as everyone slowly began to find their seats. An older lady who had volunteered to watch the little ones this week, headed quietly up the stairs.

Minutes later, after the blessing of the bread and wine and an opening prayer, the Worship Team led half an hour of singing and praise and worship. When they were done, Elders Liam and Fred, wearing their *tallits*, opened the cabinet mounted on the wall behind the podium. Together, they removed the 300-year-old Torah scroll from the Ark, which they gently placed on a special table, and began unrolling it to this week's Torah portion.

When Orlando had finished reading the pertinent parts in Hebrew, Liam strained to lift the Torah scroll high into the air as Fred recited liturgy. Then he and Fred rolled it up and replaced it in its protective cover - the "Mantel" - to prepare it for its traditional trek around the synagogue.

Everyone stood, except for the aging Elder Leroy who remained seated in his wheelchair, and began to file out from among the pews to stand against the walls in a great circle to await the Torah procession, which would allow them to touch the Word of God.

Today, instead of doing the honors of carrying the scroll around the room himself, Liam handed it to Fred with a nod and a smile - an act that brightened Fred's dour face, as his ego was still suffering from the loss of his job.

Rabbi Orlando fell in behind Fred; and Liam - who called Chad over from the sound system to join them - followed suit. Their first stop was before old Leroy who smiled as Fred bent down to allow him to touch the Torah with a trembling and withered hand. Seconds later, the little procession was making its way around the room, allowing everyone who wished to do so, to touch the Torah scroll before it was replaced into the Ark.

"May I ask a question?" Rex called out when the procession was about to reach him. He stood rigidly against the wall, wedged between Lora and Harry.

The interruption stopped Fred in his tracks and he simply stood, rooted to the spot, appearing quite annoyed.

Peering around Fred who was cradling the Torah like a baby in his arms, Orlando cast an irritated glance at Rex. "Of course, brother," he said. "What's your question?"

"Well, I'm wondering what this is all about," Rex said tersely. "I saw y'all doing this last week, and didn't join in because I'm not going to worship some scroll. Is that what you're doing here? Or what? What is this, exactly?"

"Oh, no, no, brother!" Orlando said patiently, his voice coming across low and soothing and quite melodic. "It's just a tradition that allows people to be reverent toward God's Word, that's all."

"Well, why don't you carry a *Bible* around, then?" Rex declared. "That's God's *whole* Word!"

"Well, these old Torah scrolls were handwritten by the scribes," Orlando explained. "Torah – those first five Books of the Bible – consists of the original Word of God. It contains the words He spoke directly to His people. The rest of the Bible is just basically history, prophecy and commentary...and, of course, the Gospels."

"God, you guys have some weird customs – taking that Torah thing for a walk, running around in those over-sized scarfs and beanie caps! Good God Almighty, why does this need to be done? In my mind, all we need to know is that Jesus died! Why do you guys keep adding to the Word?"

Becca, having had quiet enough of the nonsense, shot a piercing gaze across the room. "Rex," she said, her voice slightly raised, "would you please just be quiet so we can finish with the Torah procession?"

The big cowboy started to respond, but Lora leaned over to touch his arm, an expensive gold bracelet dangling from her wrist. "Rex, we don't worship the scroll," she said sweetly. "We worship God and His whole Word. This is just a nice thing to do, us getting to touch His Torah. It's just a tradition. Everybody has a Bible, but not everybody has a 300-year-old Torah scroll. You'll get the hang of it, don't worry."

Smiling appreciatively, Rex rewarded her with affectionate gaze. Returning his attentions to Orlando, he said, sounding almost giddy, "This woman is so wise! I just love her to death! If ever you decide you don't want her anymore, you can send her my way."

Becca's face burned with anger and, try as she might, she couldn't hold it back. "Rex," she cried, "that was totally inappropriate and disrespectful! You're talking about the Rabbi's wife, for heaven's sake!"

Lyle Hickman, a long-time member of the congregation who happened to be standing near Becca, leaned over to get her attention. "Sweetheart, let the men handle this," he whispered with a wink. "Women don't need to worry their pretty little heads about this kind of stuff."

Becca threw him a questioning glance. "Well, then, why didn't *you* say something to him?" she snapped. "He was way out of line!"

"Yes, he was, but I'm sure the Rabbi will deal with him. He doesn't need your help, or mine. Okay?"

The patronizing smile did not escape Becca and she shuddered at the thought that Orlando was planning to make Lyle an Elder. He had mentioned it in passing at the last Elders and Deacons Meeting. She personally didn't care for Lyle, as he tended to be a touchy-feely chauvinist who had a high opinion of himself. But somehow, he had managed to fool the Rabbi into viewing his unsavory attributes as leadership qualities.

Rex's belly laugh filled the room. "Oh, sweet little Reba," he said loudly enough for all to hear, "don't go getting your panties in a wad. I'm just kidding around. You people are so danged *serious* in here! Sheesh, loosen *up*!"

Becca's eyes flashed as she glowered at the person who, in her opinion, had been sent by Satan himself to cause trouble in the congregation. "Well, since you can't seem to take God and the Bible seriously" she snapped irritably, "perhaps you need to find yourself some church that won't mind you behaving like you're in some cowboy bar, raising heck!"

"Raising heck?" he said, chuckling. "Raising *heck*? Oh my god, that's funny!" Gazing down at Lora, he said, "Did you hear that, sweetheart? Becca doesn't want me raising heck in here! That's hilarious!"

"Good lord," a woman next to Becca whispered. "You asked for that, you dummy!"

"Rex, the very least you could do," Liam cut in, "is to show a little respect by keeping your comments to yourself until we're done with the Torah procession. Can you do that much, please?"

"Whoah, y'all, slow down!" Rex said, twisting his face into a comical mask. "I'm sorry if I peed on y'all's parade, but I like to ask questions as soon as they come to mind. Perhaps I should remind you I'm a Gentile, not subject to your Jewish ways."

Orlando, who had been quietly listening to the exchange, cleared his throat. "I think we all need to calm down and get back to business," he proclaimed loudly. "Fred, please proceed...."

"Well, can I say one more thing?" Rex interposed, his voice was deep and low and authoritative. "There's something urgent I really, *really* have to do."

"What is it now?" Orlando said impatiently.

All eyes were fixed on the tall man as he took a step forward and turned to face Harry, who had been standing unobtrusively beside him.

"Buddy," Rex said loud enough for everyone to hear, "I know nobody else around here has the guts to tell you, but you stink!" Straightening to his full height, he loomed over Harry like some gigantic shadow, and it was clear that he was in charge and relishing the spotlight.

"I've made this place my new church home," he went on, "and I don't want to feel like I'm sitting in a sewer every week. Therefore, I want you to go home right now and take a shower. Don't be showing your face in this place again until you're clean. Got it?"

Harry's face reflected utter shock. His mouth opened and then quickly closed. Finally, he muttered something about God, but Rex refused to back down.

"No, I don't want to hear any God stuff!" Rex snapped, his deep voice echoing in the sanctuary. "I'm gonna give you a choice: You can either leave of your own accord, or I pick you up and put your butt out that door. Do you *comprende*, pardner?"

"But I'm just following God's instruction," Harry countered.

"I don't care if you have a signed letter from the President of the United States!" Rex said. "Get out! *Now!* Go home and bathe! And don't come back until you do!"

Harry, noticeably embarrassed, gaped at Rex and then glanced toward Orlando for help. When nothing happened, he straightened, cleared his throat, and headed wordlessly out the door.

Time stood still as all eyes turned toward Orlando. No one uttered a sound; no one dared move as they waited on him for direction. Suddenly, someone started clapping; and moments later, the entire room burst into applause. Several people gathered around Rex to shake his hand.

Liam made his way around Orlando to relieve Fred, who appeared ready to buckle under the weight of the Torah scroll. "I think we can forget about the procession," he said quietly. "Let's put it away and get Orlando to start the teaching."

Becca watched anxiously as her husband returned the scroll to the Ark. She knew Liam was just as upset as she was over the events of the last few minutes.

Not only had Rex been allowed to disrupt the Torah procession while the Rabbi stood helplessly by like the weakling Lora said he was, but he had managed to become the congregation hero by being mean and condescending to a man who clearly suffered some mental issues. Worst of all, nobody seemed to mind....

Things were not looking good, she thought to herself. Things had quickly gotten out of hand and, after synagogue, she fully planned on talking to Liam about the possibility of leaving this place to find a new congregation.

But that was not to be because, before dismissing the group after the teaching later that afternoon, Orlando called Liam and Becca up front to announce, quite out of the blue, that he was making Liam assistant Rabbi, effective immediately.

"It's clear I need help running this place," he said as all eyes were riveted on him. "And I can't think of a better man for the job, than our brother, Liam, here! He's actually more of a Rabbi than I am, because he graduated from a traditional *yeshiva* and is an ordained Rabbi. Beit Yisrael needs him!"

The applause was absolutely deafening. Liam, too stunned to speak, simply stood beside Orlando, mute and bewilder-ed.

"As for our sister, Becca," Orlando continued, placing a fatherly arm around her shoulder, "I'm putting her in charge of setting up my new *yeshiva*. Beit Yisrael is ultimately going to become a place of learning and producing new Rabbis. Nobody is better qualified than our very knowledgeable sister, an expert writer and journalist who has made her living in the public relations field."

Becca and Liam glanced helplessly at each other as the congregation again broke into wild applause for the third time that day.

"This is truly a day of celebration," Orlando said brightly as he stepped off the platform to join the congregation. "Everyone, please stay afterward, as Sister Annie has prepared a very special meal for us! Halleluyah, let's go upstairs and celebrate!"

"Well," Liam whispered in her ear once the gaiety died down, "it seems we've been bamboozled into staying. So much for leaving this place, huh?"

"Well, I don't know about your, but I'm really quite upset about this," Becca replied irritably. "God only knows that Beit Yisrael is sorely in need of some competent leadership; but Orlando really should have discussed this with us, first!"

Liam broke into a huge grin. "Sweetheart," he said, "he knows we would have turned him down!"

Chapter 9

The sins of the father....

Ezekiel 18:19 "Yet you say, 'Why should not the son suffer for the iniquity of the father?' When the son has done what is just and right, and has been careful to observe all my statutes, he shall surely live. 20. The soul who sins shall die. The son shall not suffer for the iniquity of the father, nor the father suffer for the iniquity of the son. The righteousness of the righteous shall be upon himself, and the wickedness of the wicked shall be upon himself. (ESV)

* * * *

Becca found herself trembling with anticipation as she passed through the gates of the Jefferson City Correctional Center where her brother, Ray, had been incarcerated for the past nineteen years. It had been at least seven years since she last saw him - partly, because Ray had become more and more closed off with every visit. Toward the end, he was almost impossible to talk to, and Becca finally quit trying.

The truth was, their rift grew bigger after Becca "got saved." At first, she was disappointed to discover that Ray didn't share her excitement about God and the Bible. But, it didn't take long to realize that those without the Holy Spirit in their hearts could not possibly understand. What's more, every day she came to realize to a greater extent that, unless God Himself opened someone's eyes to His Truth, there was no way to spark their interest.

And so, ultimately, even her occasional letters to Ray were met with hostility, as he made it perfectly clear in very colorful language that he wanted nothing to do with God. As a matter of fact, one of his final responses to Becca had been: "Where the hell was your God while Dad was sexually abusing us?"

Becca's reply had come straight from the heart: "Ray," she wrote, "As strange as it sounds, He was right there with us! The bottom line is, He allows men free will; the *choice* to do things His way, or not. Unfortunately, the choices of others often impact us, and you and I happened to be at the mercy of Dad's personal, sick choices! God allowed us to experience all that pain and agony in hopes of reaching us while we were at our lowest point so He could bring us into a closer relationship with Him. It worked for me, but obviously, you have too much hate in your heart to accept His offer. My prayer for you, Ray, is that He will change your mind one day."

Ray's curt response was that he couldn't accept a God who would allow bad things to happen to good people, and that was that. They hadn't corresponded since - and she was relieved when he agreed to her request for a visit after the New Year. There were some things about the past that she needed answers to, and she was hoping Ray could help her out.

After undergoing the routine mandatory security check and body search at the entrance of the visitors' lounge, she took a seat at one of the round, one-piece, "molded" steel table/bench combination, to wait for Ray. Several people were already in the room, either waiting for "their" inmate, or already engaged in animated conversations with them -

all under the watchful eyes of the two guards stationed near the entrance, behind a tall counter.

While she waited, her mind returned to her poor, lost younger brother. At the age of thirty-eight, Ray had spent exactly half of his life in prison. He had another twenty-five to go before being eligible for parole on his conviction of statutory rape and murder.

Becca agonized over the fact that Ray had blindly followed in Klaus-Dieter's footsteps. Instead of using the pain and the rage of his abusive past as a learning experience and recognizing the damage a pedophile does to a child's psyche, and then doing everything in his power to prevent it, Ray had grown up to become just like his father! His actions had ultimately landed him in prison for impregnating a 12 year old girl and then killing both her and her 15 year old brother for threatening to expose him.

The whole situation was too depressing for words; and while Becca truly did not want to subject herself to anymore of Ray's barbs about God and the Bible (or whatever else he chose to dish out), she simply had to see him in hopes of clarifying some things in her own mind.

Trying to deflect the black mood that was threatening to ruin her day, she turned her thoughts on Liam's sudden and unexpected ordination. Both she and Liam had been angry at first, because they knew it was yet another manipulative ploy on Orlando's part to guilt them into staying. To his credit, however, Orlando had been undeniably wonderful with Liam, coaching and teaching him all he needed to know about running a synagogue.

And in the meantime, Chad had been a tremendous help, and Orlando had even appointed one more Elder – the chauvinistic Lyle Hickman – a macho, patronizing, over-friendly bear of a man with a full "Fu Manchu" type mustache and a domineering personality that Becca found nauseating. Becca had voiced her reservations about Lyle in one of the Elders and Deacons Meetings, citing the fact that she had personally seen him verbally abusing women. But Orlando didn't agree with her assessment, suggesting that Lyle was simply "an old school kind of a guy who felt overprotective toward women."

Be that as it may, Lyle had served to help relieve the pressure of Liam's workload. As a matter of fact, Lyle and Chad had taken so much work off of Liam, that Liam had finally been able to find the time to post Orlando's teachings on the Internet. Unfortunately, there was yet no money coming in, but Orlando remained hopeful.

Her heart skipped at beat when someone appeared at the door marked "Prisoners' Entrance". Disappointed to realize it wasn't Ray, she watched the man submit to the mandatory body search by a guard stationed at the door. Seconds later the young man, his face aglow with anticipation, crossed the room to hug the two elderly folks who had come to visit.

Shortly thereafter, a tall, bent, middle-aged man entered and stood with practiced indifference while the guard frisked him. To Becca's surprise, the man approached her table, and it was only then that she realized it was her brother.

Extremely emaciated – almost skeletal - Ray appeared years older than his chronological age. His short hair, formerly dark blond, was now completely gray; and on his lined and ashen face he wore a pair of clunky, black-framed glasses.

Those things, coupled with the bright orange prison jumpsuit, made for a very ghoulish presence, like something out of a Halloween horror story.

"Ray?" she exclaimed in total surprise.

"Yeah, it's me." He sounded very old and tired. Rather than to wait for an obligatory hug, Ray took a seat across from Becca, folded his hands on the table and produced a wan smile.

"To spare you the embarrassment of having to ask," he said, "yes, I have AIDS and I'm dying. I got it from my best buddy. He died last month."

Becca's mouth dropped as she ogled her brother in disbelief. "Oh, God," she finally managed as the tears began to flow. "I don't know what to say…. Is there anything I can do?"

"Sure," he said coolly. "You can stop crying and ask your God to cure AIDS. And hell, while you're at it, you can also petition the warden to allow us to smoke indoors."

"Oh, God, Ray…."

"No biggie," he went on stoically. "I view all this in a positive light because I've figured out a way to escape prison...in a pine box."

An awkward silence ensued as the siblings sat and stared at each other. Becca wanted more than anything to just hug her brother until the end of time, and she suddenly found herself wishing she knew him better. Once close as children, the only thing they had in common now was memories of the trauma they had been forced to endure at the hands of their father. Today, brother and sister were reduced to mere strangers examining each other across a cold, hard steel table, trying to figure out ways to have a meaningful conversation.

"So, what exactly are you here for?" Ray demanded pithily, his tone accusatory and impatient. "I don't see a Bible in your hand, so I'm guessing you didn't come to proselytize."

"Don't be such a snot!" she replied, not bothering to hide a renewed surge of tears. "I *miss* you! And I want you to talk about our childhood, because it seems there are huge chunks missing that only you can fill in. Just talk about our childhood, that's all I'm asking. I promise not to talk about God or the Bible today."

Ray quietly listened to her explanation about the visions Rex Lambert had somehow brought about, then straightened in his seat, and leaned back to place his hands on the bench. For a moment, it appeared as though he was going to get up and leave; but instead, he sat there, staring off into the distance, as if in deep thought.

"I'll be honest with you, sis," he finally said. "I don't remember much, either. Just the basics. I don't *want* to remember! Why should I? The past is the past. What happened, happened. Who cares?"

"Well, okay, but can you just start talking, and I'll ask questions as I think of them?"

Huge veins and tendons in Ray's neck popped out when he shrugged his shoulders. "Yeah, I guess. Buy me a cup of coffee and I'll see what I can come up with."

Becca rose and - fishing around in her jacket pocket for some loose change, which was the only thing she ever brought into the prison, besides her car keys and drivers' license - she waited her turn in the short line at the coffee vending machine.

"Okay," she said, plopping two black, steaming coffees onto the table. "As I said, my initial contact with Rex caused me to see a face with a tattoo, so I guess we can start off with me asking, did Dad have a tattoo on his cheek?"

"Strange that you can't remember that," Ray remarked with a snuffle. "I remember every damned feature of his! Geez...Klaus-Dieter was this spectacular Aryan god with the most intense green eyes you ever saw. There was a scar on his right cheek where a tattoo used to be. He told me he used to have a Swastika tattoo when he was young, but Mom wouldn't marry him until he agreed to have it removed."

"So, he was a *Nazi*?"

"Hell, I don't know if he was a Nazi, or not. He was in the German army, that's all I know. That, and the fact that he hated Jews more than anything. Maybe he was just a sympathizer. Who cares?"

Pondering what she had just learned, Becca remained in deep thought for some moments and then sadly shook her head. "Well, then," she said, "there's my confirmation. It *was* Klaus-Dieter's face I saw on Rex that day...."

"I'm absolutely amazed that you can't remember him. That is just too weird."

"Well, we have no pictures, Ray. Our family albums were burned in the fire, and Grandma and Grandpa destroyed all pictures of him when he disappeared. They had some of Mom, but none of him."

Ray took another draw on his coffee and then sat and stared at his cup for several long moments. Then, eyeing his sister, he rested his chin on the palm of his hand and mumbled something about not being in the mood to tear open old wounds. But then, suddenly – as if some obstacle had been cleared away - the words came tumbling out in rapid succession.

His face, as he recounted certain aspects of his childhood, was filled with anguish and frustration. He grimaced as he mentioned the "crappy, creaky old house on that twenty acres of cedars and underbrush and rocks outside of Ash Grove" where they grew up. He lamented how he and Becca were basically slave labor for Klaus-Dieter who insisted he was merely instilling them with "a good and noble German work ethic." Becca was his "chief cook and bottle washer and house maid," and Ray was his little farm-hand, learning to plant vegetables, milk their one and only cow (who was severely beaten whenever she didn't behave), and shovel manure and mend fences.

Every memory, it seemed, was fraught with raw emotion, and the only time Ray's countenance softened was when he spoke about their mother's parents - "Grandma and Grandpa Coursey who lived just down the road from us" - whose home had been a safe haven whenever their parents fought and argued.

"They were really good to us," Ray said sadly. "Too bad they were so old. Wish we could have had them for a few more years."

As he spoke, Becca often found herself wondering whether his memories were real, or sifted and recreated in a mind that had grown progressively more enraged and bitter with the passage of time.

There was a far-away look on Ray's face as the memories kept flowing. "I remember we had a bull that ol' Klaus castrated by putting this fat rubber band around its testicles with a pair of pliers. The lack of blood flow was supposed to make the sac fall off after awhile. And, wow, sis! Remember how he used to castrate the pigs with a razor blade? He would tie the pig's front feet together and suspend them on a hook in the barn and then just start slicing while the pigs screamed their heads off. God Almighty, what a sadist he was! And I'll never forget how he beat me within an inch of my life once, when I accidentally kicked the damned milk bucket over! God, I hated him so much...."

Lowering his head, he shuddered and emitted a forceful snort of disgust - a habit he had picked up from his father.

Becca had always disliked that about Ray...that silly snorting habit. He had taken on way too many of Klaus-Dieter's mannerisms over the years. The difference was, except for his natural blond hair and his mannerisms, Ray didn't really resemble his father at all. He didn't resemble anyone in their family, for that matter. And this new Ray – thin, gray and sickly, was a total stranger.

"He was a plumber, for Christ's sake!" Ray went on. "The way he always acted, you'd think he was President of the United States or something!"

He took a huge swig of his coffee, and then stared into his cup as if some residual memories were hidden there. "He reeked with Aryan arrogance! Ol' Klaus was just a blue-collar worker, but in his own eyes, everybody was beneath him. Even Mom, who worked her butt off all the time. Christ, she brought in more money than he did!"

Becca nodded. "Do you remember how he was always putting down Americans? Americans, the USA – everybody and everything was beneath him. Nothing could hold a candle to Germans and Germany. *Deutschland über alles!* Yet, on the other hand, he hated Germany...."

"I know! He made no sense sometimes. According to Mom, he used to love America, and he couldn't wait to live in Ash Grove and be near her parents. She told me once that their life was 'heaven on earth' until she let it slip that she was Jewish, one evening during some drunken brawl they had when you and I were little. You were like five or six and I was still a baby. She said Dad was proud of the fact that she had landed some prestigious secretarial job in Springfield. But that all ended the day she let the cat out of the bag about being Jewish! Suddenly, she was the devil in person."

"Mom told you all that?"

"Yeah. You don't recall any of this? You were sitting right next to me in the kitchen when she told us."

Gripped by a mixture of anger and regret over her memory lapses, Becca frowned and shook her head. "I don't know why I can't remember that. But you know what I find really weird? We never saw anything Jewish in our house, or in Grandma's house! They weren't practicing Jews, so what was Dad's problem?"

The look on Ray's face reflected disappointment. "Hmm," he said, "I guess you also don't remember that Mom was *adopted*? The Coursey's weren't her natural parents. They always made sure she knew of her Jewish heritage, but they raised her Christian. Well, I guess you could call it Christian, I don't know. They weren't really into God and all that malarkey."

Becca's eyes widened. "Yes!" she cried as if a window had suddenly been opened in her mind. "I had completely forgotten that! Mom was adopted! Oh, Ray, that's just bizarre! Oh wow, he made us all suffer, just because Mom had Jewish blood! Why the heck didn't he just leave her?"

"Are you kidding?" Ray cackled, grinning. "He stuck around to make her miserable!"

"Strange that someone could be so full of hate...."

"Well, yeah...I guess he stuck around because he didn't have any family in Germany. None that he ever talked about, anyway. He actually had a pretty good life with Mom – and she made a lot more money than he did, and so he stayed."

"Well, why didn't she leave him, then? She could have left!"

Ray's hoarse yet piercing laughter brought a few stares. "She did, sis; she *died*!"

Becca blinked rapidly as she pondered his words. "I know," she said, "and that's actually another question I had. How did Mom die?"

Her words were drowned out by Ray's sudden, harsh coughing fit. Years of smoking three or four packs of cigarettes per day seemed to have taken their toll, and Becca wondered why he had even taken up the habit, since both their parents had smoked and the house was always filled with a stinking blue haze.

"Wow, that sounds bad, Ray!" Becca exclaimed once the coughing subsided.

"I know, so don't even go there," Ray warned, his eyes becoming tiny slits. "I'm dying, anyway, and so I don't need another damned sermon from you. You've never smoked, so you have no idea how addictive it is."

Becca could tell his mood had suddenly changed. In an instant, he had turned into Klaus-Dieter, angry and raging over nothing. "I know," she said, "and I'm sorry. I was merely making a comment."

Tossing his sister an agitated glance, Ray stuffed his hands into the pockets of his jumpsuit and glowered. "You always have to ruin everything," he said with an air of dejection and frustration. "And I think it's a little sick that you wanted to come here and talk about Dad's endless arguments with Mom and her Oven Fodder offspring who gave him his damned *Fahrvergnügen!* God…."

Oven fodder! You don't deserve the air you're breathing!

"Ray, please don't be angry. I just need to know what's causing my nightmares, so I can start healing from my past…."

"So you're really dying to rehash how often we were told that he wished he himself could have shoved her ass into one of the ovens at Bergen-Belsen! God…I've got his mantra imprinted on the inside of my eyelids! His endless 'If only I

114

had done that before she sucked me into marrying her, then she wouldn't have had the chance to spawn you ugly, no-good, rotten kids!'"

"Okay!" Becca said forcefully. "You're getting nasty now, and I don't feel like hearing it. Let's just drop it, then! I'm sorry I bothered you."

A corner of Ray's mouth rose to form a smirk. "Well, you started it! And isn't nice to know that the Oven Fodder was at least good for something? We were able to ease Dad's pain via those warm and fuzzy 'family affairs' on his bed whenever Mom was out whoring around...Oops, I mean, when she was 'working late'!"

The smirk intensified, giving him a cold and sinister look. "But hey," he went on, "it was all in the spirit of that good ol' *Fahrvergnügen*, wasn't it? Oh yeah...the joy of driving that thing home! Ram! Bam! Thank you, ma'am! Dad certainly had his share of *Fahrvergnügen* out of us! Yessirree!"

Becca felt the blood drain from her face and she squirmed uncomfortably on the hard bench.

"What's the matter, sis?" he asked. "You look like you just ate a green persimmon."

"Oh, knock it off, Ray!" she half-shouted. "Mom was *not* a whore. She often worked late because we needed the money and she was unhappy at home. And for that, he berated her. I do remember that much!"

"Not a whore? Oh boy, you're so damned ignorant! I can't believe how dense you are! Haven't you ever wondered why we didn't come along until they were married for twenty years? Have you really never wondered why Mom was never able to get pregnant until she started working at that company?"

"Ray, come on!"

"And haven't you ever wondered how come you never got knocked up while Dad was messing with you all those years? Take off your rose-colored glasses, big sister! We're not his kids!"

"Oh, stop it, Ray!"

"What's the matter? Truth too painful? Or will it mean that Klaus wasn't actually committing incest; and consequently, that God of yours can't be too mad at him?"

Becca felt as if she had just been kicked in the gut. "...You're *sick*, Ray!" she cried.

"No. I'm a realist!" Ray squinted as he leaned back and pulled his lips into a vicious grin. A rogue tear slid hard and fast along his cheek. Suddenly, he crossed his skinny arms and leaned forward on the table so far that his chin was nearly touching. From that odd position, he peered up at her and smiled.

"Speaking of messing around, I always meant to ask you: Did you enjoy our little trysts with Dad."

Becca recoiled. "What?" she cried in disbelief.

"Well, did you? I bet you did."

"...Have you lost your mind?"

The chatter in the room died down and out of her peripheral vision, Becca could see that several people had begun looking in their direction.

"Well, big sis, you could have ended our misery by telling on him, but you didn't! Why didn't you?"

Becca stared at him, mentally kicking herself for bothering to come here. "Ray, what are you doing?" she said quietly. "What is wrong with you all of a sudden?"

"What's wrong with *me*?" he replied icily. "I'm rotting away in jail – no, I'm *dying*! - and you're out there having a wonderful life. *That's* what's wrong with me!"

"Okay, that's it. I'm leaving...."

"Aw sis, come on," he said mockingly, reaching across the table stop her. "Let me ask you just one more thing before you go, okay?"

"What?" she snapped. The look in his eye clearly said he was up to something, and she tried to brace herself.

Ray smiled as he patted her hand and gazed lovingly into her eyes. "My sweet, darling, perfect sister," he said. "I'm just wondering how many of your church friends know that the little pew-warming Miss Goody-Two-Shoes has been married five times and had two abortions before she found her Prince Charming? I bet you've never told anyone that. They all think you're a saint, don't they?"

Becca shrank back in horror as an all-consuming rage slammed along her spine. "You *Schmuck*!" she cried indignantly, rising to her feet with such a force that it nearly caused her to lose her balance. "You...you're pure evil, Ray!"

"And you're a whore, just like your mother!"

"And you're a sick pervert, just like your father! Unlike you, at least Klaus-Dieter wasn't evil enough to kill anybody!"

"Is that so?" Ray yelled defiantly. "I guess you don't remember that, either, huh?"

"Remember what?"

Two guards suddenly appeared, seemingly out of nowhere. One of them stood next to Becca, demanding that she leave; the other physically pulled Ray from the bench and began herding him toward the Prisoners' Entrance.

"You worthless religious hypocrite!" she heard Ray yelling over his shoulder. "You're the reason I'm in here! You didn't save me from Dad! I'm in here because of *you*!"

* * * *

Out in the parking lot, Becca collapsed into the driver's seat of her car and sobbed. The tears came fast and furiously as overwhelming grief wracked her body. Her whole world had just fallen apart! Not only had she learned that her brother was dying of AIDS, but he also blamed her for his lot in life!

This new knowledge hurt to the core; it pricked her soul and she briefly found herself wishing she could die. Dying would be the only way to end the intense pain.

And Klaus-Dieter wasn't her biological father? That was inconceivable! It was ludicrous!

But, it truly stung to know that her loving grandparents were not her biological grandparents because Mother had been adopted....

She sat there for what seemed an eternity, glued to the seat, too numb to move. It had been a mistake to come here. Nothing was resolved. All her visit had served to do was to tear the scabs off old wounds, and cause some new ones.

Her thoughts centered on Liam and for a moment, she longed to be in his arms; but even he wouldn't be able to take away this pain and guilt. Nor could he change what happened in the past.

In all honesty, she didn't deserve to have someone comfort her while her poor brother was all alone, dying in prison with no one to care for him.

The mental anguish was too much to bear, as she replayed the afternoon's events in her mind. What could she have said or done differently? How had she allowed the conversation to degrade like that? Why did Ray suddenly become unglued and attempt to lay all the blame on her, knowing she had been just as helpless against Klaus-Dieter as he?

"I'm sorry, Ray!" she cried into the confines of the car as bitter tears streamed down her cheeks. "I'm so sorry! Oh, God, please don't let my brother suffer anymore!"

It was dusk when she finally rousted herself to start the long drive home. As she backed out of her parking slot, she realized she never got a chance to ask Ray the questions she needed to ask....

Chapter 10

The Bergen-Belsen connection

Matthew 7:7 Ask, and it will be given to you. Seek, and you will find. Knock, and it will be opened to you. 8 For anyone that asks will receive, and that seeks, will find. And to him that knock, it will be opened to him. (AENT)

* * * *

Becca's eyes fluttered open. Pale moonlight lay in slanted windowpane patterns across her bed. Someone was in the room; she could feel his presence.

Seemingly out of nowhere, a dark silhouette loomed above her, its eyes peering at her with white-hot intensity.

"Baby killer!" it yelled! "You're a no-good little Jewish whore!"

She screamed as the hatchet swung down onto her swollen, pregnant belly....

Becca cried out in pain as her rump hit the floor. She sat, dazed, peering into the darkness until the realization hit her that she had awakened from yet another nightmare. Seconds later, Liam was down in the floor with her, hugging, cajoling, asking her if she was okay. A wet nose nuzzling her face revealed that Spike was there, too, worried about his Mom.

Heart hammering in her temples, she simply sat, gasping for air. Somewhere in the back of her mind, she realized she had wet herself.

* * * *

It was 3:47 on the dot when Liam put on the first pot of coffee. By 6 a.m. Becca was still talking, crying and spilling her soul as dawn broke to usher in a new day. "I'm so sorry," she kept repeating. "So sorry...."

Physically and emotionally drained by the time she had arrived home from the prison yesterday, she had collapsed into the bed, foregoing supper and avoiding any discussion about her visit with Ray, despite Liam's curiosity. She simply couldn't bring herself to talk about it then.

But now, she couldn't stop talking.

The nightmare, she told Liam, was nothing more than her guilty conscience meting out the punishment she felt she deserved, kicked off by the memories she had long suppressed, along with the hateful barbs Ray had seen fit to bestow upon her.

Leaving nothing out as she talked, she recounted for Liam the entire conversation with Ray, including his venomous, hate-filled reminder of her two abortions.

"I was just six weeks along both times, but I had bonded with my babies!" she confessed, as bitter tears fell. "I just couldn't bring myself to allow an innocent baby to be born into this awful world, Liam! I...I was afraid to tell you, you were marrying a murderer! I was so young and stupid...."

To her surprise, Liam understood, assuring her without condemnation that he would never hold it against her. "After what you went through," he told her, "it's perfectly understandable that you chose not to have kids."

"But still, that's no excuse," she cried. "I didn't know God back then, or I would never have done it. "I was so awful, Liam!"

"You weren't awful, sweetie. You were a product of your environment."

Becca seemed inconsolable as the confessions flowed. She told him not only of her abortions, but about the sexual hang-ups she spent years trying to overcome, and the interchangeable lifestyles – one consisting of rampant promiscuity and the other of total abstinence, depending on her moods at the time.

"Until I got saved," she related, "I was a basket case, driven by a muddle of fear, rage and confusion. I didn't know who I was supposed to be. There have been days when I hated my mother more than my father, because she never figured out what was going on. She didn't save me from him! That's why I so desire to lead a holy life now...I know what I've done and I just want to be all I can be for God, now! And people are beating me up for it, accusing me of being 'holier-than-thou'...."

Liam never interrupted, allowing her to talk until she was spent.

"I can't trust men," she admitted at one point. "Not even you. You didn't know this, but I was even feeling apprehensive when your grown son came to our wedding…but I soon realized you weren't anything like my father. I saw nothing sexual between you and Jason…and trust me, I was watching very closely! I'm so sorry, Liam…."

Holding her close as she cried, he prayed with her and made a solemn promise that he would love her, no matter what. By the time he left her side to get ready for work, she was feeling spent, but very much relieved. As painful as it had been, it seemed this terrible episode was God's way of helping her to heal from the inside out.

An eternity passed before Becca was able to move from the sofa; and the only reason she rose was because Spike stood at the door, barking to be let out. It was well after Liam was gone; and, at his urging, she had done as he suggested, and called in sick. She was in no mood to interact with anyone today.

After a shower, she fell into bed and, with Spike at her feet, she slept soundly for a few hours.

"Maybe you should try Googling him!"

"…Wha…?" Becca awoke with a jolt.

Lora's suggestion – spoken a couple months back at one of the "Friday Afternoon Hen Sessions" – had been forgotten, mainly because there was no reason to bother. Klaus-Dieter was a nobody who had accomplished nothing in his life. He had been an obscure plumber, and not a very good one, at that. There was no reason for him to be on the Internet….

However, driven by curiosity - after a late breakfast consisting of some Cream of Wheat and toast - Becca padded to the office she shared with Liam, brought her computer to life, and typed in her father's name.

To her surprise, there were indeed some random people named Klaus-Dieter Behringer on the Internet. But what grabbed her attention was a list of Nazi war criminals on a Jewish website.

It took her several seconds to realize that the man pictured in the old, fuzzy black-and-white photo above the write-up, was her father.

The hair at the nape of her neck rose as she read:

> Klaus-Dieter Behringer: Member of an elite Nazi Waffen SS hit squad for two years during World War II. Due to "behavior problems" he was eventually relegated to prison guard duty at Bergen-Belsen, and ultimately discharged from the Army when counseling failed to help.
>
> Behringer was born to a Dutch father and German mother in Hannover, who moved to the Netherlands while their child was still an infant. After Germany invaded the Netherlands, a then 18-year-old Behringer joined the Waffen SS after seeing a recruiting poster signed by Heinrich Himmler, offering the possibility of becoming a police officer.
>
> Once his penchant for "going above and beyond" in brutality and his love for torturing prisoners (which included rape of men, women and children) was discovered, Behringer received counseling and was passed along to different

concentration camps during his time in the Army. His final assignment was at the Bergen-Belsen Concentration Camp where he was fired just prior to its liberation in early 1945.

Behringer married an American woman and moved to the United States after World War II. American authorities were informed by the German government of his violent crimes and asked to keep him under tight surveillance. He lived quietly in Ash Grove, Missouri, until the mid-Seventies when he disappeared after the murder of his wife, Rachel, and is suspected of living under an assumed name.

If he is still alive today, he would be in his mid-nineties. If you have any information about the whereabouts of Klaus-Dieter Behringer, please contact your local law enforcement officials, or the Simon Wiesenthal Center ASAP.

Becca gawked, open-mouthed and in stunned disbelief, at the computer screen as she read and re-read the bio. That her father was a Nazi war criminal was beyond comprehension; it was too much to bear.

And her mother was *murdered*? That must have been what Ray had alluded to yesterday….

But wait! Yes…it *was* true! That was the morning her mother had walked in on her and Klaus-Dieter, and….

The low moan that formed at the back of her throat, turned into an anguished wail; and suddenly, when the memories came pouring in with crystal clarity, she was writhing on the floor, howling, barely able to breathe....

* * * *

It was early morning when Klaus-Dieter Behringer - the German immigrant who had had the good fortune to escape his past by marrying an American female soldier who brought him to the United States - climbed into bed with his 14 year old daughter Rebecca.

It had been several weeks since their last liaison, and Becca had hoped that perhaps he had finally grown tired of her. But, here he was again, reaching under her nightgown, pawing at her like some desperate animal looking for scraps.

"Fahrvergnügen time, Schatzi!" he said, his voice a hoarse whisper. "Time for some pile-driving good fun!"

She cringed when he touched her chin, which was a routine of his before every sexual encounter. She hated his touch; she hated his smell. She hated his German accent. And she hated that horrible "Fahrvergnügen" word...but she didn't protest because she knew from experience it would be futile. School was out and Daddy would have access to her throughout the day now, for the next three months. There was no use in fighting it. Fighting against him didn't work.

She had heard Mother leave for work a few minutes ago, and Ray wasn't home because he had spent the night at Grandma's house. He probably wouldn't be home until later in the day.

Turning her head to avoid her father's cigarette breath, she closed her eyes and waited for it to be over. As always, she wanted to cry but she knew from experience that crying would result in being knuckled on the forehead or, at the very least, berated.

A noise behind them startled Becca, but Klaus' head was in the way and she couldn't see. Could it be Ray already?

"What the hell is going on here?"

It was her mother's voice resonating loudly in the room. Her voice sounded as if she was gargling with ground glass. It literally sent shock waves into Becca's bones.

Klaus-Dieter recoiled in horror. Launching himself off Becca and landing in an awkward standing position, he stared, disheveled, naked and red-faced, at his wife.

"Rachel," he said breathlessly.

Heart in her throat, Becca sat up and pressed herself against the headboard, pulling the covers up to her chin as she sat, quietly quaking.

The silence was deafening as her mother stood there, gawking in disbelief at the scene before her; horrified eyes darting back and forth between husband and daughter.

Suddenly, Rachel's eyes narrowed as she angrily snatched a potted plant from a wrought-iron stand beside the door, and hurled it at Klaus-Dieter's head. It glanced off his shoulder when he ducked to the side, and crashed onto the floor, spreading shards and black dirt around the room. "What have you done?" she screamed.

Klaus-Dieter's Adam's Apple bobbed as he swallowed. "I thought you…left for work," he managed. His hands were trembling and sweat had begun to form on his face. It was the first time in her short life that Becca had seen her father like this. It felt good to see him speechless and terrified….

But in an instant, his whole appearance changed; he looked like someone possessed with a demon - and the thing that was both her father and yet not, suddenly and without warning, lunged forward to grab Rachel's arm. "You better calm down, you dirty Jewish bitch!" it growled, its voice menacing and low. It was Klaus-Dieter's voice, yet it wasn't, and Becca watched, horrified by what she was being forced to witness. She felt as if she were dreaming.

Her father's hold was thwarted when Rachel stomped on his bare foot with a high-heeled shoe, and then dropped him to the floor with a well-placed knee in his manhood.

Becca sat, wide-eyed and unmoving as she beheld him writhing naked and vulnerable at her mother's feet. How many times had she fantasized about this moment? How long had she waited for her mother to come to the rescue?

Tears of gratitude began to flow as she realized that years of fervent and desperate prayers had finally been answered! "Mommy?" she cried.

Rachel's face was a twisted portrait of rage as she turned toward her daughter. "Don't 'Mommy' me, you little whore!" she spat. "How long has this been going on?"

Becca shrank back in confusion. Why was Mommy angry with her? "Since forever...." she replied, her voice small and high.

"Forever? Speak English, you little moron! How long, Becca?"

"...I don't know, Mom. He started doing it when I was five...."

Rachel glared down at her daughter with a vengeance. "Liar!" she screamed. "You expect me to believe that?"

Becca never had a chance to respond because she suddenly found herself being yanked from the bed by the hair and dumped unceremoniously onto the floor, beside her father.

"You little whore...." she heard her mother yell. "How could you do this to me?"

"No...ask Raymond!" Becca cried in self-defense. "Ask Raymond! He does it to Raymond, too!"

The look on Rachel's face reflected pure shock, and for a second she simply stood there, her eyes wide open, unblinking, totally confounded, bewildered, confused.

Klaus-Dieter moaned as he painfully began to rouse himself. "Jewish...bitches!" he growled between clenched teeth. "Gonna kill you both...."

Rachel let out a howl that made Becca's blood curdle. Without another word, she kicked her husband in the head, causing him to rock backward.

Seconds later, she was on top of Becca, choking the life out of her. "Liar!" she wailed. "He's no pedophile! You seduced him, you sick little whore! This is your fault!"

"Mommy...." Becca managed, but there was no sound coming from her lips.

The last thing she remembered before passing out was the sound of her mother's neck breaking as Klaus-Dieter's fist connected with her forehead.

Chapter 11

Becca remembers....

Luke 8:17 For nothing is hidden that will not be made manifest, nor is anything secret that will not be known and come to light. (ESV)

* * * *

Becca's headache was absolutely blinding. Tears streamed down her face in torrents as she slumped to the floor of the office. It was all coming back now; every sordid detail of those awful memories her mind had suppressed from that terrible day: Mother walking in on them; Mother's surprising reaction toward her and subsequently trying to kill her; waking up next to her dead mother in a stinking dumpster in Springfield, behind the Steak and Shake, where Klaus-Dieter - believing them both to be dead - had dumped their bodies.

After that, he returned home to set the house on fire and then he disappeared forever. That was how young Becca and her brother Ray had come to live with their grandparents....

Now, for the first time in decades, it was suddenly all so clear. The memories were painful, but at the same time, it was a relief to finally remember!

The Courseys had suspected that Klaus-Dieter had killed Rachel, and that he had attempted to kill Becca; and they suspected that he was the one who had burned the house down; but there was no tangible evidence. And, Becca, the only survivor, had amnesia and couldn't remember anything about that day. How convenient for Klaus-Dieter Behringer!

When the doorbell rang, her first inclination was to ignore it because she did not have the energy to move. But Spike's incessant barking was grating on her frayed nerves, and so she roused herself and discovered a worried looking Lora trying to peek through the front door's ornate window.

Seconds later, she found herself in Lora's arms, sobbing uncontrollably.

"Honey, what's the matter?" Lora asked with great concern. "Please tell me!"

"I remember," Becca sobbed. "I remember, I remember!"

Lora gently led her to the sofa where she listened attentively and with fervent interest as Becca related the events of that fateful day. Her face, for once, reflected genuine love and concern for her friend.

After she was done telling her story, Becca watched Lora head to the kitchen to fetch a couple glasses of water. Lora was truly a good friend, and Becca wondered how she could have ever had doubts about her. Yes, she had some "rough edges" and she often seemed to shove God into the background; but perhaps she was merely in need of some understanding and gentle guidance. Teary-eyed and remorseful, Becca smiled up at her friend when she returned to the living room.

"I can't believe he left you in a dumpster to die next to your dead mother!" Lora remarked, lowering herself onto the "love seat" across from the sofa where Becca rested. "My gosh, girl, how horrible! I just cannot wrap my head around that. That is an absolutely amazing story! And I can't believe your mother would turn on you like that. I can't believe you turned out so normal. Oh, Becca, I would have never guessed you had been through something like this!"

Becca nodded, her face reflecting profound sadness and grief. She had never dared to think of herself as being special for having "gone through" tough times. To her, "abnormal" was simply "normal." It was what she grew up with; she was used to "abnormal." But, it seemed foreign to think of her life as having been "abnormal"; and the mere thought made her feel guilty and disloyal.

She even felt guilty about the fact that she was telling her story to Lora. Liam should have been the first one to hear it.

Swiping at a tear, she said, "I'm normal because Grandma and Grandpa took us in when Dad burned down our house and disappeared. As ridiculous as it sounds, that whole bizarre incident helped spring Ray and me from our father's clutches. My grandparents were the only stable influence in our lives. At least part of our childhood ended up being normal."

"Well, that apparently didn't do your poor brother any good, since he ended up in prison. Oh my gosh, why didn't you ever mention any of this before?"

"Well, it's embarrassing to tell people you have a brother in prison, or to talk about how your father sexually abused you! It's not something you sit around and discuss. Ray and I never even told Grandma and Grandpa! Back in those days nobody talked about that kind of thing. Who would have believed us? It was just too weird and too painful and we both did our best to just forget about it."

"Yeah, but you could have told me and Annie. We're your friends! If you had talked this out sooner, maybe you would have remembered all this a lot sooner, and gotten it out of your system!"

"Maybe. But, Lora, the thing about sexually abused children is, down deep, they believe it's their own fault, somehow. I honestly thought I had *done* something to cause my father to want me sexually. So did Ray. We talked about that, once, eons ago. Logically, we knew better, but there's something down deep. It's hard to explain."

The two women were sitting quietly with their thoughts when Becca suddenly remembered it was a workday. Lora admitted that she had seen Liam at a drive-thru where he was "grabbing some lunch," and he had told her that Becca was home today, not feeling well.

"So, I decided to trust Jennie to run the store by herself, and I took the afternoon off, and here I am," Lora chirped. "...Okay, so, what are you going to do now? Are you going to call your brother to tell him?"

Becca shrugged. "I don't know. He clearly wants nothing to do with me. We'll see. I do know one thing, though," she went on as she shifted in her seat and pulled her legs up under herself. "I now know for sure why Rex Lambert reminds me of my father!"

Lora smiled as she carefully lowered her water glass onto the coffee table. "I've been meaning to talk to you about that," she said carefully.

"Well, Lora, I'm sorry; I know you're totally infatuated with Rex, but I'm just telling you how I feel! Rex reminds me of my father!"

"Okay, but you told me your Dad was this German, blond god. Well, Rex is dark and swarthy, Becca. It makes absolutely no sense that he would remind you of your Dad, so you really need to let that silliness go."

"Yes, I know. It's weird and I don't understand it, myself, but the fact is, he *does*." Saying a silent prayer, Becca cast a hopeful glance at her friend. In light of the horrendous day she had had, she truly didn't feel like getting into an argument about R. B. "Rex" Lambert.

"I guess it's mostly his eyes," she explained, hoping Lora would accept the clarification. "They're not the same color as my father's, but he scrunches them up into these little slits sometimes and when he does that, he reminds me so much of him. My brother Ray does that too, and it drives me crazy! Plus, Rex is loud-mouthed and pushy, and he's got some of the exact same mannerisms as my father had. I know it sounds crazy, but it's like they were made from the same mold or something."

"Well, they weren't!" Lora snapped. "Think about what you're saying, Becca!"

"I know exactly what I'm saying! And I'm sorry it offends you, but I feel how I feel."

"Okay, fine. But, it's time to get over it now. Honestly, I wish you'd get off of Rex's case. He's not that bad, and he's certainly never done anything to you! Geez, he's been at Beit Yisrael for five or months now! It's time for you to give him some slack. You've proven to yourself just now, today, that the issues from your past have absolutely *nothing* to do with Rex!"

Becca frowned. The warm and fuzzy feelings she had felt for Lora just a few minutes before, were quickly beginning to recede. "Be that as it may, we can't change that it was *his* behavior that kicked off a series of events that led to what happened to me today! You can't change what happened or how I feel about it, so why are you defending him?"

"Because I think he's a great guy! You should be grateful to him for helping you to uncover your repressed memories!"

"Grateful? He's an ungodly person who causes trouble and pits people against each other!" She wanted to add "he's demonic and I believe he was sent by Satan to destroy Beit Yisrael," but she kept the thought in check.

"Becca, you don't know him like I do!"

"Which means what, exactly, Lora?" she asked quietly.

"...Nothing! I just like him, that's all. We've gone out to lunch a couple times and talked, and...."

"You what?"

"Oh, there you go again, being Miss Holier-Than-Thou! It was just lunch, Becca! Nothing more."

Silence filled the room as Becca peered at Lora through hooded eyes. "'Just lunch'," she said, making no effort to keep the sarcasm out of her voice. "Does Orlando know?"

Lora's eyes flashed. "He doesn't need to know!"

"Really? You see no problem as a married woman, going out to lunch with some guy – especially the very person who's been upsetting the *shalom* at our synagogue?"

"I don't have to justify myself to you!"

"Well, okay, then, since we're being honest, here, you need to know that people are talking."

"Well, they can't be saying much because they don't know anything!"

"They have eyes and can see you and Rex pawing at each other, and they have ears to hear you and Rex chatting at the back of the room during the service. They may not 'know anything,' but you two are certainly giving the appearance that something is going on. People aren't stupid, Lora!"

Lora started to respond, but instead, she dropped her gaze and inhaled sharply. "Well," she said irritably, "I don't care what people think – including you. You're not my keeper. What Rex and I do is none of your business, okay? And I couldn't care less about what Orlando thinks, either!"

"Do you honestly believe your behavior lines up with Scripture?"

"Oh, shush! I'm sorry if you don't want to hear it, but Orlando has proven himself to be just another big, dumb Mexican, and I'm sick of him…."

"Oh my gosh, Lora!"

"...So sick of him that I'm going to ask him for a divorce. Rex is my friend and I like him! I mean, I *really* like him...Perhaps I even love him! If people can't handle that, they can leave the synagogue."

Becca gawked at her friend. Rendered temporarily dumbfounded and reeling from the events of this whole strange, eventful day, she simply sat there, mutely shaking her head. Any guilt about her torn feelings for Lora had vanished.

"*They* can leave the synagogue?" she said incredulously. "So people have a problem if they don't approve of your ungodly behavior? Lora, listen to yourself! You're sitting there telling me you plan on divorcing Orlando and carrying on with Rex while remaining at Beit Yisrael, right under Orlando's nose – and you expect me and everyone else to simply accept it, or leave?"

Lora pursed her lips. "Beit Yisrael is my church home, Becca," she finally said. "I don't know what I'm going to do, yet, but don't you worry about it, okay? This is *my* business!"

"Fine. Well, I pray you won't do anything stupid. Try to remember that God hates divorce."

"Give up the preaching, Becca!" Lora shouted. "I'm sure God doesn't want me to be in an unhappy marriage, so don't presume you may judge me!"

"I'm not judging you! My gosh, I'm just trying to get you to see that what you're doing goes against what the Bible says. Have you never read or studied the Torah?"

Lora's face turned an angry bright red as she examined Becca. "Oh, yeah, the Bible!" she shouted. "That's all you ever talk about! The Bible, the Bible, the Bible and Torah, Torah, Torah! Well, I guess you overlooked the part where God commands us to love one another!"

"What do you mean?"

"I love Rex! Just as the Bible commands. *Love* one another!"

Becca rolled her eyes. "Oh my gosh, Lora! There's a difference between loving and being *sexual* with our brothers and sisters! I'm sorry, but you're crossing the line! Good grief! Since Rex started attending Beit Yisrael, your skirts have become shorter and your cleavage more pronounced, and people are noticing. I don't care how you want to justify it; the plain and simple fact is, that is *not* how God wants His women to dress or behave!"

Lora, visibly annoyed, sprang to her feet and glared down at Becca with a vengeance. "I didn't come here to get a sermon from you today," she said. "I came to see how you were doing, and this is my reward? Wow! Some friend you are! I don't believe this! I'm outta here."

Snatching her purse from the coffee table, she turned on her heel and headed out the front door, leaving Becca sitting there with her mouth agape, feeling baffled and angry.

* * * *

Several minutes passed before Becca finally stirred. The house seemed much more peaceful with Lora gone. She was saddened to see that Lora had proven herself to be just another lukewarm believer who kept God in a box and removed Him only whenever it served her purpose. She was exactly the type of person who would be vomited from Yeshua's mouth upon His return....

"Father," she whispered, "please forgive Lora and cause her to somehow recognize that she's off Your Path."

A lone tear slid down her cheek as she prayed. She felt sad for the world, because most people, it seemed, weren't interested in knowing God. They liked to chat about God and the Bible, but they when it came to a real relationship that included obedience and actually doing His will, they scattered like cockroaches.

The sound of the garage door opening indicated that Liam was home, and she rose to greet him at the door. There was a certain spring in her step and she realized that something had changed. She felt lighter somehow, free and unencumbered - and happy. Yes, oddly *happy*!

She was happy because she was finally free from the trappings of her past. Free from Klaus-Dieter, freed from the suppressed memories that had clouded her mind....

She was simply free now, and it felt great.

Standing there by the door, waiting for Liam to appear, she basked in the glow of a few scattered sunbeams that made their way through the skylight.

"Thank You, Yahweh!" she cried out loud. "Thank You...."

When Liam walked through the door, she flew into his arms, crying tears of happiness.

Chapter 12

That small, still voice

---

2 Corinthians 11:14 There is nothing surprising in that, for the Adversary himself masquerades as an angel of light; 15 so it's no great thing if his workers masquerade as servants of righteousness. They will meet the end their deeds deserve. (CJB)

* * * *

"Honey, I'm so sorry I wasn't here for you," Liam whispered when Becca related the afternoon's events. "I should not have gone to work this morning.

"It's not your fault," she said. "You couldn't have known."

Liam shifted on the couch and took a drink from his water glass. "My God, what you went through! It's absolutely beyond comprehension!"

"Well, I guess the good news is, I survived to tell about it."

"My God...."

They sat silently for several minutes, just holding hands and basking in each other's presence. Becca knew Liam would have given anything to have helped her make it through one of the most agonizing days of her life. That, alone, made her love him even more.

"Lora shouldn't have been the first one to hear all this," Liam said softly. "Especially since she's so cotton-pickin' wishy-washy. I hope she doesn't ever try to use it against you."

Becca straightened in her seat. "Do you think she will?" she asked, heart in her throat. "I really don't want people to know...."

"Sweetheart, I don't know. All I know is that she's not exactly stable."

"Well, neither is Orlando, in my opinion."

"I know." Sighing heavily, Liam leaned against the back of the sofa and rubbed his eyes with the palms of his hands. "God, I don't know what to do, Becca," he said. "In all honesty, I don't want to stay at Beit Yisrael anymore. I've been fed up for awhile now. I mean, I love the people and the fellowship, and I love honoring Yahweh's Torah. But, oh my gosh...."

"...The nonsense is overwhelming," she cut in, finishing his thought. "I know, babe. Orlando is a weak leader, full of tolerance for silliness, lewd behavior and scripture twisting. Yet, at the same time, he thinks Beit Yisrael is going to become some big, mega-church!"

"And he's forcing me to help him make that pipe dream come true. He's been using me to death, ever since he discovered I'm good with computers and willing to serve until my last dying breath."

"Well, he's got us trapped now. If we leave now, we'll let the people down."

"I know. I know. We definitely are trapped. We should have listened to that small, still voice when we had the chance!"

Liam suddenly jumped to his feet and pulled Becca into his arms. "You know what we need?" he asked, giving her a quick peck on the lips. "A vacation! Let's just hit the road tomorrow morning and just drive."

"Where to?"

"I don't know. We'll start with my Mom in Boone and take it from there."

"She doesn't like me."

"I don't care. It's time for you two to meet. Let's just go, okay? We need to get away."

"I'll go pack right now," she said with a bright smile.

Chapter 13

Liam's torment

Romans 12:19. *And be you not avengers of yourselves, my beloved: but give place to wrath. For it is written: "If you do not execute judgment for yourself, I will execute judgment for you, says Elohim. 20. And if your adversary be hungry, feed him: and if he be thirsty, give him drink. For if you do these things, you will heap coals of fire on his head." 21. Do not be overcome by evil; but overcome evil with good.* (AENT)

* * * *

The afternoon was drawing to a close when Liam pulled into the driveway of his mother's house. It had been a long drive to Boone, Iowa, but the trip was necessary on several levels: Both Liam and Becca needed to get away from Seymour and all the endless work and craziness of the last few months. Becca, who was enjoying her new lease on life, needed a little "getaway" to help her unwind and get re-centered. And – last but certainly not least – Liam needed to do something about his mother, Nola, who had been steadily withdrawing from his life. The fact that her birthday was coming up was a perfect excuse for a visit – although she had done her level best to keep Liam and Becca from coming.

"Well, here we are!" Liam exclaimed as he opened the door to allow Spike to jump out and do his business. "Behold, my famous childhood home."

Becca feigned interest as she gazed at the small, white box of a house that squatted forlornly on a neglected corner lot on Linn Street. She had been married to Liam for nearly three years, and neither his mother nor his sister had ever made any real effort to welcome her into the family. They had both made it clear they wanted nothing to do with her, so, meeting his mother now was kind of anticlimactic. But, unfortunately, there were some extenuating familial obligations and there was nothing that could be done about it, except to make the best of a proverbial bad situation.

And so, wishing to please her husband, she pasted a smile on her pale and tired face as they headed to the front door.

When Liam's mother finally answered on the fourth ring of the doorbell, she seemed more agitated than happy. "Oh, it's you," she said with a scowl as she brushed some gray hair out of her face. "I thought you wouldn't get here for at least another couple hours yet."

"Hi, Mom!" Liam said, wrapping an arm around Becca's shoulders. "We're happy to see you, too! This is my bride, Becca."

Nola flinched and stiffened as Becca took a step forward to give her a quick hug. "It's so nice to finally meet you!" Becca crooned, hoping this would be the first step toward winning the old lady over.

"Well, yeah…come on in," Nola said hesitantly. "I'm makin' some iced-tea. But don't let that dog in. I don't like animals in the house."

"It's okay, Mom. He's totally house-broken," Liam assured her.

"Well…put him in the back yard. I don't need him jumpin' around on my furniture."

Liam gazed at Becca and shrugged. "Sure, Mom," he mumbled as he turned on his heel and headed around the corner to let Spike into the fenced-in back yard.

The first thing Becca noticed about Nola's house was that it smelled "old." It was tiny, dark and dank. An ancient and worn leather sofa rested against a wall immediately to the right. In order to pass into the house, she was forced to maneuver around a rectangular wooden coffee table that had been stationed directly in between the sofa and television set on the opposite wall. From there, one could either go straight ahead into a kitchen, dining-room and laundry room combination; or turn to the right, down a short hallway that led to the bedrooms.

Following her mother-in-law's lead, Becca headed straight into the kitchen to take a seat at an old, square dining room table.

"I smell food cooking, Nola," she said. "Can I help you do anything?"

"No, no. You guys just sit down. I've got it all taken care of. It's gonna be awhile, anyway."

As Liam entered through the back door, he put his foot out to prevent Spike from coming in. "You stay out here for a little while, buddy," he admonished. "Mom and Dad will be right inside, don't worry."

He leisurely sauntered over to the counter where his mother was pouring tea, and gave her shoulders a quick squeeze, then turned to join Becca at the table. "So," he said, beaming at his wife, "now you know where I grew up. What do you think?"

"It's sweet and quaint, honey."

"Very diplomatic!'

Nola moved around the kitchen like a person who was much younger, fetching glasses, setting them on a tray and pouring the iced tea she had retrieved from an old refrigerator. Once she approached with the tray, she quickly set the glasses in front of Liam and Becca, then took one for herself. She placed the last one across from Liam in front of an empty chair.

"Expecting company, Mom?" Liam asked.

"Yeah, I'm the company." The husky voice came from the dark hallway that led toward the bedrooms. Seconds later, Liam's sister, Donna, emerged. Dressed in a faded gray sweatshirt and blue jeans that did their best to cover an ample rear end, she made no effort to say "hello" or to bother embracing her younger brother. The look on her face as she took a seat, was one of haughtiness masquerading as pleasant.

Becca watched her husband's countenance drop briefly, but then he recovered and smiled. "What are you doing here, sis?" he asked cordially. "I thought you were back in West Virginia."

"Well, that's what you get for thinking, little brother," she replied with a smirk. "Divorces take time. A lot has happened since the last time we spoke. The divorce will be final soon and Darrell said he's leaving our house in a couple weeks. He's giving me everything, including the house, my car and alimony, so I'll be all set."

"Well, good. I'm happy for you."

"No, you're not. Don't pretend."

"I'm not pretending."

"Oh, shut up! I know how you feel about me having been married six times. I know you liked Darrell and think I'm a jerk for leaving him!"

"Donna, come on...."

"No, you come on! Now since you have 'found God' I know you think I'm just your 'lost sister' going through another divorce!"

"That's not true," Becca cut in. "Liam is my fifth husband, Donna, so I can assure you, he's not judging you about the number of times you've been married."

Liam's face turned crimson as he shot his sister a disapproving glance. "I'm not here to argue with you or to pee on your territory," he said. "We came to visit Mom. We had no idea you were here, or we wouldn't have come, because you and I can't be in the same room for five minutes without getting into a fight. This trip is for rest and relaxation, not stupid sibling fights and petty rivalry."

Becca, gauging the combat in Donna's eyes and desiring to diffuse her next comment, smiled at her. "It's great to finally meet you, Donna," she said tenderly. "I bet if we all calmed down, we could make this a great visit!"

Liam's blue eyes sparkled as he beheld his wife. Lifting his glass to toast her, he presented her with a grateful smile and said, "Just one of the many reasons I love you so much, my sweet forever bride!"

Donna snorted. "Forever bride…Yeah. That's what the last one thought, too."

Becca bit her bottom lip as she straightened. She had promised herself to be "a voice of reason" in case she was ever to fall into Donna's clutches. But she found that after just a couple minutes in the presence of this loud-mouthed and abrasive creature, she had already had her fill. She had actually already had her fill of her sister-in-law just a few months earlier, when Donna had made that callous "I can't stand to see you happy" comment….

"Well," she countered scathingly, "Liam's ex would have been a 'forever bride' if she hadn't committed adultery and had someone else's kid and walked out on Liam and their son! So, is there a reason you brought this up, Donna? Or do you just want to fight? Because, if you want to fight, I promise you, it will get ugly!"

"Honey, don't…." Liam said, but she ignored him.

"So, if that's where you're headed, Donna," she went on, "I can tell you right now, you won't win! I'll play nice as long as you behave yourself, but if you plan on ruining this visit for us, you are going to be very, very sorry! I've had more than my share of craziness over the last several months, and I am done! Got it?"

The look on Donna's face was priceless. Her mouth worked as if she was about to say something, but then she thought better of it and simply crossed her arms and scowled.

Liam, red-faced and now very angry, emitted a huge sigh of frustration as he addressed his mother. "Mom," he said, "this is really unacceptable. It was unfair of you to not have bothered to tell me Donna was still here. We haven't even been here for half an hour, yet, and already we're engaged in World War Three!"

Nola kept her gaze downward and seemed to be contemplating a reply. It was clear she felt trapped. "So," she said after some moments, "how long are you guys planning on stayin'?"

"Just for the weekend. Mom. I told you that already!"

"And where are you planning on staying 'just for the weekend'?" Donna asked in mocking tones.

"What do you mean? We're staying here, in my old room, where I always stay when I visit."

"Oh, no...no!" Nola blurted. "No, no. Your room's a mess."

"Why? You knew we were coming. How much work is involved in changing the sheets and dusting and vacuuming one little room?"

"Well...you and your sister don't get along and I figured you wouldn't want to stay at the house."

"We didn't know she was here! You didn't tell us!"

Although Becca had tried hard for Liam's sake to hold her tongue, she found her anger escalating. "We would have been happy to make reservations at some hotel, if you had only said something," she muttered, trying very hard to keep her voice even and calm.

"Why are you guys gangin' up on me?" Nola yelled.

"Nobody is ganging up on you, Mom...."

Nola blinked stupidly as she examined her daughter-in-law from across the table. "You don't have to have a reservation around here," she said. "This is not some big, booming metropolis. There's plenty of hotel rooms."

"Yeah, but not every hotel accepts pets!" Liam said.

"Well, you didn't have to bring your dog. You could have put it in a kennel!"

"Spike is not an 'it'...And we don't ever kennel him because he has severe separation anxiety," Becca cried angrily. Getting into a fight with her in-laws was the last thing she expected, and she was close to tears. These days it seemed there was a battle waiting to happen around every corner.

Liam, recognizing that his wife was dangerously close to her rage threshold, reached over to take her hand. "It's okay, sweetie," he interjected softly. "We don't have to go to a hotel. I'm happy to clean my old room, myself."

"Nuh-uh!" Donna said, shaking her head and gazing smugly at her brother. "The room is full of my stuff. We've been using it for storage. It's stacked with my personal possessions from West Virginia. I brought a bunch of stuff because I didn't know whether or not I would be going back home."

Liam's face reflected shock and disbelief. "And neither one of you could be bothered to tell us this *before* we came?" he barked.

"What can I say? We seem to have a major communication problem, and I guess it just slipped our minds."

"You know what?" Becca cried shrilly. "I have a perfect solution: We'll find a hotel room this evening and then we'll just go somewhere else tomorrow. Boone doesn't have to be our only vacation destination, honey. Problem solved. I don't force myself on anyone, and it's clear we're not welcome here."

The room fell silent for some moments, as everyone waited for someone else to say something. While Becca wished she and Liam could simply head out the door and leave these people behind, she also knew she would never forgive herself if she didn't at least give her mother-in-law a chance to redeem herself.

"So, Nola," she said, breaking the awkward silence, "instead of feeding us here today, why don't you just come with us to find a hotel and, after we've unloaded our suitcases, we will take you out to dinner for your birthday. Is there any place you'd like to go?"

Pasting on a sweet smile, she waited for the old lady's response. She couldn't help but notice that Liam looked just like her – the high forehead, the brilliant blue eyes framed by dark lashes and eyebrows. There was a very strong family resemblance in both Liam and his sister who clearly took after their mother – Donna more so than Liam, despite her dried-out, bottle-blond hair. The difference was that Donna and her mother had similar dour dispositions that tended to convey negativity, while Liam radiated a quiet intelligence fused with common sense and an ability to reason with clarity. She silently wondered how someone as sweet and bright and loving as Liam could possibly have been raised in this mad-house....

"No, I don't want to eat at any restaurant," Nola replied. "There are no good restaurants in Boone. Nobody around here knows how to cook anything good."

"But Mom," Liam said, "that was going to be my birthday gift to you – dinner at your favorite restaurant."

"I don't have a favorite restaurant!"

"All right. We'll figure something else out tomorrow, then, okay? We would truly like to do something special for your birthday, though, so please be thinking about what you would like to do."

Nola, appearing to be in a quandary of some kind, suddenly rose and headed down the hallway toward her bedroom and, for a brief moment, Becca was afraid they had made her angry somehow, and she didn't want to be in the same room with them anymore. But then she emerged carrying several photo albums, and dumped them onto the table in front of Rebecca.

"Since you're part of the family now," she said without bothering to look at Becca, "you ought to know what your relatives look like."

Donna, unmistakably annoyed and disinterested, stood and stretched as she gazed down at her sister-in-law. "Well, I've seen these a million times," she said. "Don't care to go down Memory Lane with you two, so I'll just see ya later." And with that, she wound her way through the living room and disappeared through the front door.

A blessed calm permeated the house after Donna's departure. Liam's mother seemed to exude another personality when her daughter wasn't around. She had switched into a certain "travel guide" mode as she rummaged and narrated her way through the picture albums, proudly showing off each photo like some prized possession. Her favorite ones seemed to be photos of herself as a young woman. "I was so beautiful," she kept reiterating *ad nauseum*. "Every man in Boone wanted me!"

"Well, I'm glad you chose Dad," Liam said at one point, as he gingerly rescued a loose photo of his deceased father that was sandwiched sideways among the pages one of the albums.

There were hundreds of photos of the immediate family and of relatives, both dead and alive; and of Liam as a small boy and as a teenager, along with photos of his parents before they were married and during various stages of their lives. At one point – to Liam's surprise – Nola offered to let him keep every picture of himself, along with any other photos he that suited his fancy.

"Well, thanks, Mom!" he exclaimed delightedly. "Maybe I should wait for Donna to get back, so I don't accidentally take any that she wanted?"

Nola shrugged. "Just take whatever you want, and don't worry about her," she said. "She'll never know the difference because she doesn't care about these pictures, anyway. She told me she hated her childhood and doesn't need the memories in pictures or anything else."

"Why does she hate her childhood? We didn't have a bad childhood."

"Well, she seems to think she did...as a matter of fact, hang on; I'll be right back; there's something I want to talk to you about before she returns."

Liam watched his mother disappear into the hallway, then gazed at Becca with raised eyebrows. "Are you warming up to her yet?" he whispered.

"Trying real hard. She's finally being hospitable."

"Well, don't get too used to it. She can turn on a dime."

When Nola reappeared with a small, tan lockbox, she promptly placed it in front of Liam. "My bank records," she said. "I'm handling my checking account just fine, but I need you to double-check and verify everything in my savings account, and make sure they've been addin' your father's social security checks and my life insurance annuities and stuff. I've never mentioned to Donna that she's not named on my accounts or that you're the executor of my estate. I think she assumes she is, but I don't trust her. You know how she is with money!"

All heads turned toward the back door when Spike began barking furiously to be let in. He had offered the occasional bark several times before, but Becca could tell, he wasn't going to take "no" for an answer any longer.

Tossing Nola a pleading glance, she said, "He won't shut up until we let him in. Do you mind? He won't hurt anything, I promise. It's almost dark outside and he's not used to being outside so long."

Nola hesitated as she pondered something she clearly viewed as a major predicament, and then finally opened the door to let the dog in. She backed away as if she had been burned when Spike briefly stopped to offer his paw. To spare Nola any further agony, Becca called him to her side, where he stood up against the chair to lick her hand.

"I'll go out and pick up any messes he might have made in your yard, Nola," Becca offered.

"No, no, I'll go," Nola said, and was out the door before anyone had a chance to protest.

"Honey!" Liam said with an urgency in his voice when Nola disappeared into the back yard. "You're not going to believe this, but Mom has saved up nearly half a million dollars! Take a look at this page…."

Becca's mouth dropped open as she scanned the document. "How?" she whispered. "Where did she get that kind of money?"

He shook his head and shrugged. "She doesn't do anything or go anywhere. She doesn't spend money on much of anything except food and utilities. The house is paid for and she doesn't have a car. So, it obviously all goes into savings."

"Oh, my gosh! Good thing you're the executor, or else Donna would have a field day!"

"She would go through this like water through a sieve! Mom is right not to trust her." With raised eyebrow, he bit his bottom lip and shook his head. "Boy, I don't have a good feeling about this," he finally said. "Donna seems to have Mom cornered into doing her will. I don't know why, but I have a feeling that if she ever discovers this, she will manipulate Mom into removing me from all bank records, and make her the executor...."

"Well, that would be a shame."

"Sure would! Especially since Donna will squander all the money. She's kind of like Lora in that regard. She just wants what she wants, and takes what she wants, without regard to the consequences."

It was completely dark outside by the time Nola returned; and, once back inside – after returning her lockbox to her bedroom - she checked on the food in the slow-cooker, and went to her refrigerator to take out the salad she had prepared earlier in the day. Minutes later, they were gathered around the table, hungrily devouring the vegetable stew and homemade biscuits.

Donna walked in just as they had finished eating. After briefly petting the dog who greeted her, she went to the kitchen to get herself something to eat. "So, did you decide which hotel you're going to stay at?" she asked between bites.

"I'm sure we'll find something," Liam replied.

"So, how was your illustrious trip down Memory Lane?"

"Fine."

"Good. Did you choose the pictures you wanted to take with you?"

Liam craned his neck to look at his mother, who had busied herself with washing the dishes. "Yes, I did, Donna," he said. "How did you know I was going to do that?"

"Well, we need to start getting rid of stuff because we're getting ready to sell this house."

"Sell the house? *This* house?"

"Yeah, didn't Mom tell you? She's going to come and live with me in West Virginia."

Astonishment crept into Liam's face. Shocked, his gaze bounced back and forth between Donna and his mother, who still had her back to him. "Mom," he said, "would you come here and sit down, please? Why didn't either of you consult me on this?"

Nola finished wiping down the counters, then hesitantly joined them at the table. "I didn't tell you because I knew you'd be mad," she said. "I'm old enough to make up my mind what I want to do. Donna convinced me that it was time I got rid of all my old junk and moved in with her. I'm almost ninety. It's time someone took care of me."

Hurt, and too stunned to speak, Liam scrutinized his mother.

"Wow," Becca interjected to break the heavy silence that followed. "You guys are just full of surprises! Nola…take a good look at the shock in your son's face right now. How does that make you feel?"

"I don't feel anything. This is about my life, not his feelings!"

Becca shook her head. "I've waited nearly three years for one of you to reveal that you care about Liam and his well-being; but so far, nothing. We would have *loved* for you to ask us if you could live with us, but you couldn't even be bothered to *visit* us, and we're really just a few hours down the road!"

"It's okay, honey," Liam interjected, his tone sounding defeated.

"No, it's not!" she retorted. "And today, out of the blue, you tell us you're moving to West Virginia. You can't visit us because it's supposedly too far for you, but you can arbitrarily – without speaking to your son about it – sell the house he grew up in, and without batting an eye, pick up and *move* to West Virginia? And you don't care how that makes Liam feel!"

"It doesn't matter how he feels!" the old lady screeched. "It's *my* decision to make; not his!"

"You're missing the point, Nola!"

Liam suddenly reached across the table to take his mother's hand. "Mom," he said with a quiver in his voice, "this really hurts. You never mentioned that you wanted someone to take care of you. Why didn't you include me in this decision, and allow Donna and me to work things out?"

"Because all you guys ever do is fight!" she replied, drawing her hand away as if she had just touched a hot stove.

"Well, how is this going to work out in view of our earlier conversation?"

"What conversation?" Donna demanded.

Ignoring her, Liam continued to observe his mother's face, waiting for her response. "I'm waiting for an answer, Mom...."

"I don't know," she snapped without bothering to look at him. "It'll all work out."

"I want to know what you're talking about," Donna said shrilly. "What 'will all work out'?"

"Tell her, Nola!" Becca said. Her anger had finally reached that "point of no return" and right now, she didn't care whose feelings were going to be hurt. Out of her corner of her eye, she could see Spike trembling in a corner.

"I'm movin' to West Virginia, Becca!" Nola shouted. "Me. Not my bank accounts. My bank accounts will stay here."

"Bank accounts?" Donna cut in.

"Everything will stay the same. Don't worry about it! It's not your concern, anyway! This is between me and my son. You just stay out of it!"

Donna tossed her mother a quizzical look. "Mom?" she said alarmed. "What are you talking about?"

Nola rose angrily. "Liam should never have married you, you," she cried, addressing Becca. "...You smart-alecky

Jewish...person, with your weird religion. He used to be a good son until you came along! He needs to wake up and divorce you! And the sooner, the better!"

Liam's chair slammed against the wall when he rose. He started to say something; then immediately changed his mind and turned toward his wife.

"Let's go," he said hotly. "This was a horrific mistake, and I'm done. The insanity in this house just never ends and I can't take anymore. I've had enough." Turning briefly to glance at his mother he said, "Happy birthday, Mom! I hope Donna can make you very happy."

Seconds later, they were slamming the door on some unintelligible, hateful comment from Donna. "I'm done!" Liam told Becca. "I'm finally done trying. I have no mother. I never did...."

Just before they got to the car, Becca reached out to pull Liam into her arms. "You have me," she cooed. "We have each other and we have God. That's *all* we need."

Chapter 14

Trouble at the Elders Meeting

---

*2 Corinthians 6:*14 *Do not be unequally yoked with unbelievers. For what partnership has righteousness with lawlessness? Or what fellowship has light with darkness?* (ESV)

* * * *

"Hello, y'all!" Rex called out merrily as he appeared at the top of the stairs, on the second floor of the synagogue. Fingering the railing, he rose to his full height as he scanned the room, and grinned. "Hey, you didn't think you could sneak in a meeting without me, did ya?"

"Oh, this is just too much!" Becca whispered as she clasped Liam's hand under the table. "Isn't this guy ever going to give up?"

It was Wednesday evening and the Monthly Elders' and Deacons' Meeting was already in progress. The group had gathered at one of the long tables, nearest the stairwell. As always, the smell of freshly brewed coffee permeated the building.

Liam and Becca had just returned from their short vacation and, per Orlando's request, had come straight to the synagogue, without bothering to go home first. Orlando had called Liam's cell yesterday, to ask if they could curtail their "mini-vacation" to make the meeting, insisting he had "some major announcements" to make, "because some strange things have been happening around here!"

And so, here they were – Orlando at the head of the table; Liam seated directly across from him, at the far end; along with the Elders who sat on one side - Fred and Lyle; and the deacons on the other - Lora, Cassie and Becca. Annie was absent tonight because, according to Fred, she had a bad cold; and Chad had called to say he couldn't make it because one of his kids was sick. Leroy hadn't made it to the past several meetings, and people weren't expecting him anymore, anyway, because everyone knew his health was headed downhill.

"Hello, Rex!" Orlando shouted gaily...although his face reflected anything but joy at seeing the man who had become a major thorn in his side. "You're at least half an hour early...but you're welcome to join us, brother. We're still in the process of doing the formal business portion of our meeting, so you'll have to bear with us. You know everyone here, right?"

Liam scribbled something on the mini-notepad he had brought, and pushed it toward Becca. *"Why doesn't he make Rex wait downstairs until we're all done here?"* he wrote. *"He does this every month!"*

She raised an eyebrow when she saw Liam's response and scribbled: *"O is afraid of R! But sometimes I think he's more afraid of incurring Lora's wrath."*

Rex approached, cowboy hat in hand, and nodded. "Been with you all for almost seven months," he said. "I'd be in trouble if I didn't know everyone by now!"

"Well, have a seat," Orlando went on. "I know you're here because you, as always, have more questions for us - but I really want you to hold them until we're all done. We've got a lot to cover tonight, yet."

"Nice to see you folks again," Rex said as he sauntered across the room toward Liam's end of the table, to take the vacant seat next to Lyle, directly across from Cassie.

Becca scanned Orlando's face, hoping he hadn't noticed the surreptitious loving glance Rex had given Lora as he passed. But she could tell by his pained expression that he had. Lowering her eyes, she said a silent prayer and tried to push away any negative thoughts.

She and Liam had managed to have a wonderful vacation – despite the pandemonium at her in-laws' house - and she felt relaxed and refreshed. Nothing was going to get her riled up tonight; not even the knowledge that Lora was evidently still furious with her (which was okay, because she was still angry with Lora, as well, and she prayed that Lora had not approached Orlando about the divorce, yet). Lora hadn't said a word to Becca at all, and there was a distinct chill in the air.

"Well, okay then, let's continue," Orlando said. "Liam, I want you to know it's great to have you guys back! Thank you for making it in time, because we have a lot to cover, and I didn't want to have to repeat myself. A lot of strange things happened while you were gone."

"We've been gone less than a week!" Liam remarked, chuckling.

"Yeah, well...." Orlando tilted his head to one side and stared at his folded hands resting atop the table. "Hmm...Well, I guess I'll start with the weirdest thing that happened, which was that we had to change locks this past weekend because of some crazy woman. You might remember her - that eccentric lady with a peculiar name; Marianna Maher or Mayer or something like that? She's that one who wears orthopedic shoes and walks with a cane, and when you try to talk to her, she gives you the willies because she has a way of looking right through you. She's only been coming for two or three weeks, or maybe a month, at the most, I don't know exactly. All I know is she's very hard to talk to because she seems off in her own world."

Pausing briefly to take a sip of water, he produced an odd smile and dabbed at his mustache with his thumb and forefinger. It seemed to Becca that Rabbi Orlando was deeply troubled, and she wished there was something she could do or say to help him feel better. He had not been "acting right" for a couple of months now, and her guess was, Lora was at the bottom of it all. Surely, he suspected by now that his wife was having an affair....

"Okay," he continued, "so, this Marianna person thinks she's entitled to half our tithes because she is supposedly related to the original owner of this building. Unbeknownst to me or Lora, she had a locksmith come out to change the lock on our door last Sunday, and then she also broke the lock on the *pushka* and took out all the money, including the checks... which she deposited into a bank account she created as the supposed new secretary of Beit Yisrael."

There were some scattered gasps around the room and Fred, who usually didn't have much to say at these meetings, straightened in his seat and presented Orlando with a curious look.

"She had a locksmith come and change the locks?" he asked in disbelief. "Without proper identification or anything? How the heck did she manage that?"

"There's that 'heck' word again," Rex cut in with a chuckle. "Must be something in the water around here."

"I don't know, Fred," Orlando replied. "She told them she worked for the synagogue and they didn't ask any questions. They just came out and changed the locks for her, and I couldn't get into the building until I had them changed again!"

"What locksmith would do such a thing?"

The Rabbi shrugged. "All I know is that she refused to tell us who it was, and there is no paperwork, so we can't find out. I suspect it was one of the Amish. Needless to say, this Marianna will not be allowed in our synagogue again!"

"Did you press charges?" Liam asked.

Orlando scrunched his face into a painful grimace. "Well, no," he said, drawing out the words as if they had several syllables. "I...I don't even know how to begin to tell you, but...."

"Oh, good grief, Orlando!" Lora snapped. "...We didn't press charges because Marianna used her own thumb to dig out one of her eyes! She stood right there in the police station, in front of God and everybody, and just plopped it onto the floor."

"She what?" Becca cried.

Orlando emitted an impatient sigh as he tossed Lora a searing glance. "She took Jesus' words literally about plucking your eye out if it offends you," he explained. "Her eye offended her because it caused her to see our tithes and want them for herself. She's clearly sick in the head, and so we just took her to the hospital and left it at that."

While everyone else stared at Lora in wide-eyed disbelief, Rex let out a snort followed by a belly laugh that filled the room.

"It's not funny, Rex," Lora said, with a giggle. "It was really pretty gross. You should have seen it." Unable to control herself as she watched Rex writhing in his chair, she too, broke into laughter and, seconds later, Lyle began to chortle so hard, he had to leave the room.

Liam, Becca, Cassie, Fred and Orlando – they all stared at each other in stunned silence, waiting for the din to die down. None of them saw any humor in this.

Orlando, appearing quite stricken, produced a low sigh when Lyle finally returned. Reaching into his pocket, he pulled out an envelope that made a dull clanking sound when he tossed it onto the table. "Here," he said. "The new keys. Pass them around and take one. Throw away your old one."

"Can I have one?" Rex asked, grinning. He had backed his chair away from the table and was stretched out with his legs crossed at the ankles, and his hands laced behind his head.

"They're for the Elders and deacons, Rex," Liam snapped. Becca could tell he was simmering over the fact that Rex had been allowed into the meeting. Tired after driving all day, he was in no mood for any nonsense.

His face reflected grave concern as he peered across the table. "Orlando, clue me in here," he said. "I don't understand why Marianna was able to get any money out of the *pushka* on a Sunday. Lora usually takes the tithes out of it after every *Shabbat* service, on Saturday. There shouldn't have been any money in there."

Lora leaned back in her chair and yawned. "I just forgot to do it last weekend," she quipped.

"You forgot? You've been doing this every week for years...."

"I know, Liam. I just got busy, that's all!"

"Busy doing what?"

"Well, it doesn't matter," Orlando said, coming to his wife's rescue. "Turns out, it's no big deal. We got our money back, so no harm done!"

Liam shook his head. *"No big deal? Really???"* he wrote on the little notepad that he surreptitiously handed to Becca under the table.

A pained smile played across Orlando's lips as he gazed around the room. "Another thing that happened while you were gone, Liam," he went on, "was that Harry Malone came back. If you'll remember he has been gone for awhile, ever since...well, ever since Rex told him to go home and bathe."

"Hey, now, be nice," Rex muttered. "It worked, didn't it? He stopped coming and the air got cleaner in here. Now he's back all cleaned up and shaved and acting like a normal human being. You have *me* to thank for that!"

"Yes, he has cleaned up his act." Orlando added. "But, he's still behaving strangely."

Lora abruptly leaned forward to touch her husband's arm. "We should change the subject," she said pragmatically.

"I'm not finished telling the story," Orlando replied. "....Harry, uhm, he did something really crazy last Saturday."

"Just drop it, Orlando," Lora whispered. Her tone indicated that this was not a request.

"Why?"

"Well...you know...."

"No, I *don't* know! Just let me finish, okay? Sheesh! Anyway, at the end of the service, Harry came to tell me that he...*Ow!*"

A thud originating under the table caused Orlando to jump, and he reached down to rub his sore shin. "What'd you do that for?"

Lora's face turned cerise in color as she gave her husband a menacing look. "We don't need to talk about this!" she said between clenched teeth.

"Okay...what is wrong with you?"

"God, you're dumb!" she cried with a sigh as she threw up her arms. "Fine! Go ahead and spill the beans, then."

Baffled, exasperated and visibly shaken over his wife's behavior, Orlando pushed himself away from the table, and continued with his story. "Okay," he said, "maybe I'd better talk fast to keep from being attacked again! Anyway, what I've been trying to say is that Harry put an envelope into the *pushka* containing a check for fifteen thousand dollars."

Lyle let out a low whistle. "Fifteen thousand?" he said slowly. "What did he do, rob a bank?"

Again there were some scattered gasps. It was no secret that Harry wasn't a rich man, and so this new knowledge caught everyone by surprise.

"I tried to convince him to tear up that check, but he mentioned something about how God told him to give us half of the severance pay he received when he got laid off from his job. And then he turned around and walked out the door and said he'd see us next week."

Rex, still laid back in his chair, emitted a chuckle. "Cool, you guys are rich now!" he said. "I guess that means the congregation doesn't have to tithe for awhile, huh?"

"Oh, stop it, Rex, you silly," Lora said playfully. "That's exactly why I didn't want anyone to know!"

"Well, thanks for the vote of confidence! I'm hurt that you didn't tell me this! That was a pretty big thing, don't you think?"

"Why would she have told *you* that?" Orlando demanded.

"Well, Rex, I'm sorry; I guess I just forgot," Lora replied, making no indication that she had heard her husband's question. "You know I totally trust *you*! It's just not something that everyone else needs to know. We *want* people to keep tithing! It's just that...well, it's nobody's business how much the tithes bring in."

"Sure it is, Lora!" Liam interjected hotly. "I understand your concern and, while it's true that the amount of someone's individual tithe is no one's business, the fact is, the congregation *does* have a right to know our overall financial situation. And the Elders and Deacons certainly do need to know what's going on. So, unless you were worried about Rex's unauthorized presence in this meeting – because he truly does *not* have a need to know - I don't understand your desire to keep Orlando from mentioning this."

The look on Lora's face revealed exasperation. "I'm not worried about Rex at all," she snapped indignantly. "He's my friend and he has a right to know, and he has just as much right to be here as you do. I know he won't say anything, will you, Rex?"

"No, Lora," Liam countered, "Rex *doesn't* have the right to know the amount of someone's individual tithe – and I'm surprised you are actually sharing this type of thing with him! Furthermore, he does *not* have just as much right to be here as I do. This is a closed Elders and Deacons Meeting, not a free-for all, and from now on," he said, looking directly at Rex, "I'm telling you as the Assistant Rabbi, you're not invited, unless we announce that we intend to make time *after* the meeting, or if it is to be an open meeting!"

"Excuse me?" Rex began, but Liam's glare cut him off.

"It's not up for discussion," Liam snapped. "Scripture is clear about how God wants His people to behave. This is a Messianic synagogue, not a three-ring circus!"

Then, addressing Orlando, he said: "I'm guessing you tore up Harry's check? Surely, you don't plan on allowing him to tithe that much."

"Of course we plan on keeping it!" Lora interjected sharply. "He gave it to us. It's ours now. We're not giving it back."

"Really?" Liam said, tossing Orlando a questioning gaze. "You don't plan on giving it back? You do realize Harry isn't exactly mentally stable, right? Not to mention, he is unemployed and has no income. It would be completely unethical to keep that money!"

"Well, that's his problem, not ours," Lora mumbled, crossing her arms beneath an ample bosom.

Lyle cleared his throat. "Well, my dear lady," he croaked hoarsely, "since your husband is the Rabbi, I believe it's his decision to make; not yours!"

Lora shot him a warning glance, then looked at her husband for support. "God, Orlando!" she cried. "See what you've caused because of your big mouth? I told you to shut up about Harry!"

Orlando rolled his eyes and then peered off to the side at nothing in particular. "Liam," he muttered, "I'll talk to you about all this later. Let's take a quick coffee break, shall we? I desperately need a break!"

Chapter 15

The demon reveals itself

John 10:10 The thief comes only to steal and kill and destroy. I came that they may have life and have it abundantly. (NAS)

* * * *

When the meeting resumed, Orlando put on a bright smile and said, "Let's talk about something happy, now! Cassie has some joyful news for us, don't you, Cassie?"

The young lady's face flushed as all eyes turned toward her. "Oh, no – no!" she said. "We don't have to do this right now."

"Sure, we do. Please, go ahead."

The bewildered look on Cassie's face revealed that Orlando's request had clearly taken her by surprise. "Well, okay," she said, grimacing. "I'm, uh...Okay, well, I'm getting married."

Becca recoiled. *No, Cassie,* she thought. *Oh, honey, no....*

"Go on," Orlando urged, making a motion with his hand, indicating he wanted her to say more.

Cassie shook her head. "No...no, really. I can't, Orlando," she protested.

"Oh, Jesus Christ!" Rex muttered. "Just spit it out, little lady. The suspense is killing us!"

"Can you please not use that name as a cussword?" Liam barked.

"Oh, come down off the damned cross, Liam!"

"Rex, please!" Orlando begged. "Let's just allow this meeting to go on unimpeded…. Go on, Cassie, dear."

Cassie blanched. Appearing to be grappling with her emotions, she took a deep breath and said, "Okay, fine. I won't be able to hide it soon, anyway. I'm getting married because…because I'm pregnant."

Becca's breath seized and she instinctively reached for Liam's hand under the table. Unable to utter a sound, she sat, stone-faced, trying hard to breathe normally in hopes of quelling the sick feeling in the pit of her stomach.

Come here, little girl. Come to Daddy….

The room had fallen silent. No one said a word. They all stared at Cassie, whose face now glowed beet red.

"Wow," Lyle muttered. "I don't know what to say, except this is the very reason I'm glad I never had daughters!"

"Right on!" Rex replied as he leaned forward to exchange "high fives" with him.

Fred, usually silent and preferring to remain "in the background," peered across the table at Lora for her reaction to the news. But there was none. His body language revealed that he wanted to say something, but instead, he remained mum.

Cassie gazed around the room, disappointment marking her expression. "Well, thanks a lot for your lack of support, everybody," she said. "I can hear you all thinking, so, I will just say this: I don't need a sermon about how I've been sinning, so, whatever you all think about my situation, keep it to yourself, because I don't care to hear it. I'm pregnant and I'm getting married, and there's nothing you can do about it except deal with it."

"Well, regardless," Orlando said cheerfully. It's a *happy* occasion! There's a new baby on the way, and so I'm going to abide by Cassie and Rowdy's wishes to marry them under the *chuppah* this summer, outside in the gazebo."

Becca, doing her level best to appear neutral, kept her gaze straight ahead and focused on nothing in particular. Unable to hear over the angry pounding of her heart, she swallowed hard. Her mind was reeling as Cassie droned on, mumbling something about keeping her pregnancy a secret from the congregation for as long as possible....

The only thing Becca was able to see in her mind's eye, was that a naïve and immature young woman had just admitted she was marrying a convicted pedophile, and that an innocent little human being was going to be brought into their world. The thought was almost too much to bear.

She wanted to say something, but recognized there would be no point. It was too late; the deed was done. What she found most disturbing, was the fact that Orlando's presentation of Cassie's "predicament" had been very un-Rabbi-like. It was an outright lie to suggest this was a "happy occasion." He knew exactly what Rowdy was and what surely lay in Cassie's baby's future! In her opinion, he should have figured out some other way to present the news to the group, because it was certainly not "happy"; it was totally disconcerting and wrong on many levels! And it was unquestionably yet another item that Rex should *not* have been privy to!

"Well," Lyle said with a smile that was less than genuine. "I don't agree that it's necessarily a happy occasion, but I wish you well - and, honestly, I just thank God you're not my daughter because I...well, I'll leave it at that."

Fred nodded as he kept his gaze lowered. "I wish you well, too, Cassie," he mumbled.

"Oh just stop it!" Cassie snapped. "Everybody – just stop! You know you don't wish me well! I know how you all feel about Rowdy. You hate him!"

"We don't hate him!" Orlando countered.

"Oh, let's cut the crap!" Rex cut in. Eyeing Cassie with what could only be described as contempt, he let out a snort that reverberated around the room – a gesticulation that, for Becca, was reminiscent of one of Klaus-Dieter's disgusting habits.

"Since none of you pious hypocrites have the guts to say it, I will," he went on. "Cassie - what the hell do you expect from us? Your boyfriend is a damned pedophile. And now you're giving him a kid to molest in the privacy of his own home! Everybody else can pretend they're happy for you, but if I were your father, I'd kick your ass! I hope Orlando's already wiped the floor with you behind closed doors, because you deserve it!"

The room went deathly silent as all eyes bounced back and forth between Rex and Cassie - who shot from her chair as if she had been prodded with a hot poker. Mouth open and eyes wide with shock and welling with tears, she stood there, trembling. Her jaw was working, but she didn't utter a sound.

Becca spontaneously rose to place a protective arm around her shoulders. "My God, Rex!" she wailed. "My God! What is wrong with you?"

"Oh, I'm sorry, Becca," he replied, his voice dripping sarcasm. "Did my comments offend you? Be honest - you were thinking the same thing. You were sitting over there looking pretty green around the gills when Cassie announced that she was pregnant!"

"My goodness, I don't believe this!" she yelled. "My goodness! Just do us all a favor, Rex, and crawl back under that rock you slithered....!"

"Young lady, that's not very nice," Lyle interjected. "I strongly suggest you read the writings of Paul and Timothy so you can get an idea as to how women are to behave in church!"

"Back off my wife, Lyle!" Liam snapped.

Cassie stood rigidly for some moments, unable to move in the wake of Rex's insensitive and crass comments. When the color returned to her face, she turned briefly to give Becca a stiff nod; then, as the tears began to flow, she grabbed her purse and stormed from the room.

Orlando started to rise and go after her, but then abruptly changed his mind and returned to his seat. "Rex," he managed wearily. "Was that really necessary? Really?"

"This was a new low, even for you, Rex," Liam said lowly. "You just proved beyond a shadow of a doubt that you don't belong in our meetings. You don't belong in our congregation, period!"

Lora half-rose from her seat and glared at Liam. "Will you get off of Rex?" she cried, her voice high and shrill. "How dare you talk to him like that! You don't have the right to ask him to leave!"

"Actually, I do," Liam countered. "But I've been deferring to Orlando. If I had my way, Rex would not only *not* get to come to these meetings, but he wouldn't get to set foot in the synagogue, ever again! What he just did was downright despicable! How would you like it if he talked to you that way?"

There was no mistaking the obstinate look that Lora gave her husband when he started to open his mouth to speak.

Liam, who noticed the look (since he had a clear view of the far end of the table), shook his head and nudged Becca's knee with his own. She gave an almost imperceptible nod to show she understood: Lora was in charge, and Orlando was caught between that proverbial "rock and a hard place." Orlando wasn't in charge anywhere, it seemed; neither at home nor at the synagogue.

Appearing overwhelmed and exhausted, the Rabbi leaned forward to bury his head in his hands. "Thank God we're almost done, because I can't take much more," he said, his voice sounding old and worn and tired. When he looked up, he scanned every face and then slowly emitted a sigh. "I'm going to close this session by giving you the final piece of news and then we can all go home – hopefully in one piece, before anything else happens to upset us around here."

Liam scribbled a quick note and slid it over toward Becca. *"How much more of this nonsense can we take! I do NOT understand why O refuses to throw Rex out on his ear!"*

She merely raised her eyebrows and nodded, then scribbled on the notepad: *"Honey, I'm so tired of fights and arguments. Really, between the nonsense at synagogue and at your mother's house last week, I'm exhausted! I just want some peace and quiet! I wanna go home!!!"*

Reaching under the table to squeeze her hand, Liam smiled as he mouthed, "I love you!"

"…As you can see," Orlando was saying, "Brother Leroy is absent again tonight. He hasn't been able to make any of our meetings for months now, and he called me this past week to tell me he was officially stepping down as Elder. He just can't do it anymore. He can hardly even get out of bed these days, according to his great-grandson, who has been driving him to synagogue. I knew this, and that's why I made Chad and Lyle Elders a few months ago."

"Wow, cool," Rex bellowed gaily. "Make me one, too!"

"We don't need any more Elders, Rex."

"But…what if I *want* to be an Elder? Can't I at least throw my hat in the ring?"

Lora slid forward in her seat, her face glowing with excitement. "Oh, Orlando, come on!" she exclaimed. "I think it would be a great idea to make Rex an Elder! He's a quick learner."

Becca turned to get a better view of her – a view that was totally unimpeded, now that Cassie was gone. "Are you out of your mind?" she said. "You can't be serious!"

"No more Elders!" Orlando bellowed. "Rex, Lora, I'm tired. My goodness, you're pushing me to the point of exasperation! We have three Elders and one assistant Rabbi; that's plenty....Please don't argue with me about this. Let's just conclude this meeting in peace."

A coy smile played on Rex's lips. Clearly amused, he sat up and folded his arms across his muscular chest. "Well," he warbled playfully as he looked at Orlando, "I'm not leaving until you tell me you're making me an Elder!"

"Oh, for crying out loud, Rex!" Liam remarked, punctuating his frustration with a sigh. "This isn't Kindergarten; it's a synagogue!.... Orlando, honestly, this has gone far enough. I implore you to stop Rex from attending future meetings. We don't have time for his nonsense."

"Don't you dare, Orlando!" Lora shouted. "Rex has a right to be here! If you do what Liam said, I promise you, you'll regret it!"

Fred, who had been quietly listening to the exchange, suddenly sat up. Crimson with rage, he said: "What do you mean, Orlando will regret it, Lora? My gosh...he's the Rabbi; he's our leader. He's the one who is supposed to make good and sound decisions for our congregation. Rex has *not* been good for our congregation! All he ever does is cause trouble! So, how dare *you*, Lora? How dare you attempt to keep your husband from his obligations? The Book of Proverbs tells us it is better to live on a corner of a roof than to share a house with a nagging wife – and you,

Lora, are the biggest nag I've ever seen in my life! I have an outspoken wife, too, but she's tame, compared to you!"

Lora's jaw dropped. She, like everyone else at the table, was shocked to hear Fred address her this way, because Fred rarely opened his mouth about anything.

"Excuse me?" she said. "Did I just hear you correctly...."

Fred rose with a force so hard that he nearly fell over. "You know what?" he mumbled, interrupting her in mid-sentence. "Maybe Orlando has to take your constant verbal beatings, but I don't! This conversation passed the stupid stage a long time ago and I'm done wasting my time. My sick wife needs me at home. Nothing is being accomplished here, so color me gone."

The only sound for several seconds was the muffled thumping of Fred's shoes on the carpeted stairs. Lora sat in stunned silence, gawking at Orlando in hopes that he would somehow come to her defense.

But he didn't. He simply sat there, speechless and flabbergasted, rubbing his temples and shaking his head.

"Well, I guess I've been told off!" she said indignantly. "I expect his days as Elder are over with, Orlando?"

Hoping to ward off Lora's wrath, Becca broke the uncomfortable silence by attempting to reroute the conversation to the one who was responsible for the chaos, in the first place: Rex.

"Rex," she said gently, "can you not see how much damage your behavior has caused here? Everyone is at each other's throat now, so please, just go quietly, and leave us alone. This has truly gone far enough."

But Rex simply grinned as if he found the whole situation funny. "I don't know what you're talking about," he said.

"You don't? Well, okay, let me spell it out for you: You caused Julie to stop believing in God; you caused some members to doubt the validity of Yahweh's Torah; you've caused dissension among the Elders and Deacons; you were downright evil toward both Cassie and Harry, and you seem to relish causing trouble at our monthly Elders' meetings. You've accomplished what you obviously came here to do, so now it's time to leave."

Shrugging, he produced an impish grin. "Who says I came to 'accomplish' anything?" he said offhandedly. "I'm just some guy who is seeking God's Truth, and helping others learn to question things for themselves. Why is that so wrong?"

"I'm not getting through to you, am I?"

"Not really. Nothing you ever say, does. You're patronizing, condescending and forever talking that Torah stuff that I couldn't care less about. So no, you're not getting through to me. And I have to tell you," he added smugly, "you constantly referring to God as 'Yahweh' just gives me the willies!"

Becca sharply inhaled and rolled her eyes, biting her lip in the realization that she was about to lose control of her emotions. Rex, it seemed, always managed to bring out the worst in her.

"Your arrogance is truly beyond compare, Rex," she said. "I feel sorry for you because you seem driven to cause dissension. Something inside you apparently feeds on chaos, and you clearly love it! What a shame. What a waste of precious energy...."

Lyle, not stirring from his relaxed, half-reclined position with his hands folded across his abdomen, spoke up. "Oh, Becca," he said lazily, "knock it off, already! Leave Rex alone. Just stay out of it and let the men handle this."

Exchanging a short, knowing glance with Liam, she made no effort to hide her frustration. Lyle had been a thorn in her side for many months now, and his unabashed dislike of her was becoming tedious.

"Well, I guess I would let the men handle it if they were indeed handling it!" she said, trying hard to keep her voice from cracking. "But, honestly, I don't see any *man* besides my husband trying to do something about the Rex situation, do you? What have you done about Rex, Lyle? Actually, what have you done for the synagogue, besides lord your superiority and boss the women around?"

Orlando sat dumbfounded, gazing helplessly at Liam, as if hoping Liam would somehow intervene and restore *shalom*. But Liam simply smiled at his wife, and indicated for her to go on.

Lyle breathed a sigh, and placed his palms against his eyes and rubbed. "You don't get it," he finally said. "Nothing needs to be done about Rex and we're not going to *do* anything about Rex. The only thing we need to *do* is to get off his case. Rex is a good guy. He's my friend. I've been out to his ranch and watched him work his butt off to raise beef to put food on people's tables. He's no threat to anybody. He's just a good-natured good ol' boy, trying to fit in. So, he's a little overbearing. That's just part of his personality. Give the guy a break, for Pete's sake!"

"Good-natured?" Becca cried. "Did what he just said to Cassie sound 'good-natured' to you, Lyle?"

"Oh god, woman, you seriously need to study what Paul said about the female of our species being quiet in the church! Jesus, you are...."

Liam started to come to her defense, but she briefly held up her hand to stop him. "Seriously, Lyle?" she cut in. She had taken about all she was able to take out of that man, and there was no turning back now.

"*Paul* said? Really? You're going to spring Paul on me? Any true Torah observant person knows that the writings of Paul have been grossly taken out of context! But, hey, I understand. Chauvinists like yourself aren't about to read the Bible in context because it feels too good to be able to twist and abuse Scripture for your own purposes."

Rex, face aglow with a certain sadistic delight, leaned forward to poke Lyle in the ribs with his elbow. "You gonna let that woman get the upper hand in this?" he said, smirking.

Lyle grimaced and made a dismissive gesture. His face behind the Fu-Manchu had turned the color of plums, and it was clear he was enraged and doing his best to control himself. "I'm thinking Fred had the right idea," he said as he suddenly rose to leave. "I'm outta here, too."

Becca watched him head down the stairs and then angrily turned her gaze on Rex. She started to say something, but, out of the blue, the room suddenly brightened, and she realized she was about to have another one of her strange "vision" episodes. *"No!"* she thought. *"Not now!"*

Horrified, she watched as Rex's arrogant face morphed into something sinister, right before her eyes. His sneer had all but disappeared, replaced by a leering, twisted visage - the same demon she had seen on him the day he entered the synagogue for the first time. No swastika this time; just pure evil staring back at her, and glaring over at Liam.

Just as in previous "episodes," the ordeal made her feel as if the air had been knocked out of her lungs.

"Okay, Orlando," she somehow heard Lora saying above the pounding of her heart. "How much more of Becca's mouth are you going to force us to endure? Who's in charge here, you or her? Why are you not throwing her and Liam out on their ear? All they ever do is pick on Rex!"

"Oh, Lora, calm down," the demon said, its voice emanating from the deepest part of Rex's diaphragm. "It's clear that your gutless wimp of a husband, squatting there like a toad on his fat, dumb, Mexican butt, has no control over anything. It's clear that he's seen fit to allow the great and over-zealous team of Ritter and Ritter, to run this synagogue. Yes, oh *yes* - there are some seriously grave issues running rampant in this place...and Lora, honey, as you've witnessed for yourself, the problem ain't me!"

Orlando looked as if he had been kicked in the head; the pained expression on his face revealing Rex's words had cut to the quick. "Gutless?" he said. "I'm not gutless...."

"You're *gutless*, Orlando!" Rex went on. "Weak. You're a whiney, spineless excuse of a man! You can't see what's going on right under your own stupid nose. Somehow, it doesn't bother you that Liam is running this church – even though he's eminently more qualified than you could ever dream of being! And it doesn't seem to bother you that, that cute little wife of his - Little Miss Morality, who walks around with a cob up her butt all the time - is constantly strutting around and giving everybody biblical concussions to keep them in line. We can't fart in here without her coming up to us and cramming some Torah verse down our throat to show us why farting is a sin! Hell, why don't you just make *her* the Rabbi of Beit Yisrael? She would probably do a better job than you!"

"Okay, I've had enough!" Liam shouted angrily as he rose and reached for his wife. "Honey, let's just go! We're done here."

"No! Not until I finish telling this monster off!"

The demon sneered. "No, you shut up, Becca!" he replied, his voice low and dangerous. "If anybody needs to leave this synagogue, it's you! You're like some yappy little female dog snarling at everybody and biting their ankles! You're like some plague we can't cure."

"Amen!" Lora yelled in the background. "Tell her, Rex!"

The rage in Becca became unhinged, uncontrollable. Oddly, it was no longer Rex she heard, but Klaus-Dieter, taunting her, belittling her, making her feel like she was the cause of all the world's ills.

Unable to contain herself any longer, she started to dash around the table, with the intention of pummeling Rex within an inch of his life. Liam managed, just in the nick of time, to grab her around the waist to stop her.

"Monster!" she screamed as she struggled to free herself. "He's possessed! He's got a *demon*!"

"Honey, don't!" Liam whispered harshly in her ear as he held her tight. "Let's just go."

But she didn't hear him. All her focus – every cell and fiber in her body – strained to attack Klaus-Dieter's demon.

Rex visibly recoiled as he watched Becca's crazed behavior. "What?" he said, looking around for support. "What did she just say? I have a *demon*? What the hell?...."

In the background, Lora's demands for Orlando to clear the room began to grate on Becca's nerves, provoking and feeding her rage. Every bad feeling she had ever experienced in her life seemed to be reaching some kind of a crescendo in this particular moment, causing her to want to lash out and become physical.

She had never become physical before, but the antics of Rex, Lora and Lyle over the last few months had become overwhelming, too much to bear. Together, those three had managed to push her over the edge. Each in their own way made her feel "raped"...mentally raped. She couldn't get away. They, like Klaus-Dieter, had been inserted into her life; they were like an illness she couldn't shake....

Orlando, terrified and not knowing what to do, stood up and stared helplessly at the scene. "Can we all calm down, please?" he muttered nervously.

"Fahrvergnügen time, you Oven Fodder!"

Becca quailed as Klaus-Dieter's words echoed in her mind, but she remained stoic as she returned Rex's frosty gaze. In the back of her mind she recognized that this was simply another attempt on Satan's part to pull her back into her former rut. He couldn't stand the fact that God was in the process of healing her of her past, and he was desperate to drive her insane. And Rex was the perfect tool.

She knew this, but she couldn't help herself. She needed to get physical with this demonic entity that was Rex Lambert. "Let me go, Liam!" she begged as she struggled in her husband's grip.

Rex gawked at Becca as if he were examining a bug under a microscope. "And you guys think *I'm* the problem around here?" he demanded. "Look at her! *Look* at her! God almighty...."

Playing into the drama that was unfolding, he pretended to be terrified, rising from his chair and taking a small step backward, as if to get away from the crazy woman who was threatening his life. "She's nuts!" he shouted.

Becca eyes filled with tears as she watched him. All she really wanted was to be rid of this terrible plague that was Rex Lambert. All she wanted was to be free of his evil antics and the terrible emotions he evoked in her. She just wanted to be able to be part of a congregation of loving people who didn't constantly incite disorder and confusion, or prey on the weaknesses of others....

Suddenly - as if a faucet had been turned off - the sensation inside Becca's mind melted away. The room dimmed and returned to normal. Becca, still trembling, relaxed into Liam's arms. The strange episode was apparently over.

Time stood still as she and Rex stared at each other, neither making any effort to hide their scorn. Rex's demeanor had been downgraded from malicious and irate to plain angry; and, for some moments, he seemed just as dazed and confused as Becca; gazing around, as though he had just emerged from a coma.

To keep the momentum going, however, he kept backing away, pretending to be in fear for his life, finally coming to rest near the railing, where he stood like some giant pillar, his presence dominating the room. His chest was puffed out, and he stared at Becca as if she were some alien from outer space.

"Lady," he growled, "you're crazy! You're downright nuts, and I can't be around you anymore!"

"Well, then *leave!*" Liam demanded. "Nobody's forcing you to stay. The meeting's over. You ruined it. Go home and gloat!"

"You're all nuts!"

"Go, so the rest of us can leave," Becca said breathlessly. "The show's over."

Rex stood his ground for several seconds, contemplating his next move; apparently not wanting the drama to end. Finally, he opened his mouth to speak, but then changed his mind, and abruptly turned to stomp down the stairs.

"Bunch of religious freaks!" he yelled over his shoulder. "Take your precious synagogue and shove it!"

Lora let out a small yelp as she watched him disappear down the stairs. "No, Rex!" she cried as she made a mad dash to follow him. "Wait for me! I love you! Don't you leave me behind!"

Orlando, appearing totally stricken, turned in time to watch his wife disappear from view. Adam's Apple bobbing, crazily, he looked to all the world as if he were being strangled.

"I...I don't know what just happened," he whispered, gazing wide-eyed and bewildered at Liam and Becca who were now the only other people in the room. "What just happened here? Becca, what did you do?"

"What did *I* do?" she cried angrily. "The better question is, what did *you* do! You're the one who allowed things to get to this point! You...."

Her words were cut off when Liam placed his hand over her mouth. "Honey, *let's go!*" he urged as he started pulling her toward the stairwell. "We're done here. Let's just go!"

"You want to know what happened!" Becca shouted as she started down the stairs. "You allowed Satan in here; that's what happened. And he has totally destroyed us! Liam and I tried to tell you that, but you refused to listen. You reaped what you sowed, Orlando! We're done with you!"

Chapter 16

Satan is alive!

Isaiah 3:11 Woe to the wicked! It shall be ill with him, for what his hands have dealt out shall be done to him. (ESV)

* * * *

"Honey," Liam's voice sounded alarmed as it crackled in Becca's ear. "You have to come to the synagogue right away," he was saying. "I need you to be my witness when I talk to Orlando and Lora."

It was mid-afternoon the following day, and Liam had gone to the synagogue to – as he put it – "tie up some loose ends" and retrieve his personal belongings before tendering his resignation. After last night's fiasco, he had made up his mind to leave, because the never-ending chaos prompted by Rex Lambert had taken its toll. Not only had Rex managed to destroy the synagogue from within; but his presence was destroying Becca's sanity. She had been doing her best to heal, now since her memories had returned. Being around people like Rex, Lyle and Lora was severely hampering her progress. It just wasn't healthy.

Rex wasn't kidding anybody; he wasn't going to leave Beit Yisrael. Not as long as Lora was there. And Orlando was too weak to make him leave. Orlando's way of dealing with issues was to ignore them until they went away on their own. This situation could go on forever, and Liam and Becca weren't about to wait that long.

The Sabbaths, which were designed to be all about God and a weekly physical, mental and spiritual "resting" had been turned into never-ending demonstrations of disruption, disrespect and drama. God Himself had been relegated into the background, and Liam and Becca had decided the only way to restore *shalom* in their lives was to put things back into a biblical perspective - which meant they would have to flee from the evil that had permeated Beit Yisrael. Trying to fight it by themselves had not worked. It was time to go.

"What's the matter, Liam?" she asked.

"You won't believe what I found," he said with an air of excitement. "Oh, Becca, it's bad. It's really bad! I'll tell you when you get here."

Becca's brow furrowed when she hung up. Their day had already been dampened by a letter from Liam's mother bearing the disappointing news that Liam had been released as executor of his mother's estate. A simple, handwritten sticky note attached to the legal documents inside read: "I've made Donna executor. You don't need to worry about me anymore. – Mom."

"Well, that didn't take very long," Liam had commented thickly. "I knew Donna would turn Mom against me, eventually; and she did it in less than a week!"

The house phone rang just as Becca was heading out the door. To her surprise, the voice on the other end belonged to her brother, Ray.

"Hey sis," he said brightly. "Don't hang up, okay? I'm calling to apologize...."

Becca's eyes began to fill with tears of happiness. "Oh Ray," she cried as she swallowed over the lump in her throat, "I had already forgiven you!"

"No, don't be too kind. I don't deserve your forgiveness. I'm a Schmuck."

"You certainly are!"

"Yeah, I know...." His voice caught, and she could tell he, too, was crying.

"What's the matter?"

"Nothing, actually. I'm just calling to set things right between us. I was so mean to you, and after my pride finally walked out the door, I realized you didn't deserve what I dished out. I get miserable sometimes and I want the whole world to suffer with me. I...I tend to get diarrhea of the mouth, just like Klaus-Dieter used to do. I can't shut up when I'm mad."

"I know. I'm actually the same way."

"Sis, I know you suffered just as much as I did at the hands of our father, and it wasn't fair for me to suggest otherwise. I know you tried your best to protect me...."

Becca nodded. "Thank you," she managed. "I...well, just thanks. I needed to hear that."

Seconds later, she was animatedly explaining that she had suddenly remembered her past. "Ray," she cried, "it happened the day after my visit with you! I remembered what happened the day Mom was killed…Klaus-Dieter did it! I saw him do it!"

"Well…yeah," he replied. "We all figured as much. He obviously killed her and thought he killed you and was trying to dispose of your bodies…."

"No, Ray! No! That's the thing. He didn't try to kill me! It was Mom. He was trying to protect me from Mom!"

"What?"

Ray was mute as she recounted the events of that awful day when their mother had caught Klaus-Dieter in the process of raping her…of seeing her mother killed…of passing out and then waking up in a dumpster….

"I don't know what to say to that," he remarked when she was finished. "All these years I thought Dad had…Well, damn! Grandpa and Grandma and I figured something terrible had happened between you three, but I never dreamed…."

"Ray, there's more," she said, biting her lip as she considered how to explain what she had learned about their father. "I looked up Klaus-Dieter on the Internet, and he was there….Ray, he's listed as a war criminal on the Simon Wiesenthal Center's website."

Silence on the line. "War criminal?" he whispered in disbelief. "He's a *war* criminal?"

Tears fell rapidly as Becca detailed all she had uncovered, promising to run off the information to mail to him, since he had no Internet access. "It appears he married Mom to get out of Germany," she said. "Who knew, right?"

A low moan came across the line and Becca found herself wishing she were there with her brother to give him a big hug.

"Oh, God!" he said. "I wish I had known that when he came to visit me! I would have turned his butt in!"

Becca drew in a sharp breath. "Wait – what?" she cried. "He visited you? Klaus-Dieter visited you?"

"Yeah. Three or four years ago, or so. I couldn't believe it when I saw him sitting there! He's old and decrepit now, and dragging around an oxygen tank."

"He's alive?"

"Yeah. Well, he was back then, anyway. He lives in Mack's Creek, I think."

Heart in her throat and weak-kneed, Becca sank onto the living room sofa. There were spots before her eyes and for a moment she felt as if she were going to faint.

"He wasn't dumb enough to use his real name when he came to see me, sis. He was going by…let me think…Max Neumann! Said he was married to some woman named Marguerite who was a full-blooded Apache Indian squaw he met right after he and Mom moved to Ash Grove, and he had just started his lousy plumbing business. This Marguerite person had a stopped-up toilet and he fixed it and they fell in love and carried on this clandestine affair apparently for years before he married her."

"Really….!"

"He said he practically raised her son during that time. And, oh yeah, he kept talking about her blue eyes and how unusual that was for an Indian....Let's see, how did he put it? Oh! He said she had 'brilliant blue eyes set in a cream in coffee complexion' – those were his exact words. He said she was the most beautiful woman he had ever seen in his life."

"He was raising her son?" Becca muttered in amazement. "Right under our noses?"

"Yeah, that's what he told me. Kinda makes me wonder if he was raping him, too. I doubt it, though, because he kept gushing about him. Apparently the kid worshiped him, and vice-versa. He mentioned that the kid went to college and ended up being some big cattle rancher or something. I forgot exactly how he put it. Anyway, he spoke highly of this boy, which really hurt, because I'm sure he never spoke highly of us."

"...So, he was committing adultery on Mom and even raising someone else's brat? And at the same time, he kept accusing *her* of adultery! Ray, I could just scream!"

"We should scream together, sis!"

"So, did you ask the old hypocrite why he made us homeless by burning the house down?"

"Of course, I did. He denied doing it. He said he was out on a job that morning, fixing somebody's plumbing. His story was that a burglar killed our mother and he tried to kill you, and somehow that person set fire to the house. He disappeared because he was afraid they would blame him and he'd end up in prison...."

"Oh bull! Bull!" Becca cried heatedly as more tears fell. "He was there, raping me, and he killed Mom!"

"Aw, sis…if only I hadn't done a sleepover at Grandma's…."

"No, Ray! Don't you dare! It's not your fault; so don't even go there! What happened, happened. There's nothing we can do about it now."

"Dad said he couldn't handle the fact that they would put the blame on him, and since he had post-traumatic stress from his time in the German army, he wasn't prepared to deal with it, and so he ran. He kept apologizing for that."

The rage in Becca's soul grew in intensity, making it hard to breathe. It was excruciatingly painful to know there was no one to lash out at. There was no way of going back to confront her parents or make them pay for what they had done. No way to change anything at all.

"God," Ray went on, "I wish I had known then what I know now! I would have turned him in!"

"Wait a minute!" she cried. "Ray, why did he come to see you? Why did he risk that?"

"He…well, he came to ask me for forgiveness. He sat there crying for half an hour, holding my hand the whole time, and kept saying how sorry he was. He blames himself for me ending up in prison. Can you believe that? He rapes and tortures his children for years and kills their mother and burns their home down, and now he's sorry. I guess impending death tends to do that to a person."

Becca sat unmoving, stone-faced, feeling old and drained. "Well, that's good," she whispered.   "It's good that he apologized and that he realized that you followed in his footsteps."

"To be honest with you," Ray continued, "I felt like whacking the crap out of him. But he looked so pathetic sitting there with that oxygen tube under his nose, panting like a dog, that I just sat there like an idiot, telling him I forgave him. Anyway, at the end of his visit, he hugged me and left and I haven't heard from him since. As much as I hated him, I didn't have the heart to be mean to him, or anything. Judging by the shape he was in, I figured he would be dead soon, anyway."

"Well, I hope he's not, because I'm going to find him!" she said with an all-pervading resolve. "I want to hear him apologize to me, too!"

Ray's laughter sounded hollow. "Go, sis!" he said. "Let him have it!"

"Oh, you bet I will!" she cried. "You bet I will...."

When she hung up the phone, she sat for a long time, unable to move. She knew then, beyond a shadow of a doubt, that God really was healing her, one step at a time. And, in order to be fully healed, one of the things she needed to do was to face that awful demon that had held her hostage for so long....

Hopefully, dear ol' Dad would still be alive and able to recognize her when she confronted him!

Chapter 17

The Rabbi confesses

Deuteronomy 28:47 Because you did not serve the LORD your God with joyfulness and gladness of heart, because of the abundance of all things, 48 therefore you shall serve your enemies whom the LORD will send against you, in hunger and thirst, in nakedness, and lacking everything. And he will put a yoke of iron on your neck until he has destroyed you. (ESV)

* * * *

Becca's face was flushed when she arrived at the synagogue. The knowledge that her father might still be alive had energized and revived her, and she couldn't wait to confront him. This was the closure she had waited a lifetime for, and she had prayed in the car on the drive over here, for God to give her clear guidance on what to do. The last thing she wanted, despite the fact that her heart was full of revenge, was to be out of God's Will.

She found Liam and Orlando in Orlando's tiny office, upstairs, toward the back of the building, overlooking the forest. It was immediately evident by the pain in their faces that something was terribly wrong. Orlando was perched behind his desk, staring dejectedly at the pile of papers strewn across the desktop; while Liam sat in one of the ancient green armchairs, appearing concerned and sympathetic.

"Did someone die?" she asked nonchalantly as she tossed her purse onto the floor between the two armchairs.

"Worse," Orlando replied.

The old chair made a little hissing sound when Becca sank onto the cushion. "What could be worse than someone dying?"

The two men exchanged glances, neither of them apparently wanting to be the first to talk.

"Where's Lora," Becca asked.

Liam shrugged. "She refused to come."

"Okay, so what's going on?"

A visible shudder shook Orlando as he sat, stunned, peering at the papers in utter disbelief. "Your husband has discovered something in our financial records," he replied, his voice quaking. "It seems Lora has been stealing from the synagogue."

"Stealing?"

Liam gave his wife a sidelong glance. "She's been 'cooking the books' – playing with the numbers," he offered when it became clear Orlando was too overcome with grief to continue. "I decided to examine them after last night's meeting because Lora made those strange comments about Harry's fifteen thousand dollars. It's not just that she didn't want the congregation to know about it; she didn't want *anyone* to know...because she took that money and deposited it into her own, private, secret bank account. She's been transferring lots of Beit Yisrael's tithes into that account; an account nobody knew about, including Orlando."

"I trusted her!" Orlando lamented.

Liam's tone was subdued as he related that Lora had apparently been "cooking the books" for some time. The amounts she had skimmed from the synagogue's account, he explained, were usually minimal, small enough to go unnoticed by the untrained eye.

Becca was mesmerized, too stunned to take it all in. "No wonder she's been able to afford designer clothes," she whispered. "Why would she have a secret account, though? She has a thriving business in Springfield."

Orlando covered his eyes and began to sob. "I think she plans on leaving me," he replied sadly. "I've felt that for a very long time now. Even before that swine, Rex, came along. Oh, God! I knew she was greedy, and I am guilty of catering to her.... Oh Father, forgive me!"

"You haven't done anything wrong, Orlando," Liam said.

"Yes, I have! I have taken money out of the tithes, too! Lora made me do it...As you've probably guessed, she doesn't take 'no' for an answer. But, Liam, I swear, I always put it back, eventually. I didn't plan on actually stealing from the synagogue!"

Becca grimaced as she and Liam exchanged glances.

"She's been so disappointed in me," Orlando went on. "Beit Yisrael isn't growing all that much, and doesn't bring in the money we had hoped. She's been demanding I get a 'real job' - but God is my whole life! I don't want to work in the secular world."

"We understand, Orlando," Liam said. "There's no shame in having to contend with a headstrong woman. I've got one, myself!" he added, with a loving wink at Becca.

"Oh, God, I'm so ashamed!" Wiping his eyes with his sleeve, Orlando gazed at Liam. "I...I don't know how to say this, and I'm ashamed to say it, but...Lora beats me!" he admitted, his voice reflecting shame and defeat. "My wife beats me."

"Oh my God!" Becca exclaimed. "Oh, Orlando, I'm so sorry to hear that!"

"Rex is right, I'm not much of a man."

The Rabbi's words hung precariously in the air for a while; no one knew exactly what to say next. Although the news was unexpected and disconcerting, it was not surprising to Becca. Lora had certainly dropped enough hints in the Friday afternoon ladies' get-togethers about her simmering hatred for Orlando. Until now, though, she had never realized the true extent of the evil resonating in Lora's psyche.

Liam shifted in his seat. "I don't even know what to say," he said grimly. "But, really, there is no need to be ashamed. There are plenty of women who beat their husbands...."

"But, I am a Rabbi. I counsel people! I've even counseled men whose wives are just like Lora! I know what to tell them, but I can't seem to take my own advice."

"Well, it's always different when we, ourselves are going through something."

"I'm just so ashamed!"

"Well, Orlando," Liam said with resolve, "I think it's time your wife learned what shame feels like, don't you? She needs a major wake-up call! I promise you, she'll be getting it later today, when I tell her that what she's done here could land her in prison. It's only a matter of time before the IRS catches wind of this!"

Orlando reached for a tissue from a desk drawer and blew his nose. "No, Liam, please," he said soberly. "Let me take the whole blame. I'm ultimately responsible for what happens at the synagogue. As a matter of fact, if you want, we can all go down to the police station right now, and I'll turn myself in."

Liam vehemently shook his head; and, placing his hands on either side of his armchair, he pulled himself upright and crossed the tiny room to begin collecting the papers on Orlando's desk.

"Nope, that's not how it's going to happen," he replied. "This will be handled quietly between you, me, Becca and Lora. Nobody else needs to know what transpired here this afternoon. But, by the time all is said and done, Lora will know she needs a serious attitude adjustment. I certainly don't want her to end up in prison, but if she refuses to behave and comply, I'm going to press charges against her. Not you, Orlando; *her*!"

"No, brother, please!" the Rabbi begged, his eyes reflecting panic. "I insist. Please. You don't know Lora...."

"And she doesn't know *me*, Orlando! She has committed a crime – not just against the synagogue, but against God and her husband."

"No! No! Oh, this is…this is not good. This is beyond embarrassing. Brother, just please let me handle it my way. Just let me turn myself, in! Let it be all on me."

Liam remained silent as he finished gathering the documents. "Don't worry, we're not going to do anything rash," he said. "As a matter of fact, the only thing we're going to do right now is to pray together and ask God for His wisdom. After that, we are going to the bank to remove you and Lora from all Beit Yisrael's accounts! She will have to be present to do that – and you will need to let her know in no uncertain terms that if she refuses to join us, that the Sheriff will come and collect her in handcuffs."

While Liam spoke, he walked around the desk and indicated for Becca to join him on the other side of Orlando so they could pray for him.

"No, brother, please," Orlando said, his tone filled with desperation. "Just let her have the money and let me take the rap. I…I'll make up for it, somehow. I'll pay it all back."

Liam, jaw set, gently laid a hand upon Orlando's shoulder. "Sorry, Rabbi," he said firmly, "but what has to be done, has to be done. Just before Lora's name is removed from the accounts, I will tell her that she needs to transfer back from her 'secret' account all the monies she has stolen from Beit Yisrael over the years. Every penny. If she refuses, I *will* have her arrested on the spot and she will get to spend tonight in jail. If that happens, this situation will no longer be secret…."

"No, Liam…please don't do that!" The trepidation in Orlando's voice was heartbreaking, and Becca found herself fighting tears. "She'll tell Rex…oh, Liam," Orlando went on, his voice cracking, "Rex is her lover! He's very strong. Don't mess with him, please! Just let it all be."

"Rex can go fly a kite," Liam replied calmly. "If he doesn't watch out, he might end up an accessory to Lora's crimes!"

Orlando's shoulders began to shake as he sobbed. "Liam," he said hesitantly, "there's a reason I just want to go ahead and take all the blame! I'm not so innocent, either!"

"None of us is," Liam replied. "But a crime has been committed. *Two* crimes, if you count Lora's adultery."

"No! No, I mean, Lora's not the only one. I have someone, too. Lora knows."

Liam bit his lower lip as he cast a quick glance at Becca. "You have someone?" he asked, half holding his breath. "What do you mean?"

Orlando nodded. "I have a girlfriend." The look on his face revealed he was at once ashamed and relieved to be admitting his transgression.

Becca felt her jaw drop. "Hopefully, it's no one from our synagogue," she blurted before she had a chance to stop herself. She expected a scathing reply telling her it was none of her business; but; to her surprise, he simply shook his head.

"No," he said. "It's a lady from…from Webster County Baptist. You probably know her, but I can't tell you who it is. It wouldn't be fair to her."

She shook her head. "Well, I have to say, I am very disappointed in you. I understand your need for love, but Orlando...."

"I know! I know, and I'm sorry!"

"Well, good!" Becca replied stonily. She wanted to say more, but decided she was too angry. Nothing she could say or do would change anything. Having had spouses who committed adultery against her, she knew first-hand the pain and agony that resulted for all concerned.

Be that as it may, any respect she might have had for Orlando was now completely gone, vanished like a snowflake in the desert.

"She loves me for who I am," Orlando explained in desperate attempt to make Becca and Liam understand. "I needed that! Lora hasn't loved me for years."

"But you also know that God hates adultery, Orlando! It's so serious in His eyes, people used to be stoned to death for it! He *hates* divorce! Oh, my gosh, Orlando! Yeshua died to take away our past sins; not so we could continue to sin!"

"Honey, please!" Liam begged. He had paled considerably, and Becca suddenly realized that her husband was just as shocked as she. "It's...it's none of our business."

Orlando lowered his gaze. "Well, it really *is* your business," he said dolefully. "I'm your Rabbi and like everyone else, I need to be held accountable. And I failed."

"Yes, you did!" Becca snapped, her voice trembling. "My goodness...doesn't anyone around here take God and His

Word seriously? If there is someone – just one person! - I would sure love to meet them!"

Liam quietly removed his hands from Orlando's shoulder and took a small step backward to steady himself against the windowsill. The look in his eyes pleaded with Becca to stop talking.

"Well, I'm sorry, Liam," she said as the tears began to fall. "Maybe I shouldn't feel this way, but I truly believe people who claim to be Believers should take responsibility and act like it! Is that too much to expect? We're supposed to be wholehearted toward God! If we're not, then, what does that make us?"

"Hypocrites," Orlando replied glumly but with conviction. "That's what I am. I'm a big, fat hypocrite."

Heaving a great, shaky sigh, he slowly and clumsily rose from his chair and stepped out from behind the desk. "Let's just get to the bank and get this over with," he muttered. "I want this day to end."

Chapter 18

The beast roars

Ephesians 4:27 ...and give no opportunity to the devil. (ESV)

* * * *

It was nearing sunset on the following day when Orlando called an emergency Elders and Deacons meeting. He looked drawn and sickly, and it was clear that this whole situation had begun to take its toll.

Surprisingly, Lora had shown up, and was sitting in her usual place, next to her husband. Becca guessed it was only because she had been "scared straight" at the bank yesterday. During the show down, Lora had been at once exposed and cornered and forced to choose between prison or quiet, behind-the-scenes actions to resolve her predicament.

Liam's no-nonsense approach had clearly put the fear of God into her and – for the time being, anyway – she had learned some respect for authority. And so, there she was, sitting stone-faced next to Orlando; present, but refusing to make eye contact with anyone.

As was the case a couple days ago, everyone was here, except for Chad and Annie. Tonight, Lyle (who acted as if he had been severely inconvenienced) was seated near

Orlando, with Fred to his right, serving as a buffer between himself and Liam.

Fred had called Liam earlier to discuss his desire to skip this meeting and simply resign as Elder. "I've truly had it," he told Liam. "I just can't take it anymore. We used to all get along; but now, it seems, Rex has somehow taken over. I don't understand Orlando. He keeps getting more and more wishy-washy, allowing all sorts of nonsense. And what's with Lora all of a sudden? She acts like she's in charge! She's gotten way too rude and smart-alecky for my taste. Obviously, there's something going on between her and that idiot, Rex. I don't understand anything anymore, Liam. All I know is that I personally can't take much more."

Liam had agreed, and – without divulging what had transpired yesterday - suggested Fred attend this particular meeting because "something was going down, or else Orlando would not have called a special meeting."

And so, there they all were (even Cassie who had stormed out of the previous meeting) perched around the table, waiting for Orlando's "big news" to unfold.

Orlando wasted no time calling the meeting to order. It was clear that he was in no mood for any horseplay today. There was no attempt to be jovial or friendly. No smiles; nothing. He was, for once, "all business."

"First, I want to thank you all for coming," he said, hoarsely. "I'm sorry to spring another meeting on you, especially since *Shabbat* is starting shortly, but some life-changing things have come up, over which I have no control."

"I just want to make one thing clear before you start," Cassie cut in pithily. "If Rex shows up, I'm walking out and never coming back!"

"Rex isn't coming," Orlando replied. "He doesn't know about this meeting."

"Oops!" Lyle blurted, shifting uncomfortably in his chair. A blush had begun to crawl along his neck and soon his whole face turned crimson.

"What do you mean, 'oops'?" Orlando demanded.

"Well, I mean...Rex may show up. I kinda told him about the meeting."

Liam's ears perked. "You *what?*" he shouted.

"Well...Orlando called while Rex and I were chatting on the phone earlier and I had to put Rex on hold for a minute and...well, he kind of guessed what was going on."

Orlando blanched. "Please tell me that you told him not to come!" he said angrily.

"Well, I tried, but you know Rex...."

A low moan to escaped the Rabbi's throat. "I don't believe this," he mumbled.

"...I wasn't thinking when I said it. I'm sorry."

Liam emitted a great sigh as he shook his head in disgust. "Well," he said, "good thing I thought ahead. I was afraid Rex might somehow hear about this meeting, and so I took some precautions and locked all the doors."

"Locked doors won't keep that bastard out!" Cassie cried.

"Well, they'd better, or else I'll have him arrested for breaking and entering."

"Oh geez," Lyle mumbled. "You're acting like Rex is some big, bad monster."

"He is!" Becca snapped.

"Oh, woman, knock it off...."

"No, *you* knock it off, Lyle," Liam warned. "If you make any snide, chauvinistic comments tonight, I'm going to put you out!"

Lyle leaned forward and craned his neck to get a better look at Liam, at the end of the table. "You're going to put me out?" he said hollowly. "Did someone die and make you God?"

"No," Liam replied. "But I am the Assistant Rabbi, and as such, I have the authority to oust troublemakers."

Without bothering to wait for a response from Lyle, he turned his gaze upon Orlando. "I'm not playing any stupid word games tonight or allowing myself to get pulled into silly arguments that accomplish nothing," he said firmly. "Therefore, I want to go on record as having said that, unless you, Orlando, maintain total control this evening, I'm going to get up and leave. After what happened at the last meeting, I have no more patience left. Like everyone here, I am a volunteer, not a paid employee. None of us should have had to put up with what we put up with on Wednesday evening. So, let's get this show on the road and get something tangible accomplished tonight."

"And let's try to do it before Rex shows up!" Becca mumbled.

Lyle chuckled. "Gonna get up and leave, eh, Liam?" he said. "Well, son, don't let the door hit ya where the Good Lord split ya."

Orlando raised a hand to thwart the retort Liam was about to make, and then reached over and roughly grabbed Lyle by the shoulder. "Brother Lyle," he said, not bothering to hide his anger. "You might want to reconsider your attitude when you hear what I have to say. You're not doing yourself any favors by making Liam your enemy."

"What are you talking about?" Lyle snapped as he squirmed out from under Orlando's grasp.

"You'll see in a minute. In the meantime, let's stay positive and believe Rex will *not* show up."

Cassie suddenly burst into tears. "Well," she blurted, "like I said, if that monster comes, I'm leaving. I don't have to take his constant abuse! I'm not going to!"

"He's not a monster," Lora whispered without raising her eyes. "I wish people would quit saying that!"

"Oh really?" Cassie shrieked. "What do you call somebody who does nothing but mouth off and cause trouble and insult people? I'm sorry, but he insulted me! That makes him a monster, in my eyes!"

"God," Fred muttered, "here we go again!"

Orlando suddenly rose. "Everybody – stop it!" he shouted. "Be quiet! I want to start the meeting now."

All eyes were on him as he angrily plopped into his seat. There was a scowl on his face as he folded his hands on the table. "Okay, this will be quick," he said. "I've asked you all to come because I want to discuss the future of Beit Yisrael."

Casting a brief glance at his wife (who had once again resumed staring absent-mindedly at the table), he manufactured a small, sad smile. His lips quivered and, for a moment, it seemed as if he was going to cry, but then he managed to regain control.

"The big news," he finally said, "is that I'm going to be stepping down. I have come to the conclusion that I'm not fit to be your Rabbi anymore, and it's time to step aside."

The room became deathly silent. No one moved or said a word.

Clearly fighting with his emotions, he scanned each member before continuing. "After much prayer," he went on, "Lora and I have come to the conclusion that we aren't right with God right now, and until we are, we need to get out of the way and allow someone who is, to lead Beit Yisrael."

"Oh, Orlando, no!" Lyle cut in. "You're our Rabbi. You're a wonderful Rabbi! Come on, man!"

"No, I'm not. I'm not much of a man and I'm not much of a Rabbi, and I need to back off for now." With a loving look at Lora, he reached over to caress her hand.

"It's no secret I love my wife," he said, "but we've had some problems lately, and last night, after much prayer over some incidents that have recently taken place, we came to realize we need to work on our marriage more than I need to lead a congregation. That is why I am going to step down. We're even thinking of moving somewhere else. Perhaps we'll rent an RV and travel around the country. I don't know. All I know is, I can't lead a congregation right now."

Becca, holding her breath, reached for Liam under the table. Somehow, she knew what was coming and she tried to prepare herself for it.

Orlando ran a hand across his face and emitted a long sigh. "Okay," he said, his voice cracking, "so, I haven't talked to Liam about this yet, but I was hoping he would take over for me. I know he's very disappointed in me and the way things have been going lately, and I think he would be an excellent Rabbi. If nothing else, at least temporarily. I know he would restore sanity around here."

When Lyle started to protest, Orlando held up his hand to stop him.

Liam flinched. Quite taken aback and not knowing exactly how to react, he exchanged a bewildered glance with Becca.

"You don't have to answer right now, Liam," Orlando offered. "Just think it over and get back with me. If you decide you want to head Beit Yisrael, we'll come up with a date for the changeover. I would turn Beit Yisrael over to you right now, today, if you said yes! But, if you don't want to do it, then I'll have to advertise nationally for a qualified person to replace me. Of course, it would be easiest for me if you simply took over, so I can get out of the way and let the healing at Beit Yisrael begin in earnest."

Lyle groaned. Fidgeting nervously with his coffee cup, he leaned forward to address Orlando. "Well, Rabbi, here's the thing," he said irritably. "I know you seem to think Liam walks on water, but I don't. Yeah, he's the Assistant Rabbi, but I think you might be jumping to conclusions about all this. Not everyone likes him or his wife. And it seems to me, the final decision is not yours to make, anyway. I mean, doesn't the synagogue get to vote on this?"

"Yes, the synagogue gets a vote, Lyle, but this is an emergency. It's *my* synagogue and I'm stepping down, and I need a replacement! Who else is there, besides Liam? You?"

"Well, no, of course not. I just don't think Liam is qualified...."

"But, he is! Liam is actually more qualified than I. I am an ordained Baptist minister, not a Rabbi. I simply started calling myself that, once I became a Messianic believer and began shepherding Beit Yisrael. But Liam graduated from a Jewish *yeshiva*, and he is an actual ordained Rabbi. He has great Bible knowledge – a lot more than I do, actually – and I respect him."

Pausing briefly to catch his breath, he added: "Liam has many attributes that I don't have, including integrity and backbone. He's a very moral man. He and Becca live a holy life; they live according to Scripture...unlike most of us, who are just pretending."

"Well, that's fine and dandy," Lyle interjected, "but I'm going to go on record right now to nix the idea." Gazing across the table to seek Lora's support, he said, "I'm sure I won't be the only one to object, will I?"

"Lyle," Orlando countered, "you can nix all you want, but the fact remains, I'm stepping down, and the *only* one qualified to take my place is Liam. If nothing else, I'm

218

hoping he will at least agree to be the interim Rabbi. If you can't handle that, then I suggest you leave Beit Yisrael."

"Well, I *don't* like it, and so I guess I'll be leaving if he takes over!"

"I was hoping you and Liam could kiss and make up, because he will need the support of good people after I'm gone. But, if you're going to become a thorn in his side, then I would prefer you just take your attitude and get out right now! Just leave! Go! I've had all the distress and nonsense and heartache I can possibly handle, and I am *not* in the mood to fight with anyone over this issue. I want Liam to replace me. End of story!"

The conversation was interrupted by a loud, incessant knocking on the synagogue's front door. Tossing a knowing glance at Orlando, Liam rose to head down the stairs.

Seconds later, his voice echoed in the sanctuary. "This is a closed session, Rex!" they heard him proclaim loudly. "You're not invited. Go away!"

"Oh God," Becca whispered, half rising. "We need to go down and help Liam!"

"No!" Orlando admonished. "Just stay put. Let Liam handle it. It will be okay. The door's locked."

Cassie looked positively terrified. "If he figures out a way to come in, I'm leaving!" she whispered. "I can't be around him anymore!"

"If he comes in," Becca remarked stoically, "I'm going to kick his overgrown butt into the middle of next week!"

With an angry glance at Lyle, she added: "And *nobody* is going to stop me!"

Lyle shot her a searing glance that left no doubt that she wasn't worthy of a response from him.

Cassie, eyes brimming with tears, glared at him. "Yeah, go ahead and make fun of Becca," she said thickly. "The truth is, Becca has more guts in her little finger than you do in your whole, entire body! Unlike you, you pompous ass, she's got discernment and the guts to stand up for what she believes! You just rattle off at the mouth all the time! You're all talk and no action!"

Orlando raised his hand when Lyle started respond. "Everybody, be quiet!" he admonished. "Just hush! There will be no fights tonight!"

Becca nervously listened to the banter, but her heart was downstairs with Liam. Rex was not someone to trifle with and her husband was no match for a muscular rancher who was at least half a foot taller and a good seventy-five pounds heavier. Although every fiber in her being was on edge, she hesitantly remained seated, as Orlando had ordered.

She was extremely disappointed to see that none of the men were making a move to help Liam. They all – Orlando, Lyle and Fred – sat there, statue-like, motionless, as if nothing out of the ordinary was happening downstairs. In her opinion, they should *all* have been downstairs to support Liam in his efforts to keep Rex out of the building. After all, Rex wasn't just Liam's problem; he was everybody's problem!

Right now, the only sounds Becca was able to hear above the mad hammering of her heart, was Rex's muffled, angry voice outside, in the parking lot.

Suddenly, the wooden building shuddered when the heavy front door was violently kicked in and slammed against the wall. There were sounds of a short scuffle, and seconds later Rex's voice filled the building: "You think you can keep *me* from coming in, little man?" he yelled. "Well, think again, buddy!"

Sheer terror propelled Becca to her feet. To her surprise, although everyone jumped at the sound, no one made a move to get up and go downstairs to see what happened.

It was a mixture of fear and dread that propelled her toward the stairwell and hurled her down the stairs. Taking two steps at a time, she nearly crashed headlong into Rex, who was on his way up. She briefly stopped to glare at him before elbowing him aside to rush toward her husband who was sitting, dazed, in a heap on the floor against the far wall. Large and small shards that used to be the front door, were scattered about.

"Oh God, Liam, did he hurt you?" she cried as she hastened to kneel beside him.

Liam's hand was visibly shaking when he reached for his wife's face. "No, I'm fine," he said. "He broke the door and then picked me up and shoved me out of the way, that's all. I'm fine...."

Becca bit her lip to keep from crying out. She wanted desperately to run upstairs after Rex to ram one of the shards through his evil heart.

"I hate him!" she screamed loud enough for everyone in the building to hear; her voice on the edge of hysteria.

"It's okay," Liam crooned. "Calm down, it's okay."

But she wasn't listening. Her hands shook as she reached into Liam's pants pocket to dig out his cellphone. "You're going down, Rex!" she yelled as she was dialing the police. I'm calling the cops right now, you overgrown bully! You hear me? We're pressing charges!"

Just then Cassie came running down the stairs at full speed. Appearing as if she had just seen a ghost, her face was pale and her strides long, and she rushed wordlessly past, pausing slightly to duck and then step through the broken door, into the darkened parking lot.

"I hope the cops come soon," Liam said as he repositioned himself to sit up on his knees.

"It's ringing right now," Becca replied nervously.

"Rex is demonic," he said in hushed tones. "Honey, you were right...my God! You were right! I saw demons in his face. *Demons*! Truly! It's just like you said. That's the only way to explain it! The look on his face was absolutely demonic as he came bursting through that door! I thought he was going to kill me! I'm...I'm just speechless...."

The look in Liam's eye reflected something Becca couldn't quite pinpoint: A combination of fear and panic and embarrassment, wrapped in disbelief. Whatever he had seen in Rex's countenance, it had obviously spooked him.

It was a good feeling to know that someone besides her had seen those awful "demons"....

"I told you!" she replied, just as someone on the other end finally responded to her call.

"9-1-1, what is your emergency?"

"Yes, I'd like to report a forced break-in and physical assault...."

While Becca was busy talking to the emergency operator, she watched Liam – who appeared positively humiliated from the manhandling - rise and tuck in his shirt. Most men would have immediately retaliated and engaged in a physical fight when attacked. She herself would have! But not her husband. Liam was not an aggressive person. He preferred to resolve conflicts according to Scripture, specifically the Matthew 18 way, which said to take two witnesses and confront the person; and if that didn't work, take them before the Rabbi. And if that didn't work, just sever your relationship, turn it all over to God, and let them be.

She was so proud of her husband; and she had never loved him more than she did at that moment!

When she was done with the call, she handed the phone to Liam. "We going upstairs?" she said.

"You bet!" he replied with an air of confidence. Gone was the earlier expression of apprehension, and Becca knew that Rex was about to find out just who it was that he had messed with!

Chapter 19

Destruction complete....

Matthew 13:19 When anyone hears the word of the kingdom and does not understand it, the evil one comes and snatches away what has been sown in his heart. (ESV)

* * * *

Upstairs, in the loft, Rex had seated himself calmly amidst the group, glowering. No one said a word, including Lora who was carefully averting his gaze. The air was heavy and cloying, and one could literally smell the simmering fear.

Orlando turned to look when Liam and Becca entered, but apparently not knowing what to say (and clearly embarrassed) he remained mum. Fred, appearing quite sheepish as well, turned to give a brief nod. And Lyle crossed his arms and made a show of refusing to bother acknowledging their presence at all.

Motioning for Becca to remain standing by the railing, Liam crossed the room and took a seat directly across from Rex. For several long moments the men simply sat there, oozing animosity as they stared at each other.

"Liam, are you okay" Orlando asked, breaking the pregnant silence.

"I'm fine, no thanks to anyone here," Liam replied, without taking his eyes off Rex. "The big goon here threw me up against the wall after he kicked the door in, but I'm fine. Nothing's broken, except for my pride."

Orlando and Fred exchanged embarrassed glances while Lyle cut his eyes toward Rex and grinned.

"You think it's funny, Lyle?" Becca snapped, bristling. "Where were you when my husband was being tossed around downstairs? Oh, that's right – you were safely sitting on your rear end up here! So much for the *men* handling things around here, eh?"

"Oh yeah, Liam is a *real* man!" Rex exclaimed with an air of disdain.

"You wouldn't know a real man, if you fell on one, Rex! But you will as soon as the Sheriff arrives, because you're spending the night in jail! This time, you're not getting away with it."

"Ooh, I'm shaking in my boots, Becca!" he said as he lazily tilted back and raised his arms to lace his hands behind his head.

Liam, appearing oddly tranquil and composed after his ordeal, relaxed in his chair while carefully scrutinizing Rex. "I think you owe us an explanation," he said quietly.

"I don't owe you a damn thing!"

"Why are you here tonight?"

"I wanted to join the meeting."

"Why?"

"Because I felt like it."

"Well, you missed it, so your efforts were in vain."

"Oh well," Rex mumbled, shrugging his shoulders. Although he tried his best to pretend it didn't matter, the look on his face revealed otherwise.

"This was a private meeting, Rex; not a free-for-all."

"So?"

"So you didn't belong here! And you certainly didn't have a right to break the door in!"

A sneer began to form at the edges of Rex's lips, and he casually reached up to smooth his mustache. "I don't have anything else to say to you, buddy," he said. "You're nothing to me. You're not my judge nor my jury; you're just some moron who tried to lock me out of the building."

Liam grinned. "Hmmm," he said. "Yes, I guess I am. I'm also the moron who's going to have you arrested tonight. Trespassing, breaking and entering and battery…."

"Oh man, I'm really scared, Liam! I've been arrested before. It's no biggie. I'm friends with the guys down at the precinct. They all know I'm a hell-raiser. I'll be in and out of there before midnight!"

"You had no right to be here, Rex," Orlando cut in. "It was a closed session."

"Yeah, well, aren't they all."

Liam slowly shook his head. "Well, we're not going there tonight," he said. "You're not going to be allowed to run amuck around here anymore, Rex."

"It's a free country."

"That may be true, but even a free country has rules and laws to follow. Organizations have to have rules. And the rules of a Messianic synagogue - whether you like it, or not - are that Elders' Meetings are closed, unless otherwise specified. *You* had no right to try to force your way into a closed session. This is the last time I will ever tell you this, because you're finished here."

Lora, who had been silent and moping for most of the evening, suddenly came to life and reared forward to glare at Liam.

"Oh, goodie," she said with a snarl. "Here we go again with the 'you have no right to be here' rant! Well, I'm sorry, Liam, but you're just plain wrong! How many times do you have to hear it before it will sink in?"

"Lora," just stop it!" Becca cautioned.

"Rex has a right to be here!" Lora went on. "Why? Because I said so! I am the Rabbi's wife, and I like him being here!"

"Well, I *don't!*" Orlando cut in sharply. "And in case you've already forgotten, I'm stepping down, which means you won't be the Rabbi's wife much longer!"

"Oh God, Orlando - whatever!" she snapped. The viciousness in her voice left no doubt about her feelings for her husband: She hated him. "I don't really care what happens or what you think, okay? You've proven over and over again that you're a weak leader, and I can't stand the fact that you keep allowing your poster boy, Liam, to call the shots when it comes to Rex and our synagogue!"

"Well, I think you'd better start caring about what I think, Lora! And I think you'd best remember what happened over the last twenty-fours, because that is why I called this meeting this evening! The nonsense ends tonight and your silly infatuation with Rex needs to stop!"

"My what?"

Orlando roughly grabbed her wrist when she started to protest further. "Enough!" he said with a warning glance. "Don't say another word! No more stupid arguments!"

Liam quietly waited for Orlando to finish speaking, and then, peering at Lora, he said: "I'm done with the nonsense, too, Lora. You have more than amply proven that you have no understanding of, nor regard for, rules, so please don't push me, tonight! After what I've just been through, I'm simply not in the mood!"

"You just want everyone to follow *your* rules!" Lora spat.

"Sweetheart, please stop!" Orlando said, reaching for her hand.

"Don't!" she yelled. "Don't you touch me! I'm mad right now, and I'm sorry if you don't like what I'm saying, but I'm entitled to my opinion. And so is Rex, whether you like it, or not!"

A blush of anger began to creep along Liam's neck as he listened to Lora's rant. "Wow!" he said, glaring in her direction. "I guess yesterday's events at the bank weren't enough to wake you up...."

"That's totally irrelevant!" she snapped.

"Is it? Do you really want to push my buttons right now, Lora? The cops will be here any minute now, and I can certainly change my mind about pressing charges against you...."

"Don't you dare threaten me!"

"What are you talking about?" Rex demanded.

"So, all I can say," Liam went on, purposely ignoring Rex, "is that you had better behave, because you are treading on very thin ice!"

"Lora, honey," Rex cut in, "I don't know what the hell is going on, but I suggest you just go home so you don't have to listen to Liam's drivel anymore! I'd leave, too, but I have to stick around so I can get arrested."

"If anybody should leave," she yelled, "it's Liam."

"Well, you know that ain't gonna happen...."

Overcome by anger, Lora half rose to glare down the length of the table at Liam. "Don't you *dare* threaten me, you louse!" she cried. "You've had enough of me and my nonsense? Well, guess what, sweetheart, the feeling is very mutual! Rex is right to hate you – both you and your precious, holier-than-thou, prissy little snot of a wife! You are the reason the synagogue is falling apart. You're the illogical warmonger around here; not Rex!"

"Illogical warmonger?" Liam retorted, raising his voice to match her snide tones. "I'm not the one who has resorted to violence! You didn't see me breaking down the synagogue door! And I'm not the one ignoring God's commands about adultery...."

Lora rolled her eyes as she drew in a sharp breath and then dropped back into her chair. "Liam," she said with a snarl, "I would advise you to just shut up now! It's not wise to make me mad! Ask Orlando. He knows...."

"Well, I'm not afraid of you, Lora, nor am I trying to make you mad. I'm just trying to get you to understand a few things."

"Well stop it! You're not the boss of me!"

"Sweetheart," Orlando interjected, "please just sit down and be quiet...."

"Shut up, Orlando! Nobody's talking to you!" A strange look crossed Lora's face as she suddenly became perfectly still. Concentrating her attention on nothing in particular on the tabletop, she appeared to be in a trance. Or, perhaps, she was deep in thought, trying to figure out her next move....

Finally, she blinked and then turned slowly and deliberately toward Liam. Her tones were dipped in acid when she spoke.

"Liam, my dear," she said, her voice low and ominous, "I find it really ironic that you see fit to make me out to be a complete idiot with no comprehension skills; yet, you are married to the biggest lunatic in Webster County!"

"Excuse me?" Both Liam and Becca spoke the words at the same time.

Orlando's mouth dropped, and he again reached for Lora's hand. "Sweetheart!" he admonished. "What are you doing?"

The look on Lora's face was demonic, menacing. "At least *I'm* not a complete, writhing-on-the-floor mental wreck like your wife who was sexually abused throughout her childhood," she continued, launching the words like darts from the back of her throat. "At least *I'm* not dragging around some super-duper heavy baggage like your sweet Becca, who exudes this 'poor little pitiful me' attitude that absolutely sucks the life out of anybody who tries to be her friend...."

"Lora!" Orlando shouted. But she ignored him.

"*I'm* not someone who has found solace in the Bible and uses it as a weapon to force others into submitting into my ideas about God. Your little wifey, the broken vessel who turned herself into a talking Bible' to help herself feel better - she does all that, Liam. And you have the audacity to suggest *I* have mental problems?"

"Lora, I'm warning you...."

"No, I'm warning *you*! Get your own backyard cleaned up before you start digging around in mine, and stop acting like you've got authority over me! If you threaten me one more time, oh high and mighty Rabbi, I'm going to make sure everyone in Webster County will know about that sick basket-case wife of yours and her background of perversion!"

Becca recoiled, her eyes wide as saucers as she listened to the venom spewing forth from Lora's lips. Weak-kneed from the unexpected onslaught, she steadied herself against the railing and gawked, in slack-jawed disbelief, at her former friend. Clearly, Lora was referring to her near breakdown the day her memories had returned...but why would she hold it against her, or even bring it up? It had been a one-time event! It had been one of the most horrifying days of her life! Why would Lora do this to her?

"My God, Lora," Orlando said when he found his voice. "My God, I don't know who I'm married to, anymore. My God...I thought we decided as of last night to make a fresh start."

"There is no fresh start for us, you moron!" she growled. "We're done. We've been done for a long time, so just knock it off."

"But Lora...we prayed about this for hours last night...."

"Yeah, like prayer is going solve anything!" Although she tried to appear confident, her body language suddenly revealed the opposite. The crazed look in her eyes was receding, and she now seemed confused and unsure of herself.

Becca could tell that something Orlando said had gotten through to Lora and seared her conscience. She was sure that Lora knew down deep that she had been wrong to allow her anger to get so badly out of control.

Liam's face had become stony. His eyes reflected chained fury as he rose to address the Rabbi. Becca, still trembling near the railing, realized at once that her husband had finally reached his "point of no return"; and she bit her bottom lip in anticipation of his next move.

"You know what, Orlando?" he said with an authority in his voice that Becca had never heard before. "Effective immediately, I accept your offer to be the congregation leader of Beit Yisrael."

The Rabbi balked, his gaze reflecting a cross between wonder and elation. "Really?" he said in stunned surprise. "Well...that's good. Yes...very good."

"And, if it's okay with you, I'd like to take over right now, this minute."

"This minute? Well, sure, I guess so...why not? Okay. Sure. Done! Beit Yisrael is yours!"

"Great!" Liam said with a broad smile. "Then, as the new Rabbi, my first decision is to dismiss Lora as Deacon. As a matter of fact, I'm going to ask her to find another congregation, because she's no longer welcome here. Goodbye, Lora."

Lora's jaw dropped. "You can't do that...." she began in protest.

"Out, Lora!"

Lyle, red-faced and annoyed, rose forcefully. "No!" he shouted. "This is not happening! The congregation has to vote on this!"

"Hear! Hear!" Rex chimed in.

Orlando placed his hands over his face and shook his head. "Shut up, Lyle," he said irritably. "And you, Rex, keep your damned comments to yourself."

Emitting several sighs in a row, he leaned forward and folded his hands on the table. "This has been my synagogue for almost twenty years, and I'm handing it over to Liam," he said. "All the formalities can come later, but as of right now, Liam is the new Rabbi. If you don't like it, Lyle, then take your own advice and don't let the door hit ya where the good Lord split ya!"

Lora sat, mouth agape, ogling her husband, examining his face as if this was the first time she had ever seen it. She started to protest, but when the realization sank in that the world as she knew it had changed, she rose and stormed from the room.

"Come on, Lyle, let's go," she shouted over her shoulder. "We don't need to be where we're not wanted!"

Lyle stood, frozen in place, contemplating what to do next. Finally, peering down at Rex, who seemed perfectly relaxed in his seat, he said: "I think we need a mass exodus of this hell-hole. Wanna come?"

"Nahh, I'm staying," Rex replied tranquilly. "Cops are coming for me, remember?"

Once Lyle disappeared down the stairs, Liam returned his attentions to Rex. "Yes," he said, "the police should be here any minute now and you will be leaving in handcuffs. Would you like to apologize for your behavior so we can begin to forgive you for all the grief you've caused us, or do you still feel you had a right to break the door down and force your way in here?"

Rex pulled his lips into a mocking grin and shook his head. "Apologize?" he said, as if the word left a bad taste in his mouth. "Liam, you're the last person on earth I would apologize to! If anybody needs to apologize, it's you! You owe *me* an apology for locking me out!"

Car lights crawling across the far wall indicated someone was pulling into the parking lot. "It's the Sheriff," Becca said grimly. Without another word, she bounded down the steps to greet the police downstairs.

Orlando rose heavily and, lumbering over to where Liam was standing, he smiled and shook his hand. "Thank you, brother," he said, his voice sounding exceptionally tired. "Thanks for everything. I wish you well. I know you'll do great things with this place."

"I will, if it's God's will, Orlando. Without Him we can do nothing."

Rex snorted, removed his hands from behind his head, and rose. "Jesus freaks," he mumbled. "God, what a nut-house! I can't wait for the Sheriff to get me the hell out of here!"

Chapter 20

The Rabbi gives up....

Romans 1:25 *Because they exchanged the truth about God for a lie and worshiped and served the creature rather than the Creator, who is blessed forever! Amen.* (ESV)

* * * *

Becca was staring absentmindedly into her coffee cup when the house phone rang the next morning. Last night's fiasco at the synagogue had left her and Liam unable to get much sleep. She, Orlando and Liam had driven together to the Sheriff's office to formally press charges against Rex for assault, breaking and entering and trespassing. They were told that, while he would certainly spend the night in jail, he would most likely be released "on his own recognizance." After all, he had made a name for himself as a respected rancher – albeit, "a roughneck hell-raiser" - in the state of Missouri.

"You guys awake?" It was the voice of Liam's sister, Donna.

Becca turned the speaker on so Liam could hear. "*Shabbat shalom!*" she said in hopes of irritating her sister-in-law. After the way Donna had treated her and Liam during their visit to Boone last week, she wasn't going to bother putting any further effort into the relationship.

"I was hoping to catch you guys before you left for church," Donna said.

"Well, you're just in time. We've got about an hour or so before we have to leave for the *synagogue*...."

"Okay, well, whatever. I just wanted to tell you I have some bad news. Mom passed away."

Liam, who had been watching the morning's news on TV, rose and quickly joined Becca in the kitchen area. "Mom died?" he asked, alarmed. "What happened?"

"They think it was a heart attack."

Empathizing with her husband's distress, Becca reached out to touch his face while mouthing the words, "I'm so sorry!"

"Oh...Well, Donna," he managed, swallowing over the lump in his throat, "I guess she won't be able to move down to Wheeling with you, after all...."

Tears welled in Becca's eyes as she watched her husband struggle to keep from crying. Although Liam's mother had become increasingly cold and distant in her old age, Becca recognized that he still honored her, regardless – and she loved him for that. She and Liam had once discussed the issue of the Bible's command to "honor your parents" and come to the conclusion that it didn't necessarily mean we had to like them, love them even have a relationship with them. "Honor your parents" simply served as a reminder to remember that none of us would be here, were it not for our parents, and that we had an obligation to care for them in their old age, if the situation required it. Liam had tried very hard to care for Nola, but she kept rejecting him.

"What do you mean?" Donna barked. "She *was* living with me already! We had just moved to Wheeling. We left Mom's place a couple days after you guys left us. Right after we put the house up for sale."

"I didn't realize that," he replied coldly. The postmark on her lawyer's letter informing me that I was no longer part of her life, was sent from Boone. Today marks only a week since we saw you guys, so you really worked quickly!"

"Yeah, we didn't dally around, Liam! So what? Was I supposed to send letters back and forth to ask your precious permission, or something? I didn't call to get a sermon from you today! The issue is, Mom is dead, and I wanted you to know."

"So, where was she when she died last night?" Becca cut in. "Was it at your house, or in the hospital, or what?"

There was an odd hesitation on the other end before Donna responded. "I never said she died last night!" she mumbled. "She died last Tuesday, shortly after we got to Wheeling. I took her to the hospital because she had chest pains...."

"Last *Tuesday*?" Liam shouted in disbelief. "Today is Saturday. Why are you just *now* telling me this?"

"I didn't want to worry you with all the details. I took care of everything."

"What details, Donna? You didn't think I needed to know that my own mother died? What's wrong with you?"

"Liam, you...."

239

"Okay, do you think you can fill me in on the funeral arrangements, or did I already miss the funeral, too?"

"There will be no funeral. I had her cremated. She's sitting on my living room fireplace. No need for you to do anything. And that's my decision; so don't try to yell at me for it. I was taking care of her, not you."

Liam reached back to steady himself against a counter. "I'm speechless, Donna," he said angrily. "Her wish was that she would be laid to rest next to Dad in the cemetery plot they paid for back in 1989! You didn't think that I needed to be consulted in any of this?"

"What for? I'm the executor of her estate!"

"Yes. You've been that for almost a whole week now."

"Don't talk down to me!"

Rolling his eyes, he held the receiver away from his ear and shook his head. "Okay, fine," he said after some moments. "I get it, and I am done. You're totally in charge of everything concerning Mom. So, let's just wind this up, so you can put me out of your misery, okay? You know my address. You can send my half of the estate monies to the same address that the lawyer used to send me the legal documents that informed me I was kicked out of Mom's life. After that, you won't ever have to contact me again, for any reason."

"What estate are you talking about, Liam?" Donna said serenely.

Liam grabbed Becca's hand and squeezed. The look on his face said, *"Okay, here we go…she's doing exactly what I thought she would…."*

"Do you really have to ask me that?" Liam snapped. "The sale of her house and her possessions – it's half mine, Donna. Plus, she showed me her bank statement just last week. She had half a million dollars in her savings, so don't feign ignorance!"

"Hmm. Yeah, well, I'm sorry, but everything she had went for her cremation and the move to Wheeling."

"Half a million dollars worth? Donna, do I have 'stupid' stamped on my forehead, or something?"

"There was no estate, Liam. End of story."

"Oh yeah, right. How irresponsible of me to think you would be grown-up about this. Thank you, sister. You've finally revealed who you really are."

"Oh, shut up!"

"You're a vicious, mean-spirited liar and a thief. An all-around *bad* person."

"Just who do you think…."

"Goodbye, Donna. Enjoy your half and *my* half of the estate that supposedly doesn't exist."

Visibly shaken by his sister's behavior, Liam sank onto a nearby stool, slammed the phone down and buried his head in his hands.

"Idiot," he whispered. "I don't need Mom's money! I was planning on letting Donna have that money, anyway! Oh well...."

The spell of the strange conversation was interrupted by an unexpected knock on the door. It was Orlando, who came to ask Liam to take over the service this morning. He appeared totally worn out, haggard, drawn, beaten and broken.

"Lora left me last night," he mumbled as he dropped heavily onto the living room sofa. His voice was empty, devoid of emotion. "She left me for Rex. I knew she would. It was only a matter of time. Last night pushed her over the edge."

Becca and Liam sat on either side of him, touching his arm, stroking his hand; neither saying a word, but simply providing moral support.

"Brother Liam...I can't do it anymore," he said with a sigh. "I have been tolerating Lora's infidelity for years, turning my head when I saw her flirting with other men or taking money from the synagogue, all the while praying God would change her heart. He hasn't answered that prayer."

"I'm so sorry," Liam whispered. "I wish there was something I could say to take away your pain."

"Orlando," Becca cut in, "God always answers our prayers. Sometimes His silence is our answer. During those times when He is silent, it's an indication that we need to reevaluate ourselves so we can be aligned with His will again."

"Well, He's certainly been silent!"

"Yeah, but Orlando, what can He do with someone who refuses to obey Him? Nothing! He doesn't force anyone into doing anything they don't want. If someone insists on committing adultery, He's not going to stop them. We all have a choice. He couldn't change Lora's heart unless she was willing."

"I know. And she's *not* willing! Last night, when I got home, she broke down and cried – no, she wailed! And then she unleashed all of her anger on me, as if everything that has happened at Beit Yisrael was my fault. And then, for some reason, she just had to rub it in and tell me that she had not spent Christmas Day with her mother, but with Rex at his ranch. *Christmas!* My goodness, we've been Torah observant for twenty years, and suddenly she does Christmas?"

"She's clearly off Yahweh's Path," Liam said tenderly. "Talking to her has done no good. Becca has tried; and I…well, you saw what happened yesterday evening…."

Orlando's shoulders shook as his silent tears fell. "She said she bought him special 'cowboy ornaments' for his Christmas tree. Can you believe that? She has dared to go straight into the Face of God!"

Becca swiped angrily at her own tears as she exchanged sympathetic glances with Liam. Taking the Rabbi's limp hand in hers, she said: "Orlando, none of this is your fault. We know you did everything in your power to keep your wife on God's path…."

"Yes and no. It was my fault, too. I did so many things wrong. I should have done more to prevent my own stupidity and try to save my marriage!"

"What more could you possibly have done?"

"I don't know. I could have been a better, more godly husband who was actually living his faith instead of making concessions. I have failed both my wife and God!"

"No, you haven't! You're a good man, Orlando! The fact that you feel guilty about sinning proves it! The Bible tells us *most* won't be taking that narrow gate that leads to life...and we are told in Revelation that when Yeshua returns, He will be vomiting from His Mouth all those who are 'lukewarm'. Unlike you, Lora chose to be 'lukewarm', Orlando! She *chose* her own, carnal desires over Yahweh's will...and the book of Hebrews tells us exactly what happens to people who do that."

"Becca's right," Liam chimed in. "Lora is not a mature believer; that's the bottom line. All you can do is to let her go and just keep her in your prayers."

"Well, I'm obviously not a mature believer, either!"

"Come on, Orlando," Liam said. "You can't beat yourself up now. All you can do is to repent and start trying to put yourself back on God's Path."

Orlando produced a weak nod as he smiled at Liam and gave Becca's hand a grateful squeeze. "I know," he said feebly, "and I thank you, both from the bottom of my heart."

All was quiet for several minutes, each alone with his own thoughts when, suddenly and without warning, Orlando jumped up and hurried toward the door.

"Liam, thanks for your willingness to take over the service this morning," he said, briefly turning before heading outside. "I just...I just can't do it right now. Please tell the congregation that you are now the new Rabbi, and that I couldn't make it today because I don't feel well."

"We will, Orlando," Liam said. "You just take care of yourself, okay?"

Orlando's gaze dropped to the floor as he nodded. "Thank you for everything," he said. "Both of you. I love you. God bless you both forever."

And then he simply vanished, tearing across the cement patio toward his car as fast as his bulk would allow.

The sound of screeching tires sent both Liam and Becca scrambling outside just in time to see a plume of dust rising in great, billowing clouds as Orlando aimed his car down the long, winding driveway toward the main road. He wasn't bothering to make the curves as he drove; he simply tore straight across the field, picking up speed along the way.

"What the heck is he doing?" Liam muttered in alarm.

They watched in horror as the car took flight when it hit the camel-backed bridge. Soaring across the highway, it crashed loudly into the dense woods on the other side. A grayish-brown cloud of dust exploded above the trees and scattered across the horizon. A second explosion sent a fiery plume of black smoke high into the blue skies....

Chapter 21

Death in the family

Isaiah 57:1 The righteous pass away; the godly often die before their time. And no one seems to care or wonder why. No one seems to understand that God is protecting them from the evil to come. 2 For the godly who die will rest in peace. 3 "But you -- come here, you witches' children, you offspring of adulterers and prostitutes! 4 Whom do you mock, making faces and sticking out your tongues? You children of sinners and liars! (NLV)

* * * *

There was a sharp screeching sound as Chad nervously tapped on the microphone. Fred stood, pale-faced and silent beside him at the front of the sanctuary.

"Would everybody please take their seats?" Chad said somberly.

"Hey, Chadly," somebody shouted as a group in the back began to break up. "You're getting' awfully pushy in your old age!" The comment drew a few scattered chuckles and titters.

"Yeah," someone else cut in. "What are you guys doing up there, anyway? Where's Orlando? Did he oversleep again?"

"A better question is, where is ol' Rex this morning?" someone else said. "We can't start the services without one of his jokes to kick-start everything!"

More snickering….

"I don't see Lora anywhere around, either," someone else chimed in. "Or Becca and Liam. And Lyle, too! Is everybody on vacation today, or something?"

A hush fell over the crowd when Chad remained stone-faced and still. Clearing his throat several times, he gazed around the room until he was sure everyone was present and out of the restrooms.

"What's with our front door?" a teenaged boy asked. "Why is there plywood over it?"

The girl sitting next to him giggled. "I'm guessing someone couldn't wait to hear Orlando's sermon today, and was just dying to get in here early!"

Fred poked Chad in the side. "Get it over with already," he whispered impatiently, out of the corner of his mouth.

"Okay, I'm sorry for the late start this morning," Chad said, once the congregation settled down. "It's just that…well, folks…this is a very sad day. There won't be a regular service today, and you can either stay here and pray with us, or you can feel free to leave, if you want."

Clearing his throat once more, he swallowed hard and pushed on. "There's been a death in our synagogue family," he went on. "Liam called a few minutes ago to tell me that the reason Orlando isn't here this morning is because…well, there's been a horrific accident. He was killed in a one-car accident and pronounced dead at the scene. His wife, Lora, has been notified."

The room fell silent as a tomb when Chad's face crumbled. Finally, recognizing he was unable to continue, he indicated for Fred to take the microphone.

"What happened," someone demanded.

"...We...we don't know anything else right now," Fred mumbled. Like everyone else present, he was completely thunderstruck. "But as soon as we do, we'll put it up on the Beit Yisrael website, along with the funeral details and whatnot."

All eyes were on Fred as the congregation anxiously waited for more. But, like Chad, he was simply unable to speak. Not knowing what else to do or say, he joined Chad in stepping down from the platform to begin hugging those who came out of the pews to approach them.

"Poor Lora," someone said. "She must be so devastated."

"She'd be more devastated if it was Rex," someone responded forcefully and without any attempts to hide the sarcasm.

The building suddenly came alive with a strange chanting sound as Harry Malone raised his hands and began to babble: "Humminah-humminah-humminah-humminah...."

Chapter 22

Confronting the ancient beast

Deuteronomy 32:35 *Vengeance is mine, and recompense, for the time when their foot shall slip; for the day of their calamity is at hand, and their doom comes swiftly.* (ESV)

* * * *

A dying summer sun slowly yielded to a crisp Ozark evening. Becca marveled at the lovely autumn colors whizzing by as she drove along the bumpy country road. Klaus-Dieter Behringer's house, according to an Elderly man who ran the Mack's Creek Post Office, was "just on up the road a piece." As a neighborly gesture, the talkative gentleman had also added that "Max Neumann" (affectionately dubbed "Herman the German") was a "good ol' boy, a quiet, well-respected, God-fearing man who lived on a small farm with his wife, two dogs, a cow, and some chickens.

"God-fearing good ol' boy," Becca mumbled, brown eyes flashing angrily as she maneuvered around another pothole. The Klaus-Dieter Behringer she remembered was anything but god-fearing; he was the devil in person - evil, through and through; a true pervert...a pedophile who had stolen not only her virginity, but also her entire childhood. This monster had set into motion the events that led to her brother's incarceration. If he truly was living the life of a so-called "well-respected, God-fearing man," then perhaps it was time to remind him of a few things. It was payback time, some thirty years in the making!

This whole year had been a year of changes and extremes, and being able to confront Klaus-Dieter would be the icing on the cake.

It had been nearly six months since Orlando's suicide; six endless, long grueling months filled with strange happenings and revelations and surprises, peppered with sadness due to the deaths of both Orlando and Elder Leroy who died peacefully in a nursing home - ironically, on the same morning Orlando committed suicide.

Lora didn't attend Orlando's funeral. Refusing all contact from her synagogue family, she sold her business and disappeared. Rumor had it that she had moved in with Rex and was helping him run his ranch.

Liam took over as Rabbi at Beit Yisrael and, as soon as Orlando was laid to rest - with Elder Chad Kretschmar by his side - he wasted no time ridding the synagogue of anyone who wasn't serious about following biblical principles. He immediately made it clear that he wasn't interested in the number of "butts in the pews"; but, rather, in people's hearts and their desires to have a real relationship with God and to do His will. As a result, many people left Beit Yisrael for "greener pastures" – including Lyle, who hadn't shown his face since the funeral.

Fred stepped down as Elder and Annie as deacon; but they both vowed to remain members of Beit Yisrael "until the Rapture comes."

To Harry Malone's utter surprise, Liam had not only returned his fifteen thousand dollars, but also asked him to become a deacon to head up a brand new prayer ministry. Harry was overjoyed and in tears knowing that someone felt he still had something worthwhile to contribute to society. Around the same time, he managed to get himself hired at a new software development company at a fraction of the salary he had been used to, but he happily took it all in stride and thanked God for his good fortune.

Rowdy and Cassie wisely opted to leave and find a church home where no one knew about Rowdy's past. The last Becca had heard, Cassie had a miscarriage and consequently, the wedding was delayed indefinitely.

Becca – whose nerves were shattered from the events of the past year - had decided to quit her job so she could work fulltime as Liam's "right hand person" at the synagogue, helping to prepare his teachings and handling the website and all administrative duties. Her greatest desire was for her and Liam to be used by God to lead others to the Truth of Yeshua and Torah. They had spent the weeks after Orlando's death praying and promising God to lead Beit Yisrael as a godly husband-and-wife team, living their faith to the best of their ability, and being good examples for the world to see.

* * * *

Her heart pitched when Klaus-Dieter's farm came into view. The house, a wooden, two-story structure with a wrap-around porch in need of a paint job, stood tucked away in a heavily timbered area. Huge oaks and maples, now radiant oranges, greens, browns, and yellows - shaded a weed-choked yard that invaded a balding gravel driveway.

Two whooping spotted mongrels took turns bouncing off the side of her car as she parked beside an ancient rusted Ford pickup. A gray-haired old woman in a checkered apron rounded a corner of the house and shooed them away. "Hi there," she hollered. "Y'all can come on out, now. Them dogs won't bother you."

Becca swallowed. The moment of truth was finally here. In a few minutes, two lives - hers and Klaus-Dieter's - would be changed forever; thirty years of hell on earth would finally be vindicated. The urge to turn and run was tempered only by a driving desire for revenge and closure.

Forcing a smile, she pushed a strand of dark hair off her pixie face and presented a hand in greeting. "Hello, there," she said. "I'm Becca Ritter."

"And I'm Marguerite – call me Maggie," the old lady replied. "Are you a Jehovah's Witness? Because, if you are, you need to know upfront that won't work around here because my husband will verbally tear you apart. He hates religious nuts. We're Methodists, and we intend to stay that way."

Becca's laugh sounded hollow. "No. I'm actually here to see my...my father."

The woman blinked in surprise, then, finally, her tired, blue eyes – those famous "brilliant blue eyes set in a cream in coffee complexion" that Ray had told her about - lit up. Becca could tell the woman was once gorgeous, and it grated her to know that - regardless as to how dysfunctional her own family had been, and regardless as to whatever else had happened - standing before her was the very person who had helped to tear her family apart!

"Oh, my God!" Maggie cried. "It's you! It's Rebecca! My goodness, honey, Max has told me so much about you!"

"He has?"

"Oh yes! Oh, yes. He was devastated when your grandparents refused to allow him to see you kids after the…the incident."

"He tried to see us?"

Maggie's face reflected great surprise. "Yes, of course, he did – several times. I was right there in our living room listening to the conversations between him and your grandparents. They told him in no uncertain terms he'd better stay away, or else. I guess they thought he killed your mother."

Becca briefly closed her eyes to thank Yahweh for her protective grandparents. Surely, the only reason Klaus-Dieter had wanted to see her was to finish the job he had started. After all, she was the only witness.

"It was such a shame about your mother," Maggie continued. "And you…thank God you managed to survive! We were overjoyed to find out they had found you alive! Oh, my goodness, honey, what an ordeal that must have been for you! They never caught the bastard who did it, did they?"

Becca shook her head slowly as she beheld the old woman. Every nerve in her body was on edge. It was all she could do to remain calm. She *had* to remain calm and to keep her tongue in check because her rancor was not against Marguerite, but against the man who, for decades, had been duping this poor old lady standing before her.

"I've always wanted to meet you, and here you are! Lordy, lordy, won't Max be surprised to see you!"

"Yes, I'm sure he will!" Becca replied levelly. "By the way, why do you call him Max?"

Maggie cocked her head sideways. "Because that's his name," she said, matter-of-factly. "Well, Max – Maximillian – is his middle name and he's always gone by that."

"Hmmm...."

"Yes, he introduced himself as Max the very first day we met. All my former neighbors, his customers, they all knew him as Max, too. Why do you ask?"

Becca swallowed her anger and pulled her lips into something she hoped would pass as a grin. "No reason," she said. "We just never knew him as Max, that's all. When we were a family, he was known as Klaus-Dieter."

"Oh. How interesting." The look on Maggie's face revealed confusion as she turned to head into the house.

Becca's heart raced as she followed the woman up a few crumbling cement steps on legs that felt rubbery and weak. *My God,* she thought. *My God, it's really happening....*

"Who's there," a feeble voice demanded as they headed through a tiny, dark living room toward the back door. "Maggie, who is it?"

"Honey, it's your daughter!" Maggie replied as she pushed open a creaky screen door. "Your long-lost daughter has come to see you, darlin'! Come on out here, Rebecca. Watch your step, honey."

Becca stopped in her tracks when the old man came into view. Although Klaus-Dieter was a mere shadow of his former self, it was unmistakably him. Though she had mentally prepared herself for this moment, she felt the blood drain from her face. Suddenly, she was fourteen years old again, trembling in the presence of her overbearing father who now sat there, just a few feet away, peering up at her from a faded, weather-worn bench.

"You're a good girl, Rebecca! Such a pretty little thing! Come here and sit in my lap, sweetheart...."

His green eyes, once alert and fiery, were now a dull yellow-gray; his seamed and craggy face had a milky cast. A transparent plastic tube originating from a portable oxygen tank on wheels, snaked around his ears to rest under a bulbous, hawk-like nose. Despite this, he held a lit cigarette in his palsied, shaking hand.

No longer an imposing figure – much less, an "Arian god" - he looked old, small and shriveled; an invalid who was hardly able to take care of himself.

"Who are you?" he croaked irritably.

"It's Rebecca!" Maggie shouted. "The daughter you told me so much about."

Klaus-Dieter recoiled when reality sank in. He obviously wasn't expecting this. His face flushed as the raspy breathing faltered. "My...my daughter?" he wheezed. "Oh...."

You little Jewish bitch!

Becca felt faint; she stood, rooted to the spot, gawking at the man who had been responsible for ruining her entire life. It was disturbing to discover that, even after all this time, his presence still had an intimidating effect.

"Yes, it's me," she managed dryly. "How are you?"

"Old and gray and dying of emphysema. Other than that, fine, I guess."

She loathed his German accent, and suppressed a sudden urge to tell him so.

An awkward silence ensued as the three of them stared at each other in the shadows of the old porch. It suddenly dawned on Becca that she didn't know what to call him. "Dad" sounded hypocritical because they hadn't seen each other for thirty years; yet, addressing him by his first name seemed disrespectful somehow, regardless as to how she felt about him. And which name should she use since, in this household, he was known as Max?

Maggie pointed toward a chipped wrought iron picnic table on the opposite end of the porch. "We just got back from a long church program and were about to have us some fresh rhubarb pie and coffee," she said. "We're gonna skip supper altogether because we had a huge lunch. Why don't you sit down and join us?"

Becca shook her head and rubbed sweaty palms together. "I don't want to impose," she replied. "I just came by for a quick visit."

"Oh now, darlin', after all this time you'll want to stay for more than just a quick visit. You just go right on over there and have a seat and start gettin' reacquainted with your ol'

Daddy." Over her shoulder she said, "Max, you keep your little girl occupied while I'm inside, you hear? I'll be back directly."

Klaus-Dieter squinted up at Becca with questioning eyes. He started to say something, then sputtered, coughed, and spat into a yellowed handkerchief. "So, how'd you find me?" he asked. "I'm guessing Ray told you?"

She nodded.

"Ahh. Yes. I figured he would. But I didn't think you'd want to ever see me again. Not after...that day. So, what brings you after all these years? I'm sure it's not because you love or miss me. Did you come to gloat and stick a finger in my eye?"

"Sort of," Becca replied. "Don't you think you deserve it?"

"I couldn't help what happened, Rebecca. I had to disappear. They would have put me in prison."

"Well, you did kill your wife when she caught you raping your fourteen year old daughter."

Klaus-Dieter emitted a snort, made a face and raised a bony hand in dismissal. "So, what do you want from me!" he demanded.

"Oh, I don't know. An apology, maybe."

"An apology," he said, cackling. "Why should I apologize? I saved your life that day!"

"You *raped* me that day! None of that would have ever happened, if you had kept your damned hands to yourself! Mother would still be alive!"

"Keep your voice down!" he said in an angry stage whisper. "My Maggie doesn't know…."

Becca was seething; her mouth felt parched and dry. "Well, she will before I leave," she said.

Klaus-Dieter shot her a searing glance. Alarm-filled eyes bugging out, he succumbed to another powerful coughing fit. "No, don't," he wheezed when the spell subsided. "Please. Just let us go. We're old and won't be around much longer. Just leave it alone. If nothing else, just remember I protected you from your mother that day. She was going to kill you! You wouldn't be here if I hadn't stopped her!"

The conversation ceased when Maggie appeared carrying an armful of cracked cups and plates. Klaus-Dieter rose unsteadily and shuffled across the porch, oxygen tank in tow. The wheezing in his diseased lungs grew louder and more labored with each step.

Becca felt like screaming. Every nerve stood on end as she took a seat across from the man she despised to the depths of her soul. If felt strange, almost bewildering, to share a table with him after all these years.

Maggie quickly helped him to his seat, and then ducked into the house to retrieve the pie and coffee. "Sit honey," she cooed, handing her husband a large piece.

Becca tried in vain to ignore the love in Maggie's voice. The woman had no idea that she was married to a monster, or that her life was about to be torn apart by the revelation of a very nasty secret.

Be that as it may, she thought, struggling to keep her emotions under control, *what goes around comes around and it's payback time!*

In effort to clear her mind of unwanted thoughts, she quickly turned her gaze toward the rolling hills and thought of Liam, who had been against this trip. At first he insisted he come along, but Becca made it clear that this was something she had to do alone.

"Honey, listen," Liam had said when she voiced her intentions to seek revenge on Klaus-Dieter Behringer. "I know it was awful, but don't go there with hate in your heart. Yes, tell him how you feel, and let him know what a monster he was, and just get it out of your system. But be very careful, okay? Revenge belongs to Yahweh. The past is gone, and you can't change it. Judgment Day is coming. God Himself will take care of everything."

"So," Maggie said, interrupting Becca's train of thought, as she dragged over a chair to sit closer to her husband. "What made you want to see your old Dad after all these years? Did you stop hating us?"

Becca flinched. "Hating you?" she said. "I hated…Max…but until recently when my brother Ray told me about you, I didn't know you even existed."

Maggie seemed confused. "Honey," she said addressing Klaus-Dieter, "I thought you said your kids and their grandparents threw you out on your ear when you told them you were planning on marrying me after the death of your first wife. You said your kids didn't want to come and live with us, and that's why we moved to New Mexico by ourselves, with just my son."

261

Klaus-Dieter looked startled. "I don't remember telling you that," he muttered.

"Well, you sure did!"

"So," Becca said nonchalantly taking a bite of her pie, "you all moved to New Mexico, huh? Why there?" She loved knowing she had the upper hand, and fully planned to "toy" with her former tormentor for a while. It was his turn to be afraid!

"Oh," Maggie replied. "I'm originally from there. I grew up on the Mescalero Indian Reservation near Tularosa. I had ended up in Missouri with my first husband, rest his soul, and I just loved it here and considered Missouri my home. But stuff happened and I ended up marrying Max, and moving back to New Mexico. My folks were still living back then, and we lived with them for a few years until they died."

"I see. So, that's where you all disappeared to after my mother died. No wonder you were able to disappear so completely. Name change and all."

"Name change," Maggie said slowly. "Well, yes, we changed to Neumann because it means 'new man' and we wanted to get a fresh start after...well, after everything that happened. Poor Max was just emotionally exhausted, you know."

"Oh, I bet!" Becca said, with a forced smile.

"I did what needed to be done at the time!" Klaus-Dieter retorted. "I don't have to defend my actions to you."

"Well, I'm just curious, *Daddy*," Becca said, doing her best to sound as abrasive as possible. "I've always wondered whatever happened to you. Now I know. So…why did you decide to move back to Missouri, of all places? Weren't you afraid of…repercussions?"

"That's enough!" he snapped, the words lubricated by a mixture of spittle and pie crumbs. "It's none of your damned business what happened in my life. You had your new life and I had mine. End of story!"

Maggie gingerly reached over to stroke her husband's cheek. "Honey," she said, "don't get all wound up, now okay? She has a right to ask what happened to you. After all, you disappeared from her life!"

Eyeing Becca with a sweetness that could only come from an innocent and loving soul, she patiently continued relating her story. "We moved back here because my son liked Missouri," she said. "He was born here and grew up here, but came with us when we moved to New Mexico. He never liked it there, and couldn't find a decent job in those days. He tried all kinds of things, but nothing suited him. And, so, he eventually moved back here by himself to go to college at Southwest Missouri State."

"Maggie," Klaus-Dieter cut in, "that's enough reminiscing!"

"After my parents passed away," she said, ignoring her husband, "he bugged us to come back to Missouri to be near him, and so we did. Unfortunately, right after we moved back here, he got accepted into some Master's program in El Paso and then ended up involved in some big beef business out West, and he just stayed there for many years. He didn't plan it that way; it just kinda happened. Max and I decided we were too tired to move again, and so we stayed here. Of course, our son came and visited us often, but he's back permanently now, which is good, because we need someone to help us out sometimes. As you can tell, we're gettin' really old!"

"Very interesting," Becca said. "So, what's my step-brother's name, if I may ask?"

"Running Bear!" Maggie exclaimed, her voice full of pride.

"Running Bear," she mumbled to herself, wondering what they called him for short - Runny? Runner? Bear?

Eyeing Klaus-Dieter, she wondered why he hated Jews, yet loved American Indians. Whatever his problem was, it didn't necessarily seem to be racial prejudice. "Ray told me you practically raised Running Bear, even *before* you married Maggie."

"That's my business," he replied curtly. "He's a good boy and I'm proud of him! He's my one good accomplishment."

Becca's eyes flashed. "Ray and I weren't good accomplishments?"

Her only answer was another one of Klaus-Dieter's irritating snorts. She briefly thought of Ray who had picked up that silly habit.

"Of course, you kids were great accomplishments!" Maggie cried. "Max! Don't be such a hick! Goodness, Becca. I'm sorry, honey. Your Dad can be such a meanie sometimes. I'm sure you've accomplished a lot in your life, too, haven't you, sweetheart?"

"Well, I think I have!" Becca replied, doing her best to hold back the threatening tears. "I'm a journalist."

"Oh honey, how wonderful! And, I'm guessing you're married and got children of your own?"

"No, Maggie…no children." Cutting her eyes toward Klaus-Dieter, she said, "I…was always afraid they would end up raped by some pervert…."

"Raped?" Maggie said incredulously. "Why on earth would you think something like that?"

"Long story," Becca replied curtly. She simply couldn't bring herself to do this Maggie. Not yet. "But I'm married to a wonderful man," she went on. "His name is Liam Ritter and he's the Rabbi at a Messianic Jewish synagogue."

Klaus-Dieter's sluggish green eyes suddenly came to life. "A Jew?" he yelled hoarsely. "You married a dirty *Jew*?"

"Well, yes, Daddy-dear," she replied with a vicious smile. "And so did you!"

"I didn't know your mother was Jewish when I married her! She kept it from me for years."

"Yes, and when you found out, you decided to make us all miserable! Shall we discuss the many ways you did that? Or is this not a good time?"

"Maggie," Klaus-Dieter said without looking at his wife, "go do some chores."

"What for?"

Becca and I have something personal to discuss."

"...My coffee will get cold."

"Take it with you."

Maggie's expression changed from confused and hurt to indignation, then resentment. Finally, she rose without another word, tossed the contents of her coffee cup over the side of the porch, and disappeared in a huff around the corner.

Chapter 23

Crushing the serpent's head....

Ezekiel 7:3 Now the end is upon you, and I will send my anger upon you; I will judge you according to your ways, and I will punish you for all your abominations. (ESV)

* * * *

Becca glared at Klaus-Dieter, her face reflecting an unchecked fury. Myriad thoughts crossed her mind at once. "She doesn't know, does she?"

"Know what?"

"What you did to me, you pathetic pervert!"

"Watch your language! And...I don't know what you're talking about!"

"Really? Well, then let me remind you." Becca's violent trembling, as if on cue, suddenly ceased. Bathed now in unusual calm - as if someone had waved a magic wand and rendered her invincible - she graced him with a deadly smile.

"'Here little Becca, it's time for our family affair,'" she crooned, mimicking the words Klaus-Dieter used to utter, complete with his German accent. "'It's *Fahrvergnügen* time,

Becca! Time to do some pile driving into the heaven-lies!'...Sound familiar, Daddy?"

Klaus-Dieter's eyes narrowed as he pulled the dirty hand-kerchief from his pants pocket and unceremoniously hawked up a glob of oily phlegm. "I tell you, I don't know what you're talking about!" he said.

"Is that so? Well, I remember it very well – and so does Ray. He ended up in prison because of it. Your 'family affairs' ruined our lives!"

The old man balked as he fidgeted with the plastic tubing under his nose. "I never hurt you!" he muttered.

The urge to fly across the table to strangle him became overpowering. Becca balled her hands into tight fists until the feeling passed.

"Obviously, you still don't realize what you've done. You ruined my life, you Nazi freak! I was married several times because I didn't know how to have a normal relationship, thanks to you! I purposely never had kids because I don't trust men to keep their hands off of them! I had two abortions because of you! God! - You old bastard, you ruined my life!"

Cringing over her own choice of words, she immediately repented. *Oh please forgive me for my language, Yahweh!* she cried silently. *I hate him so much! Help me...please help me do this according to Your good will....*

Although she had done her best to prevent them, the tears began to flow freely now, blurring her view of the old man.

"You can't blame all that on me, for Christ's sake!" he shouted as loud as he possibly could with a voice that had seriously deteriorated with age. "You made something of yourself, so don't tell me I ruined your life."

"My career was just fine; it's my personal life that remained a mess because of what you did!"

Klaus-Dieter's eyes became tiny slits. "Why the hell don't you just get into your car and go back home?" he said. "I've got enough problems, without being blamed for yours, too. I don't need you digging into my past and accusing me of things I never did."

Becca scowled. "Things you never did?" she cried. "Oh, I see. Once you changed your name, you also decided to re-write your past! Is that because it was too hard for you to live with the fact that you raped your own flesh and blood, treating us no different than those poor victims in the concentration camps where you worked?"

Klaus-Dieter recoiled.

"Yes, I know all about your army days," she said with sadistic glee. "Your story is on the Simon Wiesenthal Center website."

Wide-eyed and surprised to discover that Becca knew his darkest secret, he suddenly pulled his lips into a vicious grin. "You know nothing!" he yelled. "Nothing!"

"It's a shame that Mom never knew," she went on. "But Ray knows, now, too. He said he would have turned you in to the authorities the day you visited him, had he only known! I fully intend to tell the whole world, including your precious Running Bear, your supposed 'one good accomplishment'...."

The old man's jawed dropped as he ogled her through watery eyes. "Well, since you know so much," he retorted icily, "you should also have figured out by now that you're *not* my daughter. Neither of you little Jewish bastards belonged to me! You want to know why? Because I had a vasectomy when I was young, because I couldn't bring myself to put children into our awful world!"

Surprise registered on Becca's face as he spoke. She vaguely remembered Ray mentioning the possibility that Klaus-Dieter wasn't their biological father, but she hadn't been willing to believe it.

"I would *not* have children," he continued heatedly. "Never! Not after what my father did, that Jewish son of a whore. He used to...he used to...do things to me when I was little...."

The old man's eyes suddenly glazed over as he fought the memories. Blinking furiously, he quickly looked away when the tears began to fall.

The only sound for several moments, as Becca tried to digest this new knowledge, was the mad flapping of bird wings nearby in the brush somewhere. It had never dawned on her that Klaus-Dieter himself might have been an abused child.

"You were sexually abused," she said breathlessly. "And your father was Jewish...."

"Yes, but *I'm* not!" he snapped. "The Bible says a Jew is one who is a Jew inwardly, and I'm *not* one!"

She repressed the sudden guffaw that threatened to burst forth. Her old man was Jewish, he had been a sexually abused child, and he had had a vasectomy! The news was at once unbelievable, hilarious and pathetic. It was almost too much to take in!

"A vasectomy," she said after some moments. "No wonder I never got pregnant."

"Yes, how lucky for both of us." he snapped. "And now you know why I was so angry when Rachel ended up pregnant with you! I was true to her until I found out that she had cheated on me! She had two bastards with her boss, behind my back! Do you have any idea how much that hurt?"

His tears suddenly came, flowing fast and hard, and his hateful, defensive look dissolved into something resembling vulnerability. "Oh my God, I loved her!" he said, snuffling. "I *loved* her! I had finally found true love and for once in my life, I was happy. She had helped me escape my awful past...."

You're a dirty little Jew whore, just like your mother!

Becca closed her eyes against the voices of the past; and, for the first time ever, she felt she understood who Klaus-Dieter Behringer, aka Max Neumann, was; and why he had turned into the monster who had so viciously victimized her and Ray.

"And that's why you got together with Maggie," she said as the puzzle of her past started to make more sense.

"Yes, I found solace in Maggie's arms when you were still a baby. I had to do something. My wife cheated on me."

Something stirred inside of Becca as she stared at the invalid perched across the table. He looked so small and delicate and doleful....

No! Becca thought, purposely pushing away the feeling. *He's a monster! He's a rapist, a hideous excuse for a human being. He needs to be punished!*

"Why did you rape us, then, if you had Maggie to release your sexual needs? Did you really think you were getting back at Mother by raping her children?"

Klaus-Dieter's breathing became uneven, tortured; he literally fought for air. "It hasn't exactly been easy on me, either," he whimpered. "I've been living in hell every damned day for 30 years now, hoping you'd never regain your memory. Actually, it's been almost half a century full of torture and guilt and wishing I'd never known you or your damned mother. You ruined my life, too! You ruined it by being born! I *had* to punish you...."

"By raping us, Klaus-Dieter? Since you knew how it felt to be raped, why did you perpetrate that same perversion on us? We were little children! We were babies!"

The wheezing intensified and he clutched at his chest. "Get out of here, Rebecca!" he yelled. "Just go home! I don't want to talk about this anymore!"

"It doesn't make any sense, what you did! Do you realize how stupid that was?"

"Go home!"

Becca's gaze was level, scorching. "Fine," she said evenly. "But I'm not leaving until you apologize. I want to hear you say you're sorry! You apologized to Ray; now apologize to me. Tell me you are sorry, and I'll leave and never darken your door again."

Klaus-Dieter appeared to be fighting within himself. "Well, I'm *not* sorry!" he finally replied, the chill in his voice deliberate and cruel. "You called me a pervert and I so have nothing to say to you! I'm *not* a pervert! I was a victim! I was hurt! It wasn't all about you, you selfish little Jewish... You have shown me no respect, whatsoever, and I want you out of my sight."

Becca rose with a force that knocked her chair backward as she angrily made her way toward the cowering figure; her eyes were bright and brimming with tears.

"You don't deserve any respect!" she said between clenched teeth. "What you deserve is to be castrated and beaten within an inch of your life! I'm sorry you were abused, but that was no excuse to become an abuser, yourself! *That's* what makes you a pervert!"

Klaus-Dieter shrank back. "It wasn't my fault, damn you – get away from me!" he wheezed as he peered up at her through watery eyes. "Satan had me back then."

The comment was so startling that she almost laughed. "Satan?" she growled, her face full of murderous rage as she continued to bear down on him. "You stupid old hypocrite! Blame yourself, if you need to blame someone. It wasn't Satan; it was all you! You gave in to that sin nature we're all plagued with! You had a choice!"

"I've paid for my sins in more ways than you'll ever know!" he screamed weakly. "I'm dying now, isn't that enough for you? You can come and spit on my grave when I'm gone."

Another violent coughing fit caused his eyes to bulge. His face, red and mottled, seemed ready to explode.

Something tugged at Becca's heartstrings as she watched the pathetic, frail figure writhing in agony. In her mind's eye, she remembered Liam's kind, spirit-filled face as he told her before she left the house earlier today, that he would bet a million dollars she wouldn't be able to lower herself to become mean and vindictive toward Klaus-Dieter.

And he was right.

Without thinking, she did something that her father used to do to her...the very same gesture that had caused the violent reaction in her the day Rex entered Beit Yisrael: She reached down to give his chin a demonstrative tweak.

"Daddy," she said, trying hard to keep her bottom lip from trembling. "You ruined my life in more ways than you could ever count. But you know what? I forgive you. And even more importantly, I forgive myself for the things I ended up doing because of my hatred for you."

Klaus-Dieter seemed temporarily dumbfounded. A tear appeared in the corner of one eye and skittered along his wrinkled cheek. Suddenly, he reached up to swipe her hand away from his chin. "Go away, Rebecca!" he begged. "Just go! I don't want you here."

Straightening, she silently beheld the old man who sat stiff and trembling in her presence, his frightened and pleading eyes peering at her through the great void that separated them.

For a long moment, she stood and simply looked at him. She hated the man...yet; he was an indelible part of her childhood. Like it or not, they had a shared past. Hurting him now, in his old age, wouldn't solve or change a thing. It really wouldn't even make her feel better. Not really. Vindictiveness was simply not a part of her personality. She had finally been able to tell him off; that's all she had ever really wanted to do....

"I just wanted to hear you say you're sorry," she said. "It saddens me that you can't even bring yourself to do that much."

The screen door opened part way as Maggie poked her head out. "You two finished telling secrets," she snapped, "or would you like the old lady to butt out awhile longer?"

A sound, unrelated to the rattling lungs, escaped Klaus-Dieter's throat. His shoulders began to shake as he once again raised bleary, pleading eyes toward the unwelcome visitor who had shaken his world.

"Fine," he said so quietly she could hardly hear. "I'm sorry."

An eternity passed before Becca was able to speak. With great effort, she swallowed the curdled spit at the back of her throat. His words had taken her by surprise; she could hardly believe he had actually apologized! Forcing a wan smile, she stepped back and stared at him.

"Well," Maggie snapped, "are you two done, or what?"

Becca continued to stare at Klaus-Dieter as she slowly backed away. "Dad and I are through reminiscing, Maggie," she said with a voice that didn't sound like her own. "I'm going to let you two get back to your pie and coffee now."

Then, suddenly and without warning, she turned and darted from the porch, running around the house to the front yard as if her life depended on it. Somewhere in the woods, a coyote howled, its voice high and shrill and lonely.

Moments later, in the privacy of her car, she collapsed against the steering wheel and sobbed. Finally exhausted, she wiped her tears with a tissue and slowly backed out of the driveway.

An unusual sensation settled over her as she drove away; a feeling she had never felt before: For the first time in her life, she felt free...relieved, released, whole.

She emitted a shaky sigh as Klaus-Dieter Behringer's gloomy old house grew smaller in the rearview mirror. Before long, it vanished completely, obliterated by the thick clouds of dust in her wake.

Ahead, a huge harvest moon illuminated the sky, casting a golden glow across the darkened horizon. She imagined Liam's sweet face in that moon; it smiled down on her, cleansing her soul with the power of love.

Chapter 24

Revelation....

Ecclesiastes 12:14 - For God will bring to judgment everything we do, including every secret, whether good or bad... (CJB)

* * *

The news about Klaus-Dieter Behringer's demise came several days later.

Becca and Liam were in the process of drinking their morning coffee when they heard it on ABC's "World News Now" news program.

"The Simon Wiesenthal Center can cross off another war criminal from their lists," the announcer said. "Ninety-six year old Klaus-Dieter Behringer who had disappeared from their radar back in the mid-Seventies, was found dead in the ashes of his home early yesterday morning, alongside his eighty-nine year old wife, Marguerite Little White Feather Neumann."

Becca watched in horror as the black and white picture from the Wiesenthal Center's website was displayed on the screen. Moments later, a couple of old photographs appeared of Klaus-Dieter in the Seventies...fuzzy pictures taken by an undercover policeman who had – according to the news caster – been assigned to follow Behringer for a time when he was suspected of being involved in the rape and murder of a small boy in Bolivar, Missouri.

The scene then switched to show the ruins of the old farm house Becca had visited a couple days before. Everything was gone except for the ancient fireplace, which stood like an old monolith among the ruins. Although the investigation was ongoing, the announcer was saying, initial reports indicated that the cause of the fire might have been a lit cigarette near the deceased's oxygen tank.

"Behringer, who disappeared in 1975 after the murder of his wife Rachel," the announcer continued as the camera returned to him, "had been living under the assumed name of Max Neumann. This information came from Behringer's stepson Running Bear Lambert, who declined an on-camera interview. We will continue to bring updates as soon as they become available."

"Running Bear *Lambert*." Becca mouthed the words just as the camera showed a glimpse of a very tall, dark and handsome, middle-aged man trying to shut his front door on the paparazzi on his front lawn.

"Oh, my God!" she cried as she jumped from the sofa. "Oh, my God, Liam! Oh, my God!"

"What?" he said, perplexed.

"It's Rex!" she screeched in disbelief. "Oh, my God! Running Bear Lambert is Rex…. Oh, my God! Rewind it, quick!"

"No! No, sweetie, it can't be!"

"Yes! Rex introduced himself to me as R. B. Lambert when he first came to Beit Yisrael! R. B. – Running Bear!"

Becca's hand flew to her mouth as she began to mentally reconcile and compare what she knew about Rex, with what Maggie had told her.

"Rex told me he had just moved down here from Albuquerque and bought a ranch in Norwood, Liam. Maggie told me her son was in the beef business 'out West' and that he recently moved back here. Oh, Liam! Running Bear Lambert is *Rex*!"

Liam's hand began to tremble and he quickly set his cup on the coffee table to rewind the segment. "Oh, my God," he whispered as he paused on Rex's half-obscured face. "Yeah, that sure does look like him…."

"Rex is my step-brother…." she stammered. Feeling her knees buckle, she quickly sank onto the sofa.

"Wow…."

The pair sat there for several long moments, incredulous, staring mutely at the screen.

"I just don't believe it," Liam finally managed.

"That is Rex on the screen. There's no doubt in my mind that's him!"

"Well…yeah, well…and what are the odds that his initials would be R. B. and his last name, Lambert? Wow! I'm – well, babe, I'm just speechless."

"Oh, Liam, he was raised by Klaus-Dieter and had all his mannerisms...No wonder he brought those visions out in me! I *knew* there something familiar about him!"

Liam nodded. "I don't know what to say. If this is true...."

"It's *true*! I know it's true! Look at the TV, honey! That's Rex! Rex, the 'Duke' is my step-brother! Oh, my God...."

Silence reigned as they stared at each other. Suddenly, Becca's eyes began to fill with tears as the realization sank in that her father had committed suicide. It had to be suicide, because she had seen how careful he had been to keep his cigarette away from the tank and the hose.

Ironically, he had chosen to burn – the very thing he had always wished on his wife and children....

Liam reached over to embrace his wife as her tears began to flow. "It's okay, sweetie," he said. "It's okay."

Becca nodded as she pressed herself against his shoulder and sobbed. It was the end of an era: Klaus-Dieter Behringer - the monster from her childhood, the man she had known as her father - was dead.

"I don't know how I should feel right now," she whispered.

"You'll sort things out, don't worry."

Suddenly, she sat up and gasped. "The media!" she cried, snuffling. "They'll find me...."

Liam blinked, then slowly nodded and retrieved his cellphone from the coffee table and handed it to her. "Might as well save them the trouble," he said.

Epilog

Four years later

Ephesians 4:30. *And do not grieve the Ruach haKodesh (Holy Spirit) of Elohim, whereby you are sealed for the day of redemption. 31. Let all bitterness and anger, and wrath, and clamoring and reviling, be taken from you along with all malice: 32. And be affectionate towards one another and sympathetic; and forgive one another as Elohim by the Mashiyach (Messiah) has forgiven us.* (AENT)

* * *

The smell of Annie's baking bread hung in the air, floating into the sanctuary to mix with the happy sounds of people's animated chatter as they waited for the service to start.

Liam stood at the podium and smiled at the congregation. Lately, there had been standing room only, and he and Chad and some of the men had been lining the aisles with plastic lawn chairs to accommodate everyone.

"Shabbat shalom and welcome to Beit Yisrael!" he said into the microphone. "For all those who are new, please look at the bulletin you received at the door, and then, when you're home, be sure to go to our website so you can learn more about who we are and what teach. All our Elders and deacons are listed there, along with their respective phone numbers and email addresses. Please don't hesitate to call or write, because we make it a point to be accessible to our synagogue family at all times...except in the middle of the night, of course. We do have our limits."

A few scattered chuckles served to lighten the mood and set the stage for the worship team who came up front to take their places behind Liam.

"Now," he went on, "you all probably have noticed we're getting a little crowded in here." More chuckles and a few amens.

"Well, you'll be happy to know that your tithes have bought a brand new piece of property in a gorgeous wooded location, a few miles down the road, just south of here. And, after much praying and searching, we have finally found a contractor we trust, to build our new synagogue. He even gave us a discount, because we've taken the advice of our favorite financial guru, radio host Dave Ramsey, and we'll be paying cash! It means there will be no mortgage payments hanging over our heads! The contractor promised me that our overcrowding problem will be resolved in approximately six months."

The worship team took advantage of the mood as the room exploded into raucous cheering and clapping. Moments later, the building was filled with loud singing and dancing and worship. Many simply stood with eyes closed, feeling the Spirit move through the congregation.

Becca was standing in the front row, deliriously happy, with her hands lifted toward the heavens. Life was so good. She never imagined it could be like this. It had been four years since Klaus-Dieter's suicide. Four years since the media descended on her, Liam and Ray with their endless questions. They had come from as far away as Australia to examine every aspect of her years under the thumb of the notorious Nazi pedophile who had tortured thousands of incarcerated Jews in Germany.

Several documentaries and two books had been produced of Klaus-Dieter Behringer's life, now that – thanks to Becca and Ray – there were some actual eyewitness accounts. It seemed the world couldn't get enough, and for a while Liam and Becca contemplated changing their names and moving to some deserted island to get away from it all.

As for "Rex" Running Bear Lambert, he had refused all interviews. The only comment he ever made publicly was to say that the man who raised him was the kind and gentle Max Neumann; he didn't know this evil Klaus-Dieter Behringer person and he wasn't about to desecrate the memory of his loving step-father.

The praise and worship at Beit Yisrael lasted for nearly an hour. It finally calmed down when Chad took the Torah from the cabinet and stood next to Liam who always made it a point to explain what the scroll meant, along with the significance of a "Torah procession."

"Rabbi," someone called out, "sorry, but I'm new to this and it feels weird. When the Torah comes around, do we have to touch it, or can we just watch it pass by?"

Liam smiled. "Great question!" he said. "The answer is no, you don't have to touch it. The procession simply symbolizes God's Word passing through the room, that's all. If someone desires to touch it as it goes by, that's fine, but you don't have to."

The man looked visibly relieved as he made a small whistling sound. "Thanks," he said. "I attended a synagogue in Springfield a few months ago and they tried to force us to do all kinds of things there. They insisted we learn Hebrew, and told my wife to keep her head covered with a scarf. And they told me I had to leave if I didn't wear a prayer shawl the whole time. I mean, I totally understand the need for Jesus and Torah; I just feel uncomfortable with some of the things certain Messianic pastors insist we have to do."

"Well, in our synagogue we realize each of us learns and grows at our own pace," Liam explained. "We won't force you to do anything. Our job is to present Yahweh's Truth and get you to read and study the Bible from cover to cover; not to beat anyone over the head with it, or insist you do extra-biblical things. We totally trust the Holy Spirit to work in you."

A few scattered "amen's" and clapping filled the room. "That's why we love you guys!" someone yelled.

"By the way," Liam continued. "I would ask that you don't call me Rabbi. Although I am a graduate of a *yeshiva*, and can legally call myself 'Rabbi' I prefer you just call me Liam. I am your congregation leader. The only one deserving of the title of 'Rabbi' is our Savior, Yeshua. Like all of you, I'm just here to serve Him. It's not about you; it's not about me; it's all about Him!"

After the Torah procession, Liam once again addressed the congregation. "Okay, everybody," he said soberly. "I need a show of hands. How many of you believe in forgiveness?"

Every hand went up.

"Okay, that's good, because throughout the Bible we see scriptures that tell us that we are to forgive. This doesn't mean we have to hang out with those who have hurt us; it simply means we are to recognize that we humans are all capable of making mistakes and doing things that God doesn't approve of. If we don't forgive, then our anger will fester and harden and imprison our minds. God can't do anything with those who concentrate more on their anger than they do on Him."

Pausing to gaze affectionately at his audience, he smiled. "Today," he said, "we are going to experience a real live lesson in the art of forgiving. We have a special guest who is going to talk about forgiveness. Lora…would you come on down now, please?"

There were several gasps as Lora Dominguez Lambert descended from the second floor and began walking down the middle aisle, toward the front of the sanctuary. Not only was it a shock to see her in the synagogue that she and Rex had nearly destroyed, but she had lost so much weight she was hardly recognizable. Sporting an expensive beige chiffon dress with big, black buttons, she stood demurely at the podium, eyes lowered as she attempted to regain control of her emotions.

"To all those who know me, I thank you in advance for not throwing rocks at me," she began. "You know what I did. And to those who don't know who I am, I was the wife of the founder of Beit Yisrael, Rabbi Orlando Dominguez."

All eyes were on Lora as she gazed lovingly at Becca. "You tried your best to steer me in the right direction," she said. "I failed you and I am sorry. Thank you for everything, including the verbal spankings you gave me. Your efforts ultimately were *not* in vain."

Wiping a tear, she scanned the congregation. "To all those who know me, please understand that I am sincerely sorry and that I am asking forgiveness for my behavior back then. I honestly didn't know what I was doing. You see, I was blinded by love. I don't know how it happened, because I knew all along that Rex Lambert wasn't a godly man; but I chose to overlook that, and I gave in to my carnal self. The Bible tells us not to associate with unbelievers and, honestly, Rex wasn't a believer. He knew *about* God and the Bible, but he didn't *know* Him. He was using the church setting to find women, that's all.

"Becca tried to warn me, but all I could see was this excruciatingly handsome, virile and charismatic man who knew how to manipulate people without even trying very hard. I denied that he was causing trouble among the Elders, sowing seeds of doubt. He was a charming and arrogant bully who enjoyed the hunt and the kill. He told me he loved to 'toy' with people, especially with religious folks. Those who didn't know their Bibles very well believed every word he said, simply because he was so charismatic."

Lora paused briefly to blow her nose and steady herself before continuing.

"I didn't even listen when my own husband confronted me about Rex," she went on. "I had fallen out of love with Orlando many years before, and was just going through the motions, pretending to be a good, godly wife. During this time I filled my empty heart with stuff – new clothes, new shoes, purses, buying whatever I wanted. I even forced Orlando to steal from your tithes - monies that were allocated for building maintenance and whatnot. And so here I was, the Rabbi's wife, stealing and conniving and ultimately having an affair with someone who was clearly sent by Satan to destroy our synagogue. I hurt my husband so badly, he committed suicide."

Overcome with grief, Lora's shoulders shook as she broke into tears. Becca left her seat to stand beside her at the podium. Hugging her old friend, she assured her that God was hearing every word, and that He would heal her hurting soul. "He loves a repentant heart, Lora," she whispered. He knows...."

When Becca began to head back to her seat, Lora quickly pulled her back. "Stay," she begged. "I need you by my side."

"The truth is," Lora went on as she held Becca's hand, "after doing much soul-searching, I realized and admitted to myself that I had made Rex my idol. I even stopped being Torah observant for him, because he refused to learn what Torah was all about. Well...God took my idol from me last Valentine's Day, when my sweet Rex died from prostate cancer. We had four beautiful years together...and the whole time, I felt guilty, because I knew I had sinned...."

Again, her shoulders shook as the silent tears fell. "I knew how he was, and why he was the way he was - and I chose to overlook it. I just couldn't let him go! And when he passed, that's when the scales fell from my eyes and I began to fully realize the impact of what I had done. Even though I have been in church all my life and I knew very well what sin was, I chose to sin. I chose Rex and his worldly charms over my relationship with God."

Becca squeezed Lora's hand as she stood and cried. "You're doing fine," she murmured.

"Second Corinthians 5:17 says, 'Therefore, if anyone is in Messiah Yeshua, he is a new creation; the old has gone, the new has come!' I now realize I wasn't a new creation when I committed all those sins. I thought I was, but I didn't have the Holy Spirit living in me. If He had been living in me, I would never have been able to do the things I did because I would have been wracked with guilt! And honestly, not to turn anybody off, but I believe it's because I have been told all my Christian life that all I had to do was to 'believe in Jesus' – that nothing else was required, because He forgives everything and anything. That is so wrong!"

"Amen!" someone shouted.

"Something *is* required of us: Obedience to His 'forever' commands! That's not just for the Jews, as most seem to think. We are *one* in Messiah, and as such, we are all responsible to know what His Torah says, and to do those things that we can!"

She stopped to swallow as a renewed surge of tears began to blur her vision. "Oh, how I miss Orlando," she cried. "I'm so sorry for what I did. He was such a good man! All he was guilty of was trying to get me to have a closer relationship with God, and I made fun of him for that...."

Lora briefly stopped talking when Becca gave her a quick hug from the side.

"I fully intend to spend the rest of my life making up for what I did against God," she said, her voice quivering. "I know He has forgiven me for my ignorance during those days when I chose to be lukewarm toward Him. And I just pray you will forgive me, too. I beg you to use my testimony as a measuring stick in your own life, because I know from experience that it's a terrible thing to fall into the Hands of the Living God. We cannot straddle the fence and pretend we're His - because there will be no sinners in Heaven…Okay, I think I'd better stop now. Thank you for listening to my story."

The room was silent when Lora finished speaking. No one knew exactly what to do in the wake of the avalanche of emotions her testimony had provoked.

Still holding Lora's hand, Becca stepped up to the microphone and smiled. "I think that deserves a standing ovation, don't you?" she said, wiping a tear.

Seconds later, as Liam joined the two women on stage, the room broke into applause.

"I just know Yahweh is smiling down on us," Becca yelled into Liam's ear. When the applause died down, she once more stepped up to the microphone.

"I would like to say something to go along with Lora's testimony," she said, turning toward her old friend. "I forgive you, Lora. I cannot tell you how happy I am that you found your way back. Your testimony is amazing."

Scanning the congregation, she blinked away some tears and smiled. "As most of you know," she went on, "I recently went through a very trying time, myself. I'm a survivor of sexual abuse at the hands of my father, the notorious Nazi war criminal, Klaus-Dieter Behringer.

"What you may not be aware of, though, is the anguish that a sexually abused child goes through during the course of his or her life. The abuse stays with you, always. All my life's decisions were based upon what happened to me, back then. I purposely never had children because I was terrified that someone might abuse them sexually. I didn't strive to make certain career advancements because I didn't feel worthy. I didn't know how to choose decent men to date, and consequently, I ended up married more than once. Like Lora, I've made some terrible mistakes, too – and most of them were because of the 'soul ties' I had to someone who abused me."

The room was completely silent as Becca spoke. All eyes were riveted on her.

"What I'm trying to say here is, that if you've been a victim of mental, emotional or sexual abuse, by all means, do seek help. But, I am living proof that the most important thing you could *ever* do is to give your life to Yahweh! He will heal you from the inside out! He is the only One who can release you from that prison. If you have never given yourself to God or accepted His Divine Messiah, Yeshua, I would ask that you please consider it doing it as soon as possible. It is, hands down, the most important decision you'll ever make in your lifetime!"

"Amen!" several peopled yelled in tandem.

"I used to pray for God to stop my abusive father in his tracks, and was disappointed when He didn't. Once I 'got saved' in that sweet little Baptist church just down the road, and realized that there was a God and that He did care, and that He had helped me make it through those terrible times...well, that changed everything! It suddenly came to me that bad things happen to good people because He gives us all the choice to do things His way, or not. He doesn't force anyone to do anything. He doesn't stop abusers from abusing. He may tweak their conscience, but it's up to them to come to Him for healing from their sinful ways.

"I had a chance to confront my father four years ago, and I realized that, all I could really do was to let go, forgive him, and turn it over to God. I'm not responsible for how he chose to conduct his life. I'm only responsible for myself. And so are you. So, if you've ever suffered abuse at the hands of someone you loved – or even if you have been the abuser - please don't hesitate to reach out to Liam and me. We will do our best to help put you on the road toward healing. We are here for you, always."

Once more the congregation broke into wild applause. Several people joined them on the stage as Becca, Lora and Liam hugged each other.

"Group hug!" Liam yelled over the din, to lighten the mood. "Everybody who wants to join us, come on up here and join in. Let's praise God today by loving each other like we love Him and He loves us. Halleluyah!

* * *

The crisp Fall air kissed Becca's cheeks as she stood in the back of the synagogue building, staring off into the woods.

Fall was coming early this year, and the leaves were already starting to turn.

The service today had been wonderful beyond measure, but also emotionally draining. Lora's testimony had brought closure on several levels. Yahweh had sent healing in many ways. Finally, there would be no more distractions. Life was simply great.

The sound of approaching footsteps caused her to turn around. Her face brightened when she realized it was the love of her life.

"Shucks, ma'am, what y'all doin' out here all alone?" Liam asked cheerily, using his best cowboy accent.

"Why are you talking like that?" she replied with a laugh. "Are you pretending you're from the Ozarks, or something?"

"As long as I can be with you, I'll pretend anything you want!" When he reached Becca, he bent down to give her a quick peck on the cheek, then gathered her into his arms. "So, what y'all doin' out here all alone?"

"Just praising God," she replied as she relaxed against her husband's bosom. "Just praising our awesome God and loving the life He gave us."

www.ingramcontent.com/pod-product-compliance
Lightning Source LLC
Chambersburg PA
CBHW062129170626
46813CB00002B/620